JINX

Also by Irma Kurtz

NON-FICTION
Malespeak
Crises
Loneliness

FICTION
Sob sister

IRMA KURTZ

Jinx

HEINEMANN : LONDON

First published in Great Britain 1993
by William Heinemann Ltd
an imprint of Reed Consumer Books Ltd
Michelin House, 81 Fulham Road, London SW3 6RB
and Auckland, Melbourne and Singapore

A CIP catalogue record for this title
is available from the British Library
ISBN 0 434 39996 5

Printed and bound in Great Britain
by
Clays Ltd, St. Ives PLC

To Elisabeth Whipp,
in friendship

ONE

Call me Marsha. How's that for a classic American opening? Spelt and pronounced, I'm sorry to tell you, in the American way, too, as in a lowlying wasteland, only flatter and less alluring than most: marsher. That's me. The name was taken from a maiden aunt, not even my own.

'A girl, Mrs Feldstein,' said the doctor who delivered me.

My mother sighed.

'Drat it,' she said.

'I had an aunt, a nice old girl called Marsha,' said the cursed doctor.

As if Marsha were not burden enough, my father then tacked on the Hebrew name, Leah. Remember your Book of Genesis, chapter twenty-nine, verse seventeen? Sore-eyed Leah was Jacob's ugly surprise. True enough, in due course she became mother of his six sons, but it was her sexy sister Rachel he had in mind all the time. So what that comely Rachel turned out to be barren. Dynasty was not uppermost in Jacob's thoughts when he watched Rachel bending to draw water from the well. Men become so dreadfully light-minded and unprincipled at the sight of a beautiful young woman, don't you find?

By the time I decided to take matters into my own hands and change my name to Jessica, raven-tressed temptress, sinuous, silky, and a threat to men, it was too late: not only was I known to teachers and classmates as Marsha, I had become Marsha — marshy Marsha Leah Feldstein, full-grown at barely five feet (lowlying) and never kissed (a wasteland), except once as a forfeit in a party-game. Scholarship and a quick tongue were not much to recommend a girl at Fiorello LaGuardia High School in Teaneck, New Jersey. I was no prize package, let me tell you, and I can't say I have ever been one. My hair is kinky, it used to have the rusty cast of a used sink scourer, but it faded to natural mouse when I was in my thirties; I am short-legged and boxy; my neck is more dodo than swan. And ever at the forefront of the inventory goes my bell-ringer, my Turkish scimitar, my flapping spinnaker, known for generations on my father's side as The Feldstein Nose. Nose first, I fell to defeat and early heartbreak. I am not one to complain, but many unprepossessing genes gather in me, eagerly it seems, after generations of dispersal. R.I.P. Here, they find a dead end: I have no siblings and no offspring. It is a little death in life when a female is undesirable to her species.

Mind you, I've grown into a tough little cookie, amusing too, if you like the type, very strong in my opinions. And I've made a name for myself; not my own name, I confess. My chutzpah was exhausted by everyday life, I'm no Helena Rubinstein, and Marsha Leah Feldstein's Beauty Products was more than I felt able to brazen out. Because of my name, my lack of looks, and the monumental Feldstein nose, I've kept what I cringe to call 'a low profile' in the beauty business where I have made my small fortune. My line of cosmetics is called, simply, Miracle Products. Miracles are what the ladies want, *n'est-ce-pas*? Miracles are what I offer and miraculous indeed would be any palpable good my products did. However, I sell my customers hope, and hope is an indisputable cosmetic. Hope is a miracle, in fact, for it triumphs over any and all evidence to its contrary. I derived much ironical pleasure in my time from concocting and advertising hope for others where I had not the slightest hope for myself.

2

Let's be honest, in this world homely women are never stars. Nobody wants my life story. Who cares where I buy my clothes? Obviously, I've had no high-class lovers: with *this* nose? Shopping and fucking are not my style. So it is as well that what I intend to do is not tell my own story, or to tell it only incidentally, while I put into order all I can remember about Jinx O'Malley: my friend Jinx O'Malley – *Vogue* magazine's 'Face of the Year' for 1957, *Time* magazine's 'Face of the Decade' in 1960. For a very long run Jinx was an icon in the eyes and hearts of lorry drivers, garage mechanics, merchant seamen, long-term prisoners and schoolboys all over the world. There were poets, too, and painters, and novelists who adored her, and set out to glorify her in their work, though that lot, nine times out of ten, ended up glorifying only themselves. Take it as read, as soon as Jinx O'Malley had her chance, she shopped till she dropped, and she had oodles of sex too, with handsome studs in fancy places, though she never called fucking other than making love. Even when Jinx's greatest days were on the wane, she would not bed a man for money or power, perhaps least of all for her own pleasure. Sex was a devotional service for Jinx; she learned erotic postures the way nuns learn forms of prayer, reverentially. With one exception, perhaps two, it was only for love that Jinx O'Malley offered up her long, silken body. She was the most beautiful woman of her age and consequently one of the most beautiful who ever lived. If my heart has not been altogether hard-boiled in the bitterness of neglect, that is partly thanks to my lovely friend, Jinx O'Malley, who had beauty enough to spare.

We met nearly forty years ago. When we became instant friends, it surprised everyone; everyone, that is, but small-minded people. Nothing surprises *them*: to be small-minded is to be satisfied by small explanations, even for miracles. Take my flatmate at the time, Flavia Jane Garvey, bluestocking and third-year poetess supreme of New York's City College. After I'd introduced Jinx to Flavia, she drew me to one side. She was wearing her 'p-word face': pious, prissy, pernickety, poached, pawky, pettifogging – 'If you want my opinion . . .' said Flavia Jane, as if there were a choice, 'a girl like that classically hangs around with a girl like you, Marsh, to make herself look good.' I had to laugh. Jinx was then emerging moist and golden from late adolescence, she was scrappily dressed and still with gawky traces, but she could not have looked better. Besides, how to explain to Flavia Jane that there was no drop of cunning in Jinx O'Malley? I wasn't sure what Jinx saw in me, or why she had immediately taken to me, but one thing I knew, it was not to make herself look good. 'Well, maybe', said Flavia Jane, who was at her most paltry and prosaic, 'she feels sorry for you.' Untrue. Pity is generally a very self-serving emotion and those who act on it are smug bigots looking for a fix. Jinx had a kind heart, one of the kindest I've ever encountered, and pity is not in the same league.

At first, I figured it had to be curiosity that drew Jinx to me: to find out what it was like to be as I was, practically invisible to the opposite sex. Curiosity is as fair a building block for friendship as any other, and a lot more promising than pity. Curiosity was the main reason I befriended Jinx; or that's what I would have said at the start. Only now do I realise that for all our evident differences of physique and psychology, Jinx and I were born with an outlandish kinship which she, on some level, recognised long before I did. Her great beauty and my extreme ugliness set us outside the common run. I was the troll and Jinx was the unicorn. Her soaring faith in love and my snuffling trepidation isolated us together, made us companions, and finally made us both sterile.

I asked Jinx once, years after we'd met and she was already famous, why she thought our friendship had begun. I put the question gruffly because, you know, I cared.

'Now, don't you fly off the handle, honey,' she said, for by that time she knew where I stood on most issues, and how touchy I could be, 'but when I was little, back home in Lafayette, I went to this carnival one time. And there was a two-dollar palmist in a tent. And she told me she saw a woman in my hand with the initial "M". She said that little "M" was going to be my life-long friend, more true to me than a sister. Well, honey, the minute I laid eyes on you and heard your name, I just knew you had to be the one.'

'Oh, spare me, Jinx!' I cried. ' You know I think all that destiny stuff is garbage.'

'That's as may be, sugar. But it's honest garbage,' she replied. And she was serious, too. Jinx could not joke, no more than she could lie; she did not know how.

TWO

Jinx and I met on one of those afternoons in October when New York enjoys its annual epiphany and dances out of torpor, as it does for a brief while every autumn, to become heaven on earth. I remember bells were ringing, which means it must have been a Sunday. It had to have been a Sunday. Working your way through school appears to have gone out of fashion, but back then it wasn't unusual for a student to wait on table four nights a week and all day Saturday, as I did, to pay tuition and rent. Sunday was the only day I would have been free to walk aimlessly along Fifth Avenue, grinning back at other pedestrians in a goofy way, and craning my neck like a hick from Ohio to look up at the skyscrapers. On that perfect day they did what they were meant to do: they scraped the sky blue, blue, blue.

It was 1955, or thereabouts; I had just started my third year at City College, and small diamonds had begun to proliferate on the ring-fingers of my classmates. My own romantic fantasies were extravagant and adventurous, but I was a realist, a *real* realist; I knew dashing heroes did not turn up in dockland bars of Shanghai and Rio to get flat-chested broads like me out of trouble – or into it, either, come to that. I was bound one day to teach high school in Teaneck, that was what my parents expected, and, realistically, I guessed that was what I'd end up doing. Realistically, how was an undersized female with a face that was half hooter going to get by if not as a teacher, or a librarian, or some timorous damn thing? So for the most part

6

I hid my barbarous daydreams deep inside my 32A chest, and I worked hard to cultivate a sarcastic inclination suited to the classroom and the ritualised torture of the under-aged. True enough, kiddies bored the hell out of me, but, on the other hand, who knew better than kike-nosed, coon-curled, marshy marsher Marsh, teacher's pet, how ignorant and in need of educating the little bastards were?

Vaguely, I was ambling towards home on 111th Street and Broadway, where I shared a flat with Flavia Jane Garvey. I was in no hurry, and I let myself be tugged from one to another stream of pedestrians, not resisting the perpetual currents that flow in New York's mid-town streets. Hurried along with an up-town surge, I was drawn to a pushcart on the corner of Fifty-sixth and Fifth where I stopped with a small crowd in front of a towering pyramid of red and green apples, crisp, bright, and bursting with seasonal juices. Each apple had been polished by hand, then strategically set with its best side out. The pedlar, like any artist forced to part with his great work, scowled at us all from behind his masterpiece, and grumbled at every sale. Suddenly, I saw his dour face relax, first in surprise, then in delight; he smiled, doffed his ragged straw hat and swept it nearly to the ground in a surprisingly graceful bow. And there, stepping out of the crowd around me was Jinx O'Malley.

Plain little nobodies like me have a complex response to real beauties. First off is a blow of desire, more passionate than any lover's longing. It arrives on the echo of prayers in front of our mirrors, back when we still had hope. Immediately afterwards, there rises in us a volatile combination of servile admiration and nearly murderous scorn for the skin-deep, and for the hare-brains who fall for it. An admixture of pure despairing envy is also there, on one level or another. But I felt no envy when I saw Jinx, no fawning slavishness, no scorn. Not then, and very rarely in

7

the years ahead, did I feel other than affection for her and, even though I do not for a moment believe myself to have a 'J' in my palm, between us from the first was a weird affinity, far beyond easy reason. We smiled straight at each other, like two old friends, and without conferring, after the briefest of introductions, we strolled to Central Park side by side, as if we had planned to meet at such-and-such a time on such-and-such a corner. In the park Jinx and I made for a bench on a quiet path facing a small thicket of trees. Anyone watching us would have assumed we came there regularly, so surely did we take possession of the place.

It was strange. And stranger still that at the time it hardly seemed strange at all to find myself so quickly in the process of making a friend. Not that I was inherently unfriendly or shy, except around men. But ordinary pursuits of husband-hunting and self-beautifying were not for the likes of me to share, and so I had no friends at college among the regular gals. As for Flavia Jane and her crowd, their grim scholarship was as alien to me as the preening of the bird-brains. With neither swots nor dimwits keen to give me the time of day, who was left to befriend? Only lame ducks. Flavia Jane brought home her gang of hyper-sensitive neurasthenics once a week, but on the several occasions certifiable schizophrenics turned up at our place for tea, it was by my invitation. The trouble with lame ducks is that they will not pull together, they are very hostile to each other as a rule, and can be acquired as friends only one at a time. Thus my circle was small: myself, and sometimes an eccentric or mad person who followed me home. As Jinx talked in her warm Southern voice I felt my heart go out to her in an unfamiliar way. I wasn't utterly struck dumb, however. On the contrary, intending to impress her with my wisdom and world weariness, at one point, after a little silence, I said, in the tradition of a City College conversational gambit: 'How perverse are we

8

Americans to call this most uplifting of seasons "the fall"! I wonder why we do it?' Of course, it was a rhetorical question which any of my classmates, Flavia Jane Garvey, for example, would have used to launch into some metaphysical meandering. 'It's on account of the leaves, honey,' Jinx said. 'Now is when they *fall* off the trees.'

She turned full on me her green eyes, and for the first time I found myself gazing upon a gorgeous lawn of cerebral vacancy that was one day going to bring America's greatest living novelist to his knees.

Apples from the pushcart broke sparkling on the tongue, like fragments of the day itself, and we said nothing for a few moments. Flavia Jane, on frisky and plebeian days, sometimes waltzed around the kitchen singing a current pop song that went: 'Either you've got, got, got it, or you don't, don't, don't.' Flavia herself had enough of 'it' to get by; I had not a vestige of 'it'; Jinx had 'it' in superabundance. When she flicked her apple core to the squirrels and sat back with arms raised to lift the long fair hair from her neck, I saw her cheekbones were widespread as eagles' wings, and her legs stretched halfway to Harlem, and I knew Jinx more than had 'it': she *was* 'it'. That was when she told me she had grown up barefoot, and I realised she meant precisely that: Jinx had no use for metaphor – the literal world held magic enough for her.

'I was number four baby,' she said, 'and number four girl. Four girls! My mama took one look at me and said, "Sweet Jesus, it has got to be a jinx!" Then my daddy comes in and he takes a good look at his number four girl, that's me. And pretty soon, he hightails it right out of town.'

I could not take my eyes off Jinx. God, she was beautiful! Her nose, oh. It was a trifle longer than *retroussée*, the septum was visible but not upturned, and the fine bone rose without the slightest deviation or bump. In all my years of professional dealings with beautiful women I never

9

again saw a nose as perfect or eyes as green and almond-shaped. Her mouth was a trifle too cushiony for the taste of the 1950s, its suggestion of lascivious idiocy was not to come into fashion for a number of years. I do not mean to imply that Jinx was stupid. She had read but one book from cover to cover in her life – 'It made me cry, honey. And where's the fun in that?' – but out of a process so little involving intellect it was perhaps technically close to moronic, she nevertheless came out regularly with observations from life that were concise and penetrating.

'Ever notice', she said, 'how many times folks have four girls in a row and then the fifth one comes out a boy? Or vice versa.' What would I, an only child, an academic, a part-time waitress, a virgin, know of such worldly matters? Only recently I read somewhere that scientists in America have noted the fifth-baby phenomenon and are writing papers to explain it.

'Well, our daddies couldn't help wanting sons, you know,' Jinx then said. 'It's deep in men. It goes back to when a man needed someone to dig his grave for him when he passed away.'

See what I mean? With no more than a single reading of *A Tale of Two Cities* for backup, Jinx sometimes made more sense than a whole lot of others I've known.

A hush settled over our part of the park, not a leaf fell; winter was on the prowl up around the Canadian border and the air itself was listening.

'My husband . . .' Jinx began, and the appearance of a green monkey out of the thicket could not have astonished me more. Her husband? Mothers' friends had husbands, older cousins had husbands, women in cotton print housedresses had husbands; my classmates were all dead set on having husbands, but none of them had one yet. How could someone a few months younger than I have a husband?

10

'I suppose my ex-husband, I have to say now. His name was Jamie, and he was the cutest thing.' Back then Jinx used to pronounce 'thing' as 'thang'. 'He was a Fuller brush salesman. And his first words when he saw me were, "Well, well, well, if it ain't a rose on the manure heap." Those were his words. And I just thought, "Well, well, well, girl, this is *it* at last." And six weeks later we tied the knot.'

A little breeze had sprung up. Jinx smiled into it and closed her eyes.

'We did it on my fifteenth birthday,' she murmured.

'Gosh.' What else could I have said? A dark green coat with a coachman's cape and a copy of *The Collected Poems of Edna St Vincent Millay* had been my own fifteenth birthday presents.

'Jamie was a Gemini,' Jinx said. 'A girl can count on Geminis for fun and trouble.'

She told me that Jamie had taken her from her home in Lafayette to New Orleans, and then up to New York where he'd run out on her only a few weeks earlier. I'd read my McCullers, my Capote, my Williams, and my Faulkner, especially my Faulkner, and I had some idea of the steamy business girls got up to in the Southland. But Jinx's matter-of-fact delivery astonished me. Events of the nature she described so calmly, had they happened to a Feldstein, would have evoked histrionics on an operatic scale.

'Love', she said, putting a little spin on the word, 'is the most important thing (thang) in a woman's life. And if it doesn't work out, that just means it wasn't meant to be.' She was wearing white net gloves that kept snagging on the rhinestones studding her see-through plastic bag. The days of designer labels were still far ahead, you understand; her suit was too summery for the season and in an uncouth, suburban shade of turquoise. 'There's always a next time,' she said, squinting at her glove and disentangling it carefully from her bag.

11

'Not always,' I dared to say. 'Not for everyone. People get too old . . .'

She drew a sharp breath. 'Never say that, Marsha. Never say "too old" or too anything for love. It's never too late for love.'

Her be-netted fingers closed on my arm and she brought close to me her face, which one day was going to drive a Central American dictator loopy with desire.

'We used to have this girl down home,' she said in a confidential tone, 'and she got herself in the family way. It was the daddy of her best friend that did it to her too.'

I held my breath. I'd read endlessly about sex, hypothetically I was a harlot, but it made me shiver to hear my new friend refer so casually to what were for me the theoretical processes of making love and its aftermath.

'What do you think that poor girl did?'

'Dropped out of school?' I suggested tentatively, and idiotically, I realise in retrospect.

'She held her stomach in for nine long months, that's what. Every minute of every day she told herself she was not going to let her situation show. And it never did. Nobody ever found out about her trouble, except she told her best friend, and her best friend told me.'

Jinx sat back and smiled happily. Was the story finished?

'But what happened?' I cried. 'Did her parents raise the baby as their own?'

'What happened was', said Jinx, 'she used her inner powers to let the bulge not show. If a girl can do that, then that has got to mean that getting old, like forty and forty-five, and all that stuff, is purely in her mind too.'

Mangy pigeons pecked wildly at our apple cores on the path. Jinx turned her radiant gaze upon them. Could it be she found them adorable? She clucked softly. Yes, she *did* think they were adorable. 'My moon's in Virgo,' she said. 'Where's yours?'

Her question was way, way ahead of its time. Back in

12

the 1950s not many of us knew we had a moon to call our own. Fortunately, I was spared the need to reply. The pigeons on the path in front of us suddenly took flight – if rats could fly, they'd do it with just such a scaly flapping – and there was a barely perceptible tensing in Jinx, hardly more than a thoroughbred's twitch at a whiff of early clover on the breeze. Approaching us were a pair of over-groomed young men in dark suits; they looked like a pair of trainee undertakers. The taller, better-looking one said: 'Hi, doll,' or something of the sort. Can anyone now believe that is actually how American men addressed pretty women in those days? The shorter man, who resembled his companion as some dogs do their masters, glanced at me, and the old familiar pain tore from my throat to my groin when, with a canine rumble of disgust, he turned his head away.

The way Jinx gave the two men in the park a swift, stunning brush-off – 'I'm not alone as a matter of fact,' she told the tall dog-walker, 'I'm with my girlfriend. And we have another appointment, if you don't mind' – ended the overture to our friendship on a high note. A young woman of the 1950s rejecting a passably good-looking man in favour of spending time with a female? It was practically unheard of, and particularly when the female was an ugly little squirt like me. Oh yes, I'd found myself a good friend, a best friend, there was no doubt in my mind after that. Later, as we were strolling together out of the park towards Columbus Circle, when she told me she was job hunting, of course I suggested right away she come to Schrafft's, the restaurant where I worked part-time, and there was a constant need for new waitresses. It wasn't much of a job but it would do until something better came along, which when a girl looked like Jinx was bound to be soon. As for a place to live, Flavia and I used the kitchen as a common room, and we had been talking for some time about converting our living-room for another boarder. There would be hell to pay with the poetess, I was quite sure. But when had she ever turned down a date in favour of me? And besides, the lease was in my name.

'We'll have so much fun,' Jinx said and, echoing what was in my mind: 'We'll be best friends.'

We were on a corner of Central Park West, the light was about to turn against us, but Jinx strode straight across the street. An approaching car skidded to a stop; the driver turned his head to follow Jinx's crossing, with a look of pained wonder such as I had never before seen on any man's face. It was like travelling in a new and exotic country. Scurrying beside her, I basked in the overflow of beauty.

THREE

Flavia Jane Garvey and I shared a fifth-floor railway apartment on 111th Street just off Broadway. To reach her bedroom Flavia needed to pass through mine, not so inconvenient as it sounds; Flavia went to bed early, she called it 'retreating into dreams', and she slept as late as she could. 'Sleep is my drug and my inspiration,' she used to say. Entry to our flat from the outside hall was directly into the kitchen that sat, alongside a dank old-fashioned bathroom, where the tender would be on a train. The front room we hardly used at all and Flavia made only a token objection when I told her I had found someone to rent it. A few days after our meeting, Jinx appeared in all her radiance. She was leading a caravan of men laden with cardboard boxes that trailed floating scarves and spilled over with pulp magazines, high-heeled shoes, paper roses, and all the bits and baubles Jinx referred to as her 'worldlies'. While the procession was going by, Flavia leaned against the refrigerator, arms folded, watching with evident disapproval.

'Mark my words,' said she at last, as if one dared not mark the words of a flatmate who had framed over her bed a letter from e. e. cummings to thank her for the very interesting poem which he was returning under separate cover. 'You are making a big mistake, Marsha Leah, and you will regret it.'

Ever since Flavia's analyst happened to mention she looked like Virginia Woolf, she had taken to wearing her hair in a bun low down on her neck. But it was early

15

morning and the bristling of uncombed tresses around her prominent black eyes gave her the weird intensity of a giant ant. She waved ghostly antennae towards Jinx's room. 'You're doing it again. You always do. No good ever comes of it. You and your oddballs. Remember the black girl who talked to Jesus? Remember the triplet who ate us out of house and home?' Looking parsimonious, piffling and puce, Flavia nodded towards Jinx's room. 'You and this girl have no common ground. This will end in tears,' she said.

Through the half-open door I saw Jinx passing back and forth, instructing her troops: a taxi driver, a policeman and an unknown male passer-by she had dragooned into service. The rumble of men's voices, for the first time since we had lived in the place, was like a new dimension.

'No, Flavia Jane,' I said, 'this time it's different.'

Jinx arrived as a woman into an encampment of children. Curtains of white and yellow polka-dot voile appeared at the kitchen window, and a pot-plant on the sill was almost enough to make you dream a garden lay beyond, instead of an airshaft half full of broken bottles and rotting rags. There was honey in the larder, a chenille cover on the toilet; on our kitchen table appeared a plastic sheet printed with roses and lilies of the valley. Every surface within reach was prettified, until only the mildewed ceiling was not covered in something bright or soft. As for our once drab living-room, Jinx turned it into a jungly bower, full of cushions and silk flowers where the temperature was perceptibly warmer than in the other rooms.

'Come in for a little visit, honey,' Jinx used to say, and unless I was studying for an exam, I always did. It was much more fun to listen to Jinx talk about men and sex and love than to sit in the kitchen while Flavia and the other City College poetastresses intoned their blank verse.

'It's like a cathouse in here,' I said admiringly, during one of my first visits to her room.

16

'You're a hoot, Marsha honey. You know you've never seen inside a cathouse in your life.'

She was propped up on her elbow out of a welter of tinsel and overstuffed pillows on the sofa-bed. She wore an orange nylon pullover and cardigan with plum pedal-pushers: it must have been a Thursday, her day off work — she always wore slacks or pedal-pushers around the flat on her day off. To my surprise, not long after Jinx moved in with us, she started taking ballet classes on Thursday evenings. 'There's mainly two kinds of little girls in this world, honey,' she explained, 'and I was never the kind who wanted to be a nurse when I grew up.'

She smiled at me and went back to reading her *True Romance* magazine. Do girls still read that junk, I wonder? Or has pulp romance been overtaken by tv soap operas? The way Jinx used to attack her magazines was more like eating than reading; sometimes she set aside a tit-bit to share with me. 'Listen to this, honey,' she said.

I threw myself into a wickerwork basket-chair she had painted gold and filled with flowery cushions. On the cover of the magazine she held, a man and woman seemed to be trying to look up each other's noses. The words 'taunted', 'slave', 'ravening beast' leapt out in bold type from the cover lines. Jinx's bedside lamp was shaded by an embroidered shawl with a beaded fringe that trembled as she leaned close and turned the pages, looking for the passage she wanted me to hear. ' "Wildfire Passion" ', she said 'that's the name of this story, and it's a good one too.'

I can still remember 'Wildfire Passion'. It was about a small-town girl called Heather and her afternoon of ecstasy with Rex, the neighbour's naughty husband: 'A mere handful of minutes stolen from time's wide orchards . . . .' Out of this single erotic encounter Heather, truly a child of the 1950s, fell from the pinnacle of respectability to end up as a good-time girl in Reno, Nevada. ' "For brief

17

though the blaze had been between Heather and Rex",' Jinx read in a trembling voice, ' "it ignited a searing, soaring con-flag-rassion of wildest wildfire passion . . ." ' Jinx looked up to make sure I'd caught the link back to the title, ' ". . . that left her heart scarred at its passing, throbbing with desire to feel again and again its sweet agony. Because . . ." ' Jinx raised one hand; shadows flickered on the wall, we could have been around a campfire in the lee of a silken tent, ' ". . . because the non-virgin . . ." ', again she looked up to make sure I was paying attention: I was, I was — ' ". . . because the non-virgin is subject to frustrations the virgin never knows." Marsha, honey,' she said, waving the magazine over her head like a banner, 'truer words were never written.'

Homelife was certainly enlivened by having Jinx around. As for my work-life, I could hardly imagine how I'd survived waiting on table before Jinx joined the staff at Schrafft's. From her first day on duty, the job became more than bearable. It was the Saturday after we'd met and New York was sweltering in the last foetid gasp of an unexpected Indian summer. Upstairs, the dining-room was cool, but there was no air-conditioning in the basement changing room, or next door in the kitchen where the massive Jamaican cooks were crashing pots and pans in the first stages of lunatic rage that by afternoon was going to be nearly homicidal. Except for the old waitresses who kept to themselves behind dazed, tragic faces, my co-workers at Schrafft's were all Irish girls with hands the size of dinner-plates; they used to come to the end of the rush hours heaving and sweating like stampeded buffalo. Because I was American-born, and most of them had no status or papers, they treated me with great caution. Also, I have to say, I'd already begun to cultivate the snappish defences of a hopelessly homely woman.

18

In the year since I'd been a part-timer at Schrafft's nobody had addressed a word to me except about work. Even our boss, the 'floor hostess', Miss Kaloczek, as soon as she was sure a runt like me could handle heavy trays, never jollied me along or scolded me as she did the others. And then, suddenly, there was Jinx, my own best friend. She fell in beside me, and we stood side by side in the line-up, while Miss Kaloczek clickety-clacked on her cuban heels, first behind us to check the butterfly bows that tied our aprons, and then down along the front to look at the cuffs of our black uniforms and our fingernails.

Jinx had waited on table in New Orleans, and before that for a few months at home in Lafayette, so she knew the ropes. On our first morning Miss Kaloczek assigned her to be my partner, and from that day on whenever I came on duty, we worked together. She was graceful, quick, generous, efficient; everyone loved her, she never quibbled over tips, or lost her temper. To swing the heavy tray and adjust for the change of balance as it was loaded and unloaded, to remember two dozen orders on the trot, then find them through the mêlée in the kitchen: it was brute work, let me tell you, and until Jinx arrived, I'd been struggling to hold my own. But after only a few hours in tandem with Jinx, the clumsy lump, marshy Marsh, whom nobody had ever chosen for a team, established a rhythm with her gorgeous new partner, and we worked together as smoothly as a pair of champion dancers. The pride I began to take in doing the job well gave me an unfamiliar confidence in myself, and looking back I see that what I learned of my own stamina and stubbornness in that period has been of more use than anything to emerge out of the cerebral cut and thrust of City College. Once again, I have Jinx to thank. And needless to mention, the tips had never been better.

Until Jinx came I'd always sat by myself and read over lunch in the basement staff room. But on the days we worked together, she slipped into the seat beside me as a matter of course. The Irish girls moved over to free a space. Were we not best friends? Conversations at home were mostly in her room, and always centred on down-home stories, usually about love. But at Schrafft's the talking was left to me, and in no time I heard myself telling Jinx things about myself I had never told anyone else. I told her about my aged parents to whom I had arrived as an unplanned, not altogether fortuitous surprise, late in a barren marriage. In my childhood home, the scales were set five pounds under, and clocks ten minutes ahead, the fruit in the bowl was wax, a shelf of books hid bottles, though my parents were practically teetotal; at home, I told her, everything lied but the mirrors.

'Not lies of omission, or lies of malice, you understand. In my home are the lies of disguise. I read somewhere that Indian parents dress their sons as little girls so evil spirits can't be bothered to steal them. That's the kind of lie we have at home. Lies of protective colouring. They're content now to think I will be a schoolteacher, for example. That looks good to them; it fits and gives no reason for concern. And for my part, I guess I'm content to believe a schoolteacher is what I'll have to be.'

'You know,' Jinx said, 'I just love to listen to you talk, Marsha. Don't you have the prettiest speaking voice?'

I had to lower my head and hide the sudden tears.

On Saturday during our break when Oleg, the handsome barman who doubled as a bookie, used to strut through the staff room, the Irish girls dug into their pockets for handfuls of sticky coins, always to back the longshots. For the first three weeks Jinx and I worked together, she did not place a bet. Then, on the fourth Saturday, she put a dollar on a horse called 'Earth Angel'. She said she liked the name. That was when I told her something I had never told a living soul, and had hardly confessed to myself: I was

20

counting pennies, saving everything I could, not for further education, as my parents were happy to believe, but to pay for a trip to Europe after I was graduated from City College.

A dinky sort of secret, you might say, but all my own. And remember, travelling to Europe was a much more serious enterprise in those days before jet planes. Crossing the ocean then could still simulate a rebirth. Deep within myself, too, it was more than a holiday I sometimes dared to envisage. Whatever sly expectations lived on in the reality all too clearly reflected in my mirror, they pointed east; on good days I could almost allow myself to believe that wise men lived in the old capitals, men who saw through an ugly woman's hide to her existential beauty.

'So, I'm saving up to go to Europe and maybe even live there.'

'But why do you want to go there, sugar?' she asked. 'Everybody there has always been dying to come here.'

FOUR

A few weeks after Christmas Jinx signed up for classes in something called 'Deportment', a mixture of posture and etiquette. It would be a mistake to imagine her lessons in ballet and deportment meant she was a bundle of energy. A shadow of indolence rippled around Jinx like a curtain on a south-facing window, and it was part of her attraction. In all the years we knew each other, I never saw her run or be out of breath. Ballet and deportment, what I used to call her classes in 'auto maintenance', were the only sign she ever gave of an ambition beyond waiting on table at Schrafft's. Jinx was not actively pursuing any career at all, only getting herself into tip-top condition for her man, when he came along at last.

'A woman's only half alive until she falls in love,' Jinx said, shimmering in the light of her bedside lamp. 'The real thing always comes along sooner or later. It will come to you too, honey. You'll see.'

My spirit flinched whenever Jinx said that kind of thing to me. Those romantic youngsters who knew that they were destined to die young? Well, listening to Jinx, I'd come to realise that's how it was bound to be with me and love. I've never been self-deluded. How could I not see that if I found a love I wanted, he was bound to be miles above my station? A short walk with my stunning friend along any city street was enough to show what men longed for in their women, and it sure as hell was nothing I had. Even if most of the jerks who tripped over their feet to stare at Jinx were going to have to settle for a lot less

22

than their dream, I was too stubborn and too proud to settle for less than mine. Intimations of unrequited love were in my bones as keen and sharp as the first ticklings of consumption in young poets long, long before the disease declared itself outright. Love was going to have to break my heart to get at me. For Jinx, of course, it was altogether a different matter. She glowed with faith. Faith was what you might call her spiritual microchip, as central to her function as good sense and industry were to mine.

Central to Flavia Jane Garvey was something beginning with 'p'. Prejudice? Flavia was discovering herself through a process of elimination, building up a body of fixed opinions to call herself; and that's a long haul. Flavia Jane would have made a hell of a feminist in the 1970s, but feminism was not yet a gleam in mommy's eye, politics was still a country for old men, and all the best young people of the 1950s wanted to be artists. We are at that point in the decade when psychoanalysis had started leaking into the humanities; psychic complaints, real or fancied, were a 'must' for any girl who dreamed of devoting herself to Art. The greater had been childhood angst, the greater it was believed became creative sensitivity. Most of Flavia's gang were in analysis and achieving preternatural degrees of sensitivity, none higher or more excruciating than Flavia Jane's. It took only the first notes of anything by Berlioz or Brahms to bring the pins out of her chignon so the electrified filaments flew wildly around her shoulders as she fell into a rapture. And she had at last achieved such a dizzy height of aesthetic discrimination she could not eat highly coloured foods, or she'd be violently sick. Her new diet of mashed potatoes, scrambled eggs, pears and vanilla ice-cream had begun to give her skin a fainly iridescent pallor that was the envy of less highly-developed Flavians.

Dear old Flavia Jane Garvey. It became a whole lot easier to smile at the thought of her after we no longer

23

shared a kitchen. She wasn't altogether a prig. She could sing all the words to 'Heartbreak Hotel', and 'Either You Got, Got, Got It . . .'; and she knew baseball batting averages from way back before she was born. I wonder if her analyst ever suggested a girl will develop such a butch skill to appease a daddy who wanted sons? I often saw her in the cafeteria shoulder-to-shoulder with campus brawn, discussing the merits of the Brooklyn line-up. One of her poems, 'elegy for a southpaw out on third' was published in the school magazine and turned up one morning framed on the kitchen wall next to Jinx's calendar of Alpine scenes. To be fair, three is a very awkward number for human beings, and after Jinx arrived, Flavia was the odd one out at home. She took to skulking around the apartment, coming out of her room only to make irritable assaults on the refrigerator for buttermilk and cold rice. Prim though she was, years later I heard somewhere that the second of her three husbands was a jazz musician. The first was her psychoanalyst. Flavia's lovelife was slow getting off the ground, but once away, it headed straight for the baroque.

The wedge that was finally to separate Flavia from our earthier element was hammered in one night in deepest winter when we were all at home together. Five Flavians had turned up to listen to their leader's epic poem in free verse, 'lament for an infant prodigy'. Before Jinx and I realised what was happening she had already started reading in the tone of controlled fury many poets favour for their own works, and it was too late to flee. I had been caught on the hop near the sink. I did not dare look again at Jinx, who was perched on a kitchen stool, her long legs entwined and her green eyes fixed on Flavia with an expression quite like horror.

'Ta-ta-tum, ta-ta-ta-ta-tum-tum,' went Flavia Jane, and then waffle, waffle, waffle, waffle, and if memory, which

24

has discarded infinitely finer stuff, serves: 'taps the toy timpany of tiny tears . . .' Flavia had warned us the work was based loosely on her subconscious recall of passing through the birth canal, but I for one was not ready for the marathon labour it turned out to be. Something, something, something, 'nursery sleep', something, something, 'where dolls and bunnies bite and bleed'; rhubarb, rhubarb, rhubarb. The acolytes were seated around the table with their hands clasped under their chins; their dark hair flowed as they undulated like fish caught in a slight current. From where I stood I watched the pages pass to the lesser pile from the one that appeared to be eternally greater. Would it never end? An age went by before Flavia's voice dropped at last, and those in the know detected a hint of landfall. 'Thrum, thrum, thrum of thor's thunder,' something, something; 'mummy, where are are you? daddy, daddy, daddy who are you? ah, life, the ragpicker's bundle!' At last, all was silent. But Flavia Jane had a sneaky way with long pauses as some had learned to their cost; nobody dared stir until her head fell forward and she sighed deeply, ejected from the other side of genius.

'Why that', said Jinx, loud and clear, 'was just awful . . . .' Quickly, I developed a cough and turned my face to the wall. 'Those poor bunnies,' Jinx said. 'And that little baby all alone in the storm. How come her mama couldn't hear the poor mite crying? That thunder must have been terrible.'

Flavians were forbidden to laugh except bitterly or knowingly, and for a while there was a strained silence in our kitchen. When Flavia Jane finally chose to speak it was in her patrician mode, purple and patronising.

'My analyst tells me', she said to the company at large, 'being born caused me traumatising guilt.'

'Fiddlesticks,' said Jinx. 'Being born is as natural as it can be. Nobody ought to be guilty for a thing (thang) like that.

25

Don't you pay any heed to what that analyst fellow says. He has a dirty mind.'

Flavia closed her eyes and spoke slowly, emphatically: 'He did not say I *was* guilty. He said I *felt* guilty.'

'For a sensitive person,' one of the vestal group volunteered, 'feeling something is every bit as bad as being it.' When Flavia turned the dreaded beam her way, she added hastily: 'It's even worse.'

A week later Flavia generously paid up her rent to the end of the term, and moved out.

'I have one last word for you, Marsha Leah,' she said the morning she left, 'if you choose your company from lowlife, you will never be an artist.'

'When did you ever hear me say I wanted to be an artist, Flavia Jane?'

'Everyone,' she replied, 'wants to be an artist.'

FIVE

It was a Monday when Jinx O'Malley was discovered for posterity. Nobody who has done dirty work for a living ever forgets the feeling of Monday. Week after week, year after year, life after life, most of humanity trudges towards the weekend, which is hardly more than a mirage before the rolling penance begins again, for us at Schrafft's and most other working stiffs, on Monday. It was a Monday, nearly forty years ago, when the beautiful Jinx O'Malley started out on her path to the big time. In the locker-room where we were changing into our uniforms, all of us except the soul-dead lifers were raising a silent prayer that the week we were condemned to begin would quickly achieve the terrible brief glory of its end. Even I, who worked full-time only during long holidays, was dumb with misery, and the Irish girls were quiet too, as they pulled their uniforms on over flesh-coloured hand-knitted vests sent from home. We were in the era when some-where around her sixteenth birthday a girl went from flat shoes and ankle socks straight into a girdle. Not for nothing was the girdle called a foundation garment: to wriggle into one, straining against nature like butterfly reverting to caterpillar, was an exercise that symbolised modesty and restraint. The girdle was truly a cornerstone of womanly estate. Only Jinx, of us all, did not wear a girdle; she said it mashed a woman's innards, but she winked to let me know there was a better, sexier reason. The Irish girls wore fierce girdles constructed out of flesh-coloured rubber and reinforced with what looked

27

like metal rods that made them appear solid under their uniforms, and as unbreachable as Fort Knox.

The colleens all adored Jinx. After we finished for the day, they used to ask her to join them for drinks, and I would trail along. The local bar they preferred was a hangout for off-duty policemen, who must have known the girls were by and large immigrants working illegally. But what the hell? They had bigger fish to fry. As soon as the men laid eyes on Jinx they turned courtly, inclined their big bullish heads, moderated their language, and offered drinks all around to the ladies. The Irish girls had signed the pledge and they drank only ginger ale, but they were obviously very much at home in the half-light of the bar, trading mildly off-colour jokes with the boys.

Oleg, the handsome barman, kept his distance after work. He had made a dead set for Jinx from the first day; there was static between them in the staff room, and clumsy *doubles entendres* about the names of horses, the weights they carried, and so on. Jinx flexed slightly and glowed whenever his dark eyes turned her way. Once, on the subway coming in to work she said to me out of the blue: 'Oleg. Isn't that a cute little name?' Then one of the Irish girls told her he was married with twin daughters, and after that, whenever drinks needed to be picked up at the bar, Jinx sent me or someone else to get them. She never bet on another horse after 'Earth Angel' or ever again said more than two words to the handsome barman. Poor Oleg. When Jinx cut him, he was denied the classic vengeance of seducing her best friend: I was too homely. But he pushed little favours my way; it was he who taught me the use of easeful drink, for example. Sometimes in the early evening he used to slip me a teacup full of dry martini. There was a ledge over the dumb-waiter where we deposited dirty dishes and I kept it up there to nip at during the shift.

We waitresses in our old-fashioned black uniforms put the finishing touch on a decor that was even then beginning to look as quaint as a superannuated ocean liner. Miss Kaloczek's job was to welcome customers aboard and usher them past the red velvet rope that separated the entry from the dining-room, then lead them in stately procession to tables that seated two, four, or six. Once they were seated she presented each of them with a big maroon leather folder. 'Schrafft's' was in gold letters on the cover, and a gilded ribbon marked the 'Chef's Thought for the Day'. Customers were mostly secretaries from nearby offices, and older women in from the suburbs for a day's shopping, bad tippers they were too, and fussy in their feeding habits. They ate their sandwiches with knife and fork. Men in general preferred greasy-spoons or restaurants where the barman knew them by name and waiters served serious food. In the early evening, businessmen drifted in, but just for drinks at small tables near the bar before they caught trains home. If a man turned up at night, it was to give the girlfriend or the better half a bite to eat before a movie. Even Jinx, when her long hair was tucked into the compulsory mob-cap, shared a degree of anonymity with the rest of us; not that it stopped a few besotted, lonely old guys from coming back again and again, to nurse a beer at the bar and hope for a glimpse of her.

There were some men who found our uniforms erotic, perhaps they were turned on by the idea of anonymous females paid to shut up and give a man what he hungered for. Although I was indisputably the plainest of the staff, I too had a brush with the type the girls used to call 'an octopus'. It was the cocktail hour on Friday, always the busiest of the week, and I had just come on duty after a seminar on the eighteenth-century novel. I was leaning across the small table to serve a rye highball to one of a pair of men when suddenly I felt a hand stroke the length of my back from waist to behind the knee. My skin quaked, not just where it was being touched: everywhere. I did not tremble, however, or spill a drop. For a long time afterwards the shimmering sensation of being stroked returned at odd moments, and it began to seem a girl could after all construct some sort of sexual and sentimental life out of such glancing caresses.

Yes, it was indisputably a Monday. The Chef's 'Thought for the Day' was tuna-loaf with tomato sauce, which was always his thought for Monday. I was working full shift, so it must have been during the Easter holidays at the fickle end of spring, late March or early April. The worst of the lunchtime rush was over. Jinx was in the kitchen picking up last orders, and I was clearing our empty tables before we went down to our own late lunch. We waitresses were not allowed food from the upper end of the menu, but Jinx had wangled minute-steaks for us both that day. The cooks were going to hide them under pinkish slabs of tuna-loaf so Miss Kaloczek, who checked our trays before we went down to the basement, wouldn't see them. The black cooks never yelled at Jinx, or kept her waiting for her orders; they favoured her over us all. Their preference for a white Southerner instead of a budding northern liberal like me was puzzling.

'It's the Mississippi, honey,' Jinx explained. 'That old river gives all us Southerners a colour of its own.'

I was hungry and looking forward to the meal ahead while I cleaned the six-seater with a damp cloth, then started setting it up again with paper doilies and cutlery. Suddenly, the door flew open and in they sailed, as if storm-driven: a flotilla of doe-eyed boys and girls, in the midst of them, high-masted and wound around and around in purple silk, wearing a purple turban and long purple gloves, was the woman called Helsinki Braw. Even Oleg, who was gifted with the barman's sang-froid, except where

30

Jinx was concerned, gaped as they swept past his station. Vision was not the only sense Helsinki assaulted, her voice was pushing lesser sounds out of its way. At the starboard corner of the room, where I stood, astonished, I could hear the clashing of bangles on her skinny arms. Without so much as a by-your-leave Helsinki went to work on the velvet rope, unhooked it and left it to dangle in her wake. Miss Kaloczek, paralysed by surprise, could do nothing.

'Isn't it lurvely? Don't you lurve it all? Isn't it too divinely lurvely,' brayed Helsinki Braw. Matrons and secretaries raised their heads in alarm to find themselves included in her transports. 'So perfect, don't you agree?' she crowed. 'Kitchy-coo. Kitchy-kitchy-coo. A flagship of past decades, darlings. It will go down with all hands on board!' The alien contingent was making straight for the table I had cleared. 'See the butter pats with itsy-itsy moo-moos on them? They won't make them like that much longer,' Helsinki said, and shivered our timbers with her laugh. Miss Kaloczek had started dutifully handing out menus; these *were* customers, after all, though of a sort never before encountered at Schrafft's. 'See the napkins?' cried Helsinki. ' "Serviettes" they call them here. Doris Dayland, ain't it? Couldn't you just die? Isn't it swell? True-blue American too. You won't get that dago horse's piss in here!' A pair of blue-rinsed dowagers in town for the day froze, knives and forks upright in their hands. Helsinki fixed me with her vulturine eyes, their flicking lids were painted purple. I noted her strong, long magnificent nose. 'Now, what do you recommend?' she asked. Before I could think of a reply, she cried: 'The tuna-loaf, *sans doute*! Oh yes, darlings. You've all gotta have the tuna-loaf. My spies tell me it's like going back to war-time and coupons. Is it not divinely kitchy-coo in here? Is it not lurvely?'

A note of uncertainty, beseeching almost, had crept into

31

her voice. In spite of her height and noise that dominated the little party, she was not the one in charge. Nor were any of the boys and girls who were looking around dimly, not yet knowing what to think; least of all was the skinny, haggard girl in an embroidered kaftan who suddenly sang throatily into the silence: 'Dance, ballerina, dance ...', and then fell back into abrupt silence. In that instant I saw him, the one to whom all the twittering had been directed; he sat on Helsinki's right at the round table. An eerie stillness was the first thing you noticed about him, the inertia of a stone, and then you saw his pallor, and finally his eyes.

'Do you like it, Tom-Tom? Hasn't your 'Sinki done good?' Anxiously, we all studied the elfin face that was so pale under fine, colourless hair. Everyone waited while his amber eyes roved slowly over our cutlery, our pitchers of iced water, our 'Chef's Thought for the Day', our swags and swoops and potted palms, our Miss Kaloczek; I winced when they brought themselves to bear briefly on me. His nose was small and bulbous, made for a teddy-bear. At last, he spoke in an accent not of a region, but of a state of mind: peevish, capricious, selfish, and very smart. His lips barely moved at all, his long-drawn vowel sounds were broken by soft hiccoughs. 'You always doo-hoo good, Sinkikins,' he said. 'You are all things wu-hunderful to me. And I think this place is really cute.'

I sprang into life, filled glasses with water, laid out extra plates, and signalled Jinx, who was just emerging from the kitchen, to bring on the bread rolls. By that time I had achieved the skills of a long-time waitress, and could pretty much predict on sight not only what customers were going to order, but how much tip they would leave. Waitresses all possess something of the gambler's fitful optimism and dollar bills came along often enough to keep hope thriving. The weirdos at our table were out of Schrafft's league; there was a hope they might tip according to some standard beyond my experience, and I wanted to give them good service. Briskly, I took the orders and Jinx came along behind me to collect the menus. Tuna-loaf for the lot of them, except for the man called Tom-Tom. 'Hot chocolate in a pot,' he said. 'And bru-hing me oyster crackers. Lots and lots of oyster crackers. They're such cute little things.' In the history of Schrafft's nobody had ever before asked for oyster crackers as a main dish. They're those octagonal salty nibbles you don't see around much these days; we used to serve them six at a time in cellophane packets, but only as side-orders to clam chowder. While I dished out the tuna-loaves, Jinx worked on the head cook to fill a bowl with packets of oyster crackers and call it a legitimate main course.

Three or four years later in 1960 or '61, *Time* magazine ran a cover story on 'the Most Beautiful Woman in the World', and in it 'Helsinki Braw (thirty-two) rag trade whiz-kid and fashion pundit' was quoted as saying she had come into a restaurant for a quick bite one day and immediately recognised, 'cheekbones to die for . . .'; whereupon, she said, she invited her waitress to pull up a chair and sit down. 'I'm Helsinki Braw,' she's supposed to have told Jinx, 'and your waiting days are over.' Good old Helsinki, she had to toot her own horn; nobody else would go near it with a ten-foot pole. In fact, I saw it happen, and it did not happen that way.

The pale man, Tom-Tom, barely said a word; the young men in his party, who all wore black jackets and jeans like his, imitated his creepy detachment as best they could, and tried to make themselves absent behind blank eyes. Once, the skinny girl blasted out a few lines of 'Beware my Foolish Heart', but she soon went back silently to pushing pieces of tuna-loaf around her plate. Tom-Tom meanwhile had opened the packets of oyster crackers and emptied them on to his dinner-plate. One by one, he was taking

33

each little cracker and turning it in the tips of his white spatulate fingers to study it intently before he added it to a growing pile on his side-plate. Jinx approached, she carried a frosted water-pitcher; light slanting through a window behind made her seem to be stepping into our world from a glowing, silvery place. Tom-Tom stopped what he was doing. He sniffed. He raised his head. In that moment which was both supernal and deeply mischievous, the avant-garde painter, film-maker and jack-of-all-arts, Tomas Blalack, found himself face to face with the most beautiful woman in the world. His eyes glittered like pieces of beer bottles on a beach. And he discovered her.

For the time being, it was enough that he had seen her, and nothing else happened. The odd group ate little, and in due course they sailed away, leaving turbulence behind and not much else, the cheapskates. When Jinx and I cleared the table, we found two quarters and a Canadian nickel shoved under Helsinki's side-plate.

SIX

Life went on in the usual way during the weeks that followed our encounter with Tomas Blalack. I worked and read, and wrote papers, and went to classes. I slept little and increasingly let my dreams off the lead to fly ahead to Europe and escape. Jinx waited on table many more hours than I, she went on reading her magazines, she surrounded the bathroom pipes with plastic ivy, she danced and deported herself; and she made ready for love. Although she'd abandoned literature without a backward glance, she loved movies, and whenever I could, I used to go with her. We both liked musicals, but I'd choose an arty French film or a tough-guy thriller, even an oater, over the melodramas Jinx liked best of all. While true love was floundering on the screen, she wept softly, and when it all ended in a dry and soulful clinch the way ninety-nine out of a hundred films used to do in those days, she'd sigh: 'Oh yes!' As easily as Jinx wept at the movies, she never cried, not with racking sobs that leave an ache in precisely the same places as wild laughter. She never laughed either, wholeheartedly I mean, in the snorting way that leaves the face unguarded and drives into it momentarily the furrows of old age. Very beautiful women do not laugh like that. Nor did Jinx wail and gibber over trifles as Flavia and I used to do. Hormonal panic of virgins in their prime was a widespread condition of the 1950s. But whatever frustrations the non-virgin was subject to that we virgins could not know, Jinx kept them under her hat. Dignity is a by-product of beauty; beauty like hers is a solemn responsibility.

35

The spring passed quickly that year. Jinx loved spring most of all the seasons, and used to fill our vases with early flowers that reek of a girl's first perfume. Later in her life when she went to southern California for the first time, she took to it from the start because of its climate. The extended springtime of the west coast which I find boneless and thick, is just the ticket for sensualists who revel in constant arousal without satiation or satisfaction; further-more, as sexpots age, the perpetual vernal body-heat gives them the illusion of being eternally young and juicy. Summer roared in early the year Jinx was discovered, with all guns blazing. Plain young women do not like summer, it's a season for those who can take pleasure in disrobing. For realists like me, autumn is better. And best of all is the great democratic northern winter, when everyone stoops and huddles against the wind, and goes out bundled up in a semblance of equality.

It was a hot morning in early summer when the letter arrived from Tomas Blalack. I found the square heavy in the mailbox on my way out to classes, and I was surprised to see that it was addressed by hand to Jinx O'Malley. She never received personal letters, neither of us did. Most people don't. The modern post is increasingly devoted to advertising and soliciting. Month after month went by when Jinx and I received no mail at all. No doubt it was Helsinki Braw who found our address for Blalack. She must have called in a favour, perhaps from someone high up at Schrafft's. Favours owed Helsinki were at the top of a feeding chain in New York where she was known as 'the barracuda'. In fact, the barracuda is a striker, and Helsinki was a swooper. Ten per cent here, fifteen per cent there, and then she'd swoop down to peck a bit somewhere else, always leaving her victims alive in case she wanted to come back again. Designers paid Helsinki to persuade beautiful people to wear their clothes in the right places; restaurateurs paid Helsinki to nudge the beautiful people their way; beautiful people paid her to get their pictures in the papers, sometimes they paid her even more to keep them out. Photographers paid Helsinki to introduce them to fashion editors, models paid to meet photographers, and they all paid her a percentage of their fees. Blalack alone never paid Helsinki a red cent. But he did her the enormous courtesy of allowing it to be put about she had influence in his court, and that was worth more than money could buy. Beyond mutual convenience, however, Blalack and Braw were bound by a shared taste for mischief on a lordly scale.

Tomas Blalack. It was he who cast aside the tortuous sensibilities of the past to establish fine art once and for all as a hedge against inflation. Just before the end of the 1950s he finished his most celebrated paintings called 'American Crackers'. The huge, bold canvases of that famous series stood the art world on its head, and kicked it in a brave new direction. He was the first creative artist to recognise the Oreo cookie as an American icon, and the gigantic image he painted of it is right now hanging at the headquarters of a computer empire in Japan. 'Graham Cracker' has pride of place at MoMA in New York, it's the first thing visitors see when they enter, the last when they leave. 'Animal Cracker II' and 'Saltine III' are at the museum in Los Angeles, only a few blocks away from this very hotel. 'Oyster Cracker I' hangs in the Musée d'Orsay in Paris, and 'Oyster Cracker II', twice the size of that one, takes up an entire wall at the Tate. Where I live in London is near enough so I walk over from time to time and look at at it — only for reasons of nostalgia, I hasten to add. To be honest, Blalack's work is too smart and spartan for my taste: it reminds me of the wrapping paper yuppies of the 1980s used to like under their silver Christmas trees. Blalack was no conman, believe me: he was a con-artist. Every painting he made, every film, every pronouncement, has been catalogued and reverenced. I wonder if Jinx held on to that first invitation from him? The handwriting was spindly and quick, in brown ink the colour of dried blood. 'Do come!!!' Blalack had written in his own hand. And: 'Bring a friend.' He signed it, 'Tom-Tom Blalack'. Even his hentracks now sell for a lot of money. But of course, not in a million years would it enter the sunny mind of Jinx O'Malley to save anything for a rainy day. There exists, or used to exist, a painting he called privately his 'Oyster Cracker III'. It was much smaller than his other works, barely three feet square, and unsigned. For the only time in his professional career he painted in oils, not acrylics, and he used a human subject straight from life. 'Life's too messy,' he told an interviewer who asked him why he preferred working from photographs or using inanimate objects. 'It jiggles,' he said. Anyone who did not know 'Oyster Cracker III' was a Blalack would never guess. I know, because I was there. And Jinx knows, of course, because he gave it to her, and it's her portrait. Blalack caught her at the moment when her beauty was absolutely true, pure, and as full of joyous promise as an unaccompanied trill of birdsong at sunrise. It was a wonderful thing. But Jinx never liked it. And in the end, she left it behind as she did so many other rare and beautiful things.

What to wear to Blalack's party was no problem for me. As the 'friend' in Blalack's 'bring a friend' I intended to wear my customary dark skirt and white blouse. Forty years on, I look down and see what I wore that night was precisely what I'm wearing now, except this skirt is cashmere and my blouse is silk. We uglies have our order too, and our habit, and our responsibility. Dressing Jinx presented a problem, however.

'Pink', I told her, 'is an immature and irresolute colour with no role to play in the life of an adult.'

'Oh Marsha, honey, where do your funny ideas come from?' she said, but she threw the offending dress to one side.

'You must have been taken to a roadshow "Carmen" when you were a kid,' I said, as we searched through her things that were thrown in a dazzling heap on the bed. 'I cannot imagine where else a sense of style like yours got its start.'

'Why, thank you honey,' said Jinx, who knew Carmen was a gypsy, and she died for love.

Finally I persuaded her to wear a navy blue sheath, the only plain dress she possessed, and not to tack a big pink silk rose on the hip.

'Trust me, Jinx,' I told her. And she did. I was trustworthy. I have always been trustworthy, as far as those who trust me are concerned.

Earlier in the century Blalack's building on lower Eighth Avenue had been a fire station, those in the know called it 'The Hook and Ladder', or sometimes just, 'The Hook'. Gossip columnists cherished Blalack and watched his every move in a steady rise to fame orchestrated by Helsinki Braw; I knew from items I'd come across in the newspapers, that he lived and worked in The Hook, and it was there he made all but a few of his 'Home Movies'.

Long before I had encountered Jinx or Blalack, Flavia Jane dragged me to a basement room near City College where one of his experimental films was being shown. 'Washing', it was called. It was a grainy, agonisingly slow exposition of a young man's chronic acne. Flavia called it a breakthrough. 'Dermatologically?' I asked. Probably.

Very few New Yorkers had actually seen one of Blalack's 'Home Movies' at the time Jinx and I attended our first party at The Hook, and none of his paintings was hanging in public galleries, nevertheless, the man in the street held an opinion on everything Tom-Tom did thanks to Helsinki's crafty manoeuvring of the press, and the foremost of Blalack's People were known too, by name and reputation.

Jinx's debut was a long time ago, many parties were to follow, and more often than not I went along with her; my memory of her first night is therefore probably a composite. I am not generalising from one party. But memory is a tight packer. Trust me. All I saw of Blalack later blended with what I observed the first time, and reinforced it. Blalack himself, for instance, was always in black and always chaste; I saw many, many times the way he cast his benediction on others who were gaudy and promiscuous, and how, as often, he denied it. Tom-Tom was slow-moving, so deeply in fear of his life he would not cross a street when he came to it, but used to stand on the corner until, with his own eyes, he had seen the light change in his favour. His followers, however, skated very close to the edge. Skinny girls tapdanced for him on ledges twelve stories up, and in the back rooms of his establishment young men grew old fast on drugs he provided, though he was never seen to take any of them himself. One otherwise unremarkable young man was driven to try his hand at DIY trepanning, another flaunted an affair with his blood sister. These were Blalack's People, and they would do whatever they could to catch his attention for a while.

SEVEN

The Hook was not dimly lit, as I had expected it to be. Yards of fluorescent tubing blazed overhead; there was no escaping the harsh light or fooling it. Jinx and I walked out of the late summery dusk into a blue-white noon, where hundreds of people, or so it seemed to me, were sweating in the glare. They stood in pairs and small groups, and glanced constantly over each others' shoulders to see who else was there. Jinx entered the immense room ahead of me and immediately there was a ripple of interest – perhaps, more accurately I should call it a lapse of self-interest – as both men and women idled momentarily in their mono-logues, and turned to look at her. She was slender and graceful, her hair was swept up into a gleaming halo, and her beauty outmanoeuvred the neon, by showing nothing but the truth: the cruel light flattered her. Her air of serenity, which is right next to kindness on the emotional spectrum, made a cool space around her. It was the en-trance not of a queen, believe me, but of an angel. And I, her earthbound attendant, rode bustling and proud in her wake.

Tom-Tom would not allow music at his parties. My guess is he foresaw enviously the days ahead when pop stars were going to be able to achieve explosive fame by using technology we in the 1950s were only starting to imagine. Back then, it was still hard to be famous in more than one place at a time, and the slow process of word of mouth on which Blalack mostly had to rely must have galled him. An unadulterated roar of many New York conversations was impenetrable, except when Blalack himself had something to say; then, bubbles of pure silence containing his words were passed from group to group along the length and breadth of the room, some of them smuggled out into print afterwards by reporters selected by Helsinki. 'What did he say? What did Tom-Tom say?' The question was being asked all around us as Jinx and I started to make our way through the crowd. A wild-eyed girl with hair cropped close to her scalp, grabbed Jinx's arm. 'Do you know what Blalack said? What'd he just say? Oh, somebody, what did Tom-Tom say?' A tall man near us had caught the message, he sent it back: 'Tom-Tom says "Silence is glamour".' he called over our heads. 'Tom-Tom said "Glamour is silent",' cried the girl. 'Isn't that the end? Isn't that too much? What did he say now? He said something. What did Tom-Tom say?' The tall man listened for a moment: 'Tom-Tom said "the cheese dip is real good".'

Not a picture hung on the raw brick walls of the big ground floor, only a few big canvases leaned against them, blank sides out. Opposite the entrance was a big spiral staircase, on each step sat a boy, or a girl, nodding over a glass of wine. Jinx and I threaded past this androgynous kindergarten to a small landing with a wrought-iron rail. There, we found a slight breeze and we could look out across the room. Blalack himself was at the far end from us near the brass pole firemen used to use as a way down from the rooms above. Behind him was a rank of fans, the cool air variety, and around him for a depth of three feet or so was a circle of empty space. A dozen of Blalack's People were ranged roughly around this dry moat, and occasionally they escorted over it a guest Blalack requested to see. The concentration of celebrities increased with proximity to Tom-Tom: beside him stood a world-famed American playwright, on his other side a familiar Hollywood actor – thought it might be Rock Hudson. Since that time I have

42

learned there ain't much in life as fruitless as close encounters with famous actors and actresses. Celebrity dazzle on the whole fades the closer you stand to it. My tiger-wife and strong right arm, my secretary – ' "Personal Assistant", Ms F, if you please' – my nearly friend and not-quite confidante, my clever, plain, ambitious Glynis, back in London at the headquarters of Miracle Products, whenever I mention movie stars I've seen up close always asks what they were really, really like? 'Shorter than you think, Glynis,' I reply, and nine times out of ten, that's a fact. Also, their heads are disproportionately large for their bodies, though whether the swelling occurs before or after fame, I do not know for sure. However, I was young once too, I must confess, and all that time ago I was absurdly thrilled to find myself in such a starry crowd.

Helsinki Braw was the only one of Blalack's inner circle not dressed in black as he was. In those days she was very skinny, and in her costume of gold lamé topped off with a turban in the same fabric, she looked as if she were streaming out of a brass lamp after five thousand years of internment. Across an eighth of a mile of seething humanity, wouldn't you know her darting eye found Jinx? She peered and stiffened. Then she snapped an order at a boy in black and I watched him bob through the crowd, coming our way, clicking his fingers to a beat all his own. 'Tom-Tom wants to see you,' he shouted up the stairs in dentalised Brooklynese. And then with us in tow he made his way back through the crowd that parted to let us pass, then closed behind us, whispering.

We stood in the presence. He stretched his mouth, said a hardly audible 'Hi', then moved his gaze away from Jinx and looked full at me. In a split second I was sized up as impartially as by a lens, and dropped so brutally I actually reeled back a step. My heart was weighed down by a sudden foreboding as I watched Tom-Tom hand Jinx over

43

to Helsinki in a way that was neither dismissive nor uncivil, but grand, condescending, affable as an emir might assign a recruit for instruction to his trusted eunuch. Helsinki Braw had the wily, byzantine proclivities of a castrated male. Her libido was a jangly thing for sure, but she watched Blalack with lovesick eyes, and when she spoke to him, it was not as I was ever going to hear her speak to other men: with them, she was either arch or butch – with him, she was daddy's creature and longing to please. When I made to follow her and Jinx, she looked down her beaky nose at me and shook her head so hard the dangling earrings bounced and tinkled. I could only stand and watch as she pulled Jinx into an office or private room of some kind off to one side, it was too far and there was too much noise for me to hear the door slam, but I saw it quiver in its frame from the impact. For an instant, I stood quivering too, the door slamming again and again in my mind.

The waiters were unemployed actors milking the room, in no hurry to serve a big-nosed nonentity the size of a shrimp. They passed me without a glance; I hadn't enough nerve to stop them and refill my glass. Gradually, I felt myself being pushed towards the edge of the party, which spat me out eventually in a far corner. The neglect of waiters and the indifference of fashionable gatherings are among the things that help make plain women turn ugly within. But on the plus side, in that entire company I alone was not concerned with the impression I was making. I decided consciously to take the view that all the flashy show-offs were performing just for me. And for Blalack, of course. Being, as I was, invisible to him, meant I could study him too with impertinence and impunity, and so even Blalack, though he did not know it, was performing just for me. The pleasures of a snoop must seem measly to principals in the action, but when you're a homely little body in a handsome crowd, you grab whatever you can to prevent yourself from going under. Prophetic inklings of a promising future as a spy stirred in me, I snuggled back half hidden by a rack of summery street-smart wraps and scarves.

Tomas Blalack was vanity beyond reckoning; he was a black hole of vanity. I watched, and saw how others were sucked to him and held by a tug he exerted on every atom of vanity they contained. The famous playwright glowed when Blalack breathed his way, and faded when he turned his back. The good-looking actor was there only for him. Otherwise he was lost in the crowd. Celebrated and beautiful people came forward to flutter around Blalack's head, delivering the juiciest of their conceits, before he brushed them away to darker areas of the room. Everywhere in his vicinity women squealed, and men tried to look blasé. Off to one side was the emaciated girl who had been with Blalack's People at Schrafft's. She was dancing alone in little circles. Every few minutes she sang into the air. I don't know whether her memory was blasted or her breath control wasn't up to much, but after a phrase or two she ran down and had to stop, sometimes with a little sob. I heard the others call her Velvet. They treated her with deference, and later I learned that the songs she warbled had mostly been made famous by her mother, a long-ago star in musical comedies and movies. Blalack smiled her way just often enough to keep her spinning.

Famous people or their children, rich people, and most of all, beautiful people, had what Blalack thirsted for; he took them in and drained the *amour propre* right out of them. As soon as he'd had enough, and there was no more, he cast the husks away to do the best they could without him: not very well at all, as history shows. A few years after Jinx's first party at The Hook, Velvet committed suicide. The famous playwright wrote a couple of duds and drank himself to death. The Hollywood actor dwindled into death slowly, horribly, in public. Most of the boys and girls in black whirled away like empty paper bags into a windy space. Helsinki Braw endured, of course, but dollars to doughnuts she never touched love again. Don't imagine Tomas Blalack was cruel. There was no more cruelty in him than there was mercy. He was not inhuman; he was a-human. Something took place at that first party to demonstrate his power, and show how very little energy he needed to exert for destruction.

It began as a commotion way back in the room, that drew closer until into the empty space ever around Blalack fell, or flew, one of the most celebrated of his People: Trans Sylvia. Yes, it was Trans Sylvia, in person; who else could it have been sparkling in rhinestones and swirling chiffon? Not many people had actually seen the Home Movie called *Blue Nineties* in which Blalack had starred Trans Sylvia, but everyone who read a daily paper held an opinion about it, and most people thought it was shocking. Granted, we were in a decade awfully easy to shock. Ordinary men could conceivably reach ripe old age back then without having seen a woman naked, not even those they were married to, and women still went to their graves never having seen a man unclothed: not that there's very much to see. The point is, in the 1950s if you had a television set, you kept it in the living-room for family viewing and most of what we watched were radio programmes with pictures. When Trans Sylvia began the notorious dance that had set conventional tongues wagging it was as alien to us then as a transistor radio would have been, or a halogen lamp. Before us was a revelation of what the future held. Trans Sylvia was dancing in time, and the disturbing tension building up in us could be exploited only by generations as yet unborn. Even Velvet shut up when Trans Sylvia started the sinuous twisting without music. I guess it was a party turn that qualified as a strip-tease; it was a dilly. The body was hairless and not commonly naked, but dressed in silvery skin, from which there rose the smell of ozone.

Perhaps I was intoxicated by the glamour and it made me fanciful, but I would have sworn a prayer of contrition was being offered silently when I saw Trans Sylvia's plum-coloured mouth moving between sheets of shoulder-length platinum hair. It was no surprise when I heard it whispered later that Tom-Tom had been displeased with his favourite who had dared to give an independent inter-view to the press about *Blue Nineties*. I think even now, at the flesh-weary end of the millennium, an audience woud be stunned by the intensity of Trans Sylvia's performance and by the dancer's unequivocal need for love and forgive-ness. Hip-bones gleamed as nobody's used to do in the well padded 1950s; between them was a glittering cache-sexe which was quite redundant: never had a body been as possessed of receptive female sexuality as Trans Sylvia's, though it was not in any familiar sense, feminine. Soon, I thought, the very skeleton under that strange pale flesh was going to take the air and then if Tom-Tom said the word, Trans Sylvia's bones would clatter, abject, at his feet. The audience swelled with the great intake of breath that precedes applause. Trans Sylvia stood, arms raised, spangled and beseeching. Our hands were meeting. And at precisely that instant, Blalack turned away. His tinny, petulant voice rang out: 'Where's some more that chee-heese dip? That cheese dip is ree-heel good.'

We laughed. 'What did Tom-Tom say? What did Blalack say?' The last thing I saw before the crowd closed in was Trans Sylvia, scrambling for tatters of chiffon cast aside during the dance. That was all there was to it. Next day it was in the papers that Blalack's recent favourite had fallen irrevocably from grace.

By about nine o'clock I heard the names of fashionable

restaurants being called from group to group, and most of the guests drifted away to the next place on their list. Tom-Tom preferred to stay at home that night, which meant his People had to stay around with him. Only during the three or four hours between six and ten in the morning when Tomas Blalack slept, was he on his own. Otherwise, members of his inner circle were always in sight of him, stoking themselves on the booze and amphetamines he supplied. Jinx told me she thought Blalack needed company around the clock because he was bored on his own and relied on others for entertainment. In my opinion, however, the reason he was unable to sit in a taxi alone, or go unattended to his bank, his doctor, his barber, was not so clear-cut, not so sane. Blalack required constant living witness to his corporeal being because without it, without his People to fence him in, the man could actually have ceased to be. He demanded his People keep an eye on him because unless they did he was in terror of disappearing in a monstrous explosion of ego. It hardly needs saying that anyone chosen to attest to the existence of a Tomas Blalack could not be just *anyone*. When the guests had finally gone, a dozen black-clad people collected around him in the big room: his inner circle of beauties and madmen. For the first time, Trans Sylvia was not among them. But Blalack intended to make up for the loss of Trans Sylvia by recruiting Jinx O'Malley, the most beautiful woman he'd ever seen.

Tom-Tom hoisted himself up to sit on the edge of a trestle-table that had been laid with refreshments and carried the debris of a luxurious spread. Jinx had reappeared with Helsinki right after Trans Sylvia's performance and he invited her to pull up one of the striped canvas deck-chairs he used instead of sofas or easy chairs. I stood off to one side where Blalack couldn't see me, and Jinx leaned back practically under his neat little patent leather shoes that gleamed like the hooves of a circus pony.

48

'Luh–huv that name. Jinx. I'm going to paint your picture, guh–horgeous Jinx.'

Eyes narrowed all around and there was a nervous shifting in the ranks of Blalack's People. But if Tom-Tom hoped to entrap her by way of her vanity, he was in for a surprise. Jinx was as unselfconscious as a rose, and as oblivious to the envy coming her way. She wore a tender smile I knew and recognised; it meant her mind had flown away, probably to the land of dark handsome lovers. Her beauty was alone and fending for itself. Delight and allegiance rose up in my heart to see how impervious she was to Blalack's flattery.

Jinx and I stayed up drinking coffee in our kitchen after the party. With surprising calm she told me Blalack wanted her to become a fashion model, and Helsinki to be her agent.

'Should I do it?' she asked me.

'Why, of course you should, Jinx. How can you ask? It's a dream come true.'

I ought to have given the matter more sober thought. Leaving The Hook, on our way to the subway, we had passed a gaunt figure, pacing back and forth on the pavement. The sight of Trans Sylvia, wild on a short tether, making anguished sounds, should have been enough to make any wise person think twice about the risks of Blalack's favour.

EIGHT

'A beautiful woman is born with a scar,' said Pfefferling to the young men. He saw them wondering. Were they supposed to laugh? Hell, they were only boys. Pfefferling was wrong to expect them to share his old-as-the-hills state of mind, or why would they be there in his lecture hall, ranked and graded and boxed like unhatched eggs, waiting for him to show them something new? So he told them: 'Beauty is a scar. It draws every eye. People don't want to stare, but they must. When a woman is young and beautiful', and Pfefferling felt his heart fly out through his mouth when he said: 'the walls have eyes . . . .'

In Light of Venus by Jacob Orben, page 132: the hero is delivering a lecture in art history at Yale while simultaneously being tormented by the disintegration of his marriage. His wife has just left him, not for another man, not in Jake's book, you can bet on that. Jake's fictional dreamboat leaves her fictional genius for existential causes, something about completion: his brilliance completes her beauty, meaning death, or something like that. In other words, his fictional wife runs out on her husband for reasons which, to be honest, would have been quite incomprehensible to the real McCoy. It was Jake's twelfth novel, patently autobiographical, and his only fake. It wasn't just that Jake overrated his wife's intellectual aspirations, which were actually nil, it was also that he underestimated her natural simplicity, and her enviable gift for living in the here and now. 'Words, words, words!' Jinx cried a few months after she and Jake were married, 'and most of them are Greek to me!' The simple truth is Jacob Orben bored his Mrs half to death. But he never bored me. More's the pity.

'Beauty is never alone, Marsha. Remember the one who "vanted to be alone"? Impossible. Any shining surface gives beauty urgent and distracting company. Even asleep in the dark, some idiot will light the lamp to have a look. The trouble is, Marsha, everyone requires some time as a snail. It's during snail-time, when we're creeping along alone, we build our resilience and our wisdom. Human beings grow only when nobody is watching. There is no other way. See what I'm leading to? A woman as beautiful as she, as Jinx, never alone, must always be unfinished. Incomplete.'

We were here in Los Angeles. Not a mile from this very hotel, this absurd palace that's painted all over pink as a mouse's ear. Whenever I must visit LA I stay here; in its pink way it is authentic. In what other city but this one could a roseate fantasy fort be taken as a serious address? Not that Los Angeles is a real city. It's a chunk of climate on a short lease, and its fame is based on shadow-plays they refer to here as 'The Industry', as if ephemera were not the name of the game. Jake and I were here in LA, it must have been twenty or twenty-five years ago, where their marriage had begun, and where it was rapidly ending. We were waiting for Jinx in the commissary of a big studio where she had a part in some dimwit spy thriller. He had finished the first draft of *In Light of Venus*, and in a few hours he was taking the manuscript back to Boston to have it transcribed by his faithful secretary. What was her name? 'My girl back east' Jake used to call her, wherever on the

51

planet he happened to be. I had booked myself back with him on the same flight; then I was travelling straight on to London.

Jinx was late again. Time was a bottomless element as far as she was concerned, hours and minutes were less than spray on its surface. 'Anything worth doing now will be worth doing later,' she used to say. Only by the greatest effort did Jinx turn up on time for work. It was no surprise she would let an estranged husband cool his heels. And I knew what was keeping her. Under me was ice so thin I heard it crackle, and a voice within cried: '*Sauve qui peut!*' Had I been unbalanced and able to delude myself there was the slimmest chance for me with Jake, I cannot even now swear that I wouldn't have told him the truth: his beautiful wife, my best friend, Jinx, was at that very moment can-oodling in a trailer on the back-lot with a third-rate English rock musician called Ziggles. But I hadn't a prayer. There was no light blinding enough to make Jacob Orben see past the nose on my face and no treachery or betrayal of a friend was going to bring him into this Leah's bed.

'Some day they'll dig up this dump,' Jake said, referring to the studio, or perhaps to the whole of Los Angeles, 'and they'll find the shards of all America's lost dreams.'

He tipped his chair back and smiled over my head. Jake was gap-toothed, like the Wife of Bath. Chaucer took it for a sign of lechery in her, but it was from my side the tongue-tip space between Jake's upper teeth looked ticklish and exciting.

'Oh what the blazes,' Jake said, following a thought he had not spoken. He brought himself forward and put his elbows on the table. 'I wish I'd found her back then and not that monster, Blalack. She's been hanging around tinselvania too long; no fault of her own. How long does it take a beautiful girl to start knowing herself only through the desire she inspires in men? Her unmitigated beauty. It

52

actually hurts to see beauty like hers. Why is beauty in a woman so hearbreaking?'

The question was rhetorical, of course. Jake was an intellectual, and they only ever ask rhetorical questions. Otherwise, I could have told him why beauty in a woman caused so much pain. Because without it, you big-brained booby, a poor girl could as well be dead as far as you are concerned. Isn't it amazing how intellectual men recognise no emotion but the one they are feeling? It's a good thing they don't feel very often, or no thinking would be done at all.

Jake turned to look through the window beside our table at the palm trees that grow in these parts like giant swizzle sticks. As soon as he was preoccupied, I dared to look at him boldly. His eyes were narrow and deep and set identically in his head; all that remained of my fond hopes had long before sunk without trace in their criminal symmetry. Mixed with the blues and greens of his eyes were tingling drops of irony, yet even so he was not able to see that while his gorgeous wife was elsewhere occupied, ugly muggins here would happily have died for him. They were calling it a 'trial separation', but everyone knew it was the end and divorce was already in the works.

'She was a deprived child,' he said. 'That's why she doesn't believe she deserves what she desires most. That's why she's doomed to push her salvation away.'

Not at that moment, o Jacob of my long and anxious nights; your wife wasn't pushing away her heart's desire at that moment: she was making a trailer shake with it.

'Slam a lid on that, Marsh,' I told myself. 'Or your goose is cooked.'

More than their marriage had failed. A year earlier, Jake had written a film for Jinx, and that had bombed, too. *Reflected Glory* it was called. I've heard it has acquired a cult following, but it was too wordy and cerebral for the time.

53

Jake blamed studio politics when it sank without trace. The truth is, however, Jinx was a terrible actress. Way back at the start of her career, Helsinki made her enrol for drama classes, but no power on earth could make Jinx take acting seriously. As soon as she opened her mouth what came through loud and clear was amazement that she, of all people, was pretending to be somebody else. It was hard luck the peak of her beauty coincided with a period in Hollywood when a modicum of talent was required to make it big. By the time the mid-seventies rolled around, when once again all a girl needed was good looks for stardom, Jinx was fortyish, still beautiful, to be sure, but past it as far as the studios were concerned. The camera loved her, and she would have been a smash in silent movies; but in the end, all she ever played were long-legged walk-on roles. Spy-master films were her professional salvation. Jake's witty, subtle script required her to portray a woman past her middle thirties which she actually was at that time, and the fact is, whatever creative energy a beauty over thirty possesses, in Hollywood she needs to use it for coming across as younger.

At last Jinx came into sight walking not very fast down the path towards the commissary. When Jake saw her, he shook his head ruefully.

'Damn it. All that sensual stuff churning around again. I should have known at my age the risk was incalculable.'

'What risk do you mean, Jake?'

'The risk of failure,' he replied. 'An ageing man who marries a beautiful younger woman and fails is a shlemiel. I did not hope to go out on such a note.'

But during the summer of Jinx's debut at The Hook it was nearly twenty years and another husband to go before she even so much as heard of Jacob Orben; remember, she was not a reader of books. She left Schrafft's, of course, and after the summer break so did I, to concentrate on my final thesis and nurse my nest-egg cautiously. In the early autumn Jinx's face started appearing on magazine covers, but her style of living hardly changed at all.

'Down home there was this girl who married a rich boy from N'Awlins, and she went to live in a big house, and everything. And three months after the wedding, didn't her husband up and run off . . . with a *man*,' Jinx said. 'Which just goes to show that nothing lasts, Marsha.'

We were at our kitchen table drinking coffee the way we always used to do even before her career had begun its rapid trajectory. 'You are perfectly beautiful, Jinx O'Malley,' I said. 'Your face is made for the camera and you are made to be admired.'

'No,' she said, and she sounded low, 'I'm made for love.'

'Don't you be disgusting!' I cried. I wanted to make her laugh. 'Don't you dare say a thing like that. Don't even think it. Women who are made for love are prone to alcoholism, masochism, and all sorts of sordid afflictions. A woman who's made for love has no future; she exists only to acquire a past.'

'Oh Marsha, honey, the way you do go on!' Jinx said in the tender way that never failed to make me weepy. 'As if it wasn't you putting those French songs on the phonograph all the time.'

'Piaf moves me, okay. Fair enough. Eleanor Roosevelt did too. Madame Butterfly. Leah from the Bible. And Cinderella's unhappy step-sisters. Those poor sad girls were all truly made for love. But not you, Jinx,' I said, 'you're made for something better.'

'Marsh, you better watch your mouth, honey. Bad things happen to girls who laugh at love. You'll see some day where it gets you, high-hatting love. Now me, I love love. And when I meet that man of mine, I'm going to love him to pieces.'

'Again?'

'Making mistakes is half the fun, honey.' She frowned, 'I wish he'd let me walk around and circulate.' She was talking about Blalack, of course. 'I don't know what he wants from me,' she said. Sexually, Blalack was not even dormant; he was simply absent. 'He gives me the whim-whams. I've seen some cute guys hanging around The Hook. But he never lets me loose to get near anyone.'

I remember that conversation because there was a party at The Hook that very night, there was always a party at The Hook and I used to tag along whenever Jinx felt she needed a friend in the crowd. Sure enough, the instant we walked in Tom-Tom called out 'Ji-hinx!' and waved her forward. She shrugged, as if to tell me, 'You see?', but obediently she did as Blalack ordered.

Now memory takes on the clarity of film. I see Jinx perfectly, she is in pink I'm sorry to tell you, but she is aglow and ravishing. Everyone in the room turns to watch her. Tom-Tom's watching her too with his evil, ochreous eyes. He looks dangerously close to being pleased with himself. Fortunately for him, along with other human failings, complacency was missing from his nature; had Tom-Tom once been pleased with himself, he would on the spot have been translated into a single dense atom of purest ego. What happened next deserved a clap of thunder, though there wasn't one at the time: not one I heard, in any case. Tom-Tom turned and made a 'come here' gesture. A young man standing behind him leapt to his side, towering over him, arms crossed pirate-style. He flashed ice-bright teeth at Jinx. Jinx faltered, and when she started to move again it was with a slight show of resistance: each step was too great a pleasure to end, each was a step closer to him. He wore jeans and a tight black T-shirt with short sleeves that showed off his shapely upper arms. His eyes were dark, his mouth was full, straight and firm. Mighty as any man could wish rose his nose. He tossed his head once,

RINGLAND LIBRARY

**RINGLAND CENTRE
RINGLAND
NEWPORT
GWENT NP9 9PS**

TEL: 273151

MONDAY	9.30-12.30	1.30-5.30
TUESDAY	9.00-12.30	1.30-5.30
WEDNESDAY		CLOSED
THURSDAY	9.00-12.30	1.30-6.30
FRIDAY	9.30-12.30	1.30-5.30
SATURDAY	9.30-12.30	1.30-4.00

Newport

twice. His hair was black and long for the time; it curled along the nape of his neck. I fancied his skin was smooth stroked one way, rough the other, and that his body would leave a grassy smell in the hollows of the bed.

'Jinx, angel-eyes, come mee-heet what's-his-name. Niccolo de Lisi. Nick.'

That was about all Tom-Tom ever again needed to say to Jinx. He had her right where he wanted her, a show-piece at his side. It was uncanny how perfectly he'd got her number. With a slumbrous gaze in his dark eye the stranger put his hand out for hers. I saw Tom-Tom and Helsinki exchange grins as the magnificent pair headed for a corner where each leaned against a wall, bodies touching as if they were hinged.

'I'm a Sagittarian,' I heard him say.

And that was that.

NINE

I had many reasons to be grateful to Jinx. Can anyone be so foolish, for example, as to dream that Tomas Blalack would have invited me on my own to The Hook and let me in on the workings of his eerie machine? Short, squat girls with big noses are not plucked out of the crowd by greedy artists, you can bet on that. I owed to Jinx the greatest adventures of my life that far. And I had her to thank for laughter, for affection, for unexpected companionship; most of all, I could thank her for my new-found courage. Come what may, because of Jinx's example, or due merely to her sympathy and presence, I knew for sure I was not going to be a teacher in Teaneck. A few thousand dollars were tucked away in my bank account, and with barely a year to go, I was already studying brochures and price-lists for trans-Atlantic liners. There was no question in my mind that Jinx and I would remain friends, but I had seen her meeting with Niccolo de Lisi, it was unmistakably love, and things could never be the same. Jinx was bound to want to move in with him. Away she would go, out of my day-to-day life along with the paper roses and the polka-dot curtains. It was a Friday night when the lovers met, and on Monday morning when I left for my classes, Jinx still hadn't come home. Love always takes first place with a woman. That's only natural, isn't it?

By the time I put the key in our door on Monday evening, sentimental reminiscence and gratitude had made me quite drunk; I was thinking that in years to come whenever Jinx needed me, I'd go to her, no matter what. Our apartment, like all the others in Manhattan, was infested with cockroaches, I heard them clatter across the linoleum when I opened the door, and even though there was no sign of them when I switched on the light, the air was stiff with alarm. I filled the kettle and made myself a cup of coffee; alone and dispirited I sat at the kitchen table. Gradually, it dawned on me that the silence in our flat was not mindless. It was the calculated silence I remembered from childhood, and it meant someone was about to leap out of hiding to scare me half to death. Suddenly, I heard a long sighing 'Aaaaah' followed by a throaty gasp. Well, even a dumb virgin was bound to have a pretty shrewd idea at that point what was happening behind Jinx's bedroom door. I waited, mouse-like and twitching, for more. There were several sharp intakes of breath, a volley of creaking springs, what sounded like a man's sob; and then there was only silence, mindless silence.

After a while, I heard laughter and scuffling, the door to Jinx's room flew open, and there stood handsome Nick, barefoot and bare-chested, the colour of lightly-done toast. His long toes were peaked like spiders' legs and gripped the floor daintily. 'Hey, you gotta be Marsha, right?' he said.

Evidently, he was an actor. Rough diamonds were big on Broadway that year, and all young actors spoke with the full-lipped mumble of Hoboken longshoremen. When Nick tossed his head, the way he had at The Hook, I saw him glance at the mirror on our kitchen wall, and I knew for sure he had to be an actor. 'Niccolo de Lisi. Call me Nick. Pleased to meetcha, Marsh.'

In the depths of heavily lidded eyes was a flicker of apprehension. Who would have believed it? A strikingly handsome man was actually afraid I wouldn't give him my approval. He wanted me to like him. I was enchanted. I

59

clasped his warm, moist hand in both of mine, and a syrupy
undulation passed up along his splendid torso. Behind him,
Jinx appeared, blazing with happiness. Through the open
door, I saw a pair of big cardboard suitcases, not hers. She
wasn't moving out; he was moving in. I was going to be
living in sin. What else do you call sharing a bathroom and
a kitchen with a man who is neither father nor brother? I
gave them both a delirious smile.

And so was established for a little while a union unknown except in music, the trio in harmony. I don't know
why it worked so well; perhaps Jinx's natural equanimity
was enough for three. Also, I posed no sexual threat of any
kind. I liked Nick well enough, but those dark eyes . . .
melting men are not my type, and never were. Not that I
have a type. Or ever had. Any thought of sex between Nick
and me was as inconceivable as mating a stallion with a
mole. At the same time, I was no lesbian to envy him
possession of my friend. Oh, I won't say I haven't thought
about sapphic love, what plain and rejected woman hasn't
at some point in her life? But two females lapping at each
other to me seems reminiscent of fringe psychotherapies
that popped up in the 1960s, fundamentally a neurotic
activity, to be undertaken with deadening earnestness. I
was happy to think of Nick and Jinx making love to each
other; more than happy. I enjoyed the sex. Sex permeated
everything: we breathed sex, we ate it. On Sundays and
other days of rest, sex emanated so thick and quick from
under Jinx's door I felt myself saturated by it. If I'd cut my
finger I would have bled sex. Sex was inside us and out; it
filled our rooms with the smell of cloves and hot tin.
Everything was painted sex, it was an eighth colour emerging from a decomposing spectrum, somewhere around
violet. At night the quiet was sexy, and in the morning,
when Jinx came out to make his coffee, her mouth looked
bruised and tumescent. While she waited for the kettle to

boil, her mind was distracted, following the trail of a tickle, and when she shivered, so did I. I'd been brought up to believe males were constantly ruttish, so it was surprising to note that desire gushed mainly from her. Especially when Nick was busy or preoccupied, let him be sitting at the table reading his paper, say, or fixing a broken radio, and she would be right there, rubbing against his back and putting her mouth to his ear, until he pushed back the chair and rose again to loving.

Jinx liked me to observe her love. Tender services to her man, with me as a witness, became rituals in service to love itself. Oh see, Marsha Leah, how buttering my man's toast is like the liquefaction of loving; note how in the way a woman irons her darling's socks (his socks!) is enacted love's steamy uncreasing. You think this batter is being beaten merely to make his pancakes, don't you, Marsha honey? And this needle threaded just to sew on his button? But these are actually donations to the sacred continuum of jobs done to be undone, and to all the sacramental tasks a woman joyfully undertakes for the greater glory of love.

'He makes me totally happy, Marsha,' Jinx often said.

Well, you know how it is: people who make us totally happy by definition can make us wish we had never been born. 'Aren't you just the funniest thing (thang), honey, when you talk about love,' I can imagine her saying, if I'd known then what I know now, and tried to warn her of the risk she was taking when she counted on any other person for happiness.

Man spoor was everywhere, and I studied it, tracking. Everything Nick did, every trace he left, was enlightening. Steel filings that materialised overnight in the basin turned out to be a dark young man's growth of beard. Sludge in the bottom of empty cups was the residue of sugar a man took, then did not stir. A man returned jars to the refrig-erator smeared and empty after he'd polished off the contents. He dropped underwear where anyone could find it, and he never cleaned any household appliance that had a drain. A man's childlike confidence that nothing about himself could in a million years be found offensive or less than adorable by his women managed somehow to be endearing. Men were not as moody as women; they had only two moods (my father had only one, a mood of mournful resignation, but he was disqualified from my study of men): as far as I could tell from watching Nick, men were either in a good mood, or a bad one. When in a good mood, he played stand-up comic in the kitchen or told long stories, usually about his triumphs over other men who had not realised what a force they were dealing with when they took on Niccolo de Lisi. Often he cast me as his straight man in routines that used Jinx as a patsy.

'Hey Marsh, gedda load of this ...' was the customary opening. Then, while Jinx blew him a kiss and twirled joyously around the kitchen: 'Has your friend got a screw loose, Marsh, or what?' Other times, however, he came in from one of his occasional jobs or an acting class and said: 'Watch out, girls, I'm in a fucking lousy mood.' Most of the time, he was a cheerful flatmate, a fair cook when the fancy took him, and even though he had no savings and was earning less than Jinx had started bringing in, he was punctilious about his share of the expenses. So little fuss and so little luggage attended Nick's moving in, it was as if he had actually materialised in answer to Jinx's prayers.

In his manly way, Nick believed the single worthy form of conversation to be argument; a verbal exchange was not worth its salt unless it entailed a possibility, no matter how slight, of ending in blows. Nick liked having me around; Jinx was so busy loving him, without me there he'd have had nobody to spar with, man to man. 'It says here . . .', he'd generally begin, and refer to an article he had just read in the paper. Whatever his opinion, I was obliged to take the opposing view. If I resisted, or tried to back off, he went on to another topic, and another, until he finally found one that engaged me. Had Eisenhower been right to send troops into Little Rock? Nick said no; I said yes. An hour later we were still arguing, while Jinx watched us nervously, not quite sure it was in fun. For me, our exchanges were like the ones encouraged among us students at City College, only Nick's 'reading of the issue' as he called his opinion, stretched into politics and the sciences as often as art and literature. Was injecting gold in John Foster Dulles going to rid him of cancer? Alchemy, I told Nick, not worth the pot they boiled it in.

'You just don't dig how it works, Marsh. These gold molecules, see? They attach themselves to the cancer molecules. And then the body gets rid of them both together.'

When he needed money, he hired himself out as a waiter, through an agency for private parties. I was pretty sure that was how he had caught Blalack's eye, though the way Nick used to say, 'Tom-Tom and me go back a long way . . .', suggested something much more intimate. Only when it came to his theatrical ambition was Nick not prepared to start at the bottom. I asked him once why he never auditioned for a stock company, or one of the off-off-off Broadway productions that popped up in Brooklyn or Long Island. After all, he had to begin somewhere, did he not?

'You see other guys all the time who didn't begin anywhere,' he replied. 'Good-looking guys, you see them in movies, you know. Tab. Rock. Lex. Flex. Those guys didn't sweat their guts out playing the sticks for twenty years before they got a break. Let me tell you something, Marsh, in my racket you gotta be in the right place, looking good, at the right time. You look good at the right time, and you think anybody gives a pardon-my-French whether you've played goddamn Hamlet or Willie Lomax? They

63

take one look and . . . wham, baby! You are a star. A big star. It's all in the way you present yourself.'

Smoothing his hair back with both hands, he walked to the mirror over our telephone in the kitchen. He turned in profile, bent his arm, made a bicep bulge.

'It's all in the presentation,' he said.

Meanwhile, Jinx's modelling career was moving fast and took an increasing amount of her time, though as labour it was not so demanding as Schrafft's. Forget protestations model girls make to the contrary: they have it easy – they need to concentrate only a few minutes at a time, and solely on themselves. They are made slothful by admiration and too much money. Most of them are cluck-brains. Anyhow, how would your average model know what hard work is? These days they start younger than ever, long before they've had any experience of life. Take it from me, modelling is a doddle compared to the things plain women do to get by. When Jinx started out, it was still the 1950s, and cosmetic technology was in its infancy. My classmates often arrived on Monday red-eyed, wearing headscarves to hide the aftermath of mistimed home perms. Botched nose jobs of the era can be seen to this day, flaring in the ruins of ageing faces. Since then, beauty has been put on sale and anyone with the price doesn't need to be homely. But there were no tinted contact lenses when Jinx was starting out, no skin peelers, or bikini-line waxers, permanent eyelash tinters, collagen plumpers, silicone grapefruit halves; there were no aerobic teachers, aroma-therapists, flesh-carvers of note, or liposuckers. We didn't even have Marsha Leah Feldstein's Miracle Products back then. In those days, beauties were more or less 'naturals' who started later and lasted longer than the current crop. Don't kid yourself modelling has ever been hard work, but in the old days, there were no hairdressers with their own assistants backstage, or 'nail sculptors', or make-up 'artists', and a girl needed to acquire at least a few basic tricks of painting and design to do the job.

A few months before my graduation from City College, Jinx let me come along to a fashion show, so I could see for myself what went on. It was a very grand event, the All Designers New York Show: ADNYS – 'ad nauseam', Helsinki called it when she sent Jinx the contract. Because I chivvied her along, we arrived early at the ballroom of the big hotel where it was to take place. Dressing-tables were set up back to back down the centre of the vast backstage area. In the frames of the mirrors were cards printed: 'June', 'Dawn', 'Ivy', 'Fawn', 'Pixie', all top girls of the season, and at the far end, 'Jinx'. Behind each station was a dress-rail from which were suspended the garments, wrapped in white dust sheets; on the floor beneath were matching shoes. In the silence backstage the hanging white sacks seemed to be gathering themselves together, like a *corps de ballet* before the entrance. Then the girls skipped in, peppering the air with 'I', 'I', 'I'. A Yorkshire terrier poked its head out of a model's squashy bag and yipped: 'I, I, I'. Several of the beauties had a little plain jane in tow to help them dress, and run out for coffee; the redhead, Fawn Ellis, had two.

Before I went out to join Nick in the audience I peeked through the curtains into the auditorium. From where I stood, I saw the catwalk extending out into space. The audience had started to arrive, like a rolling sea it covered the hundreds of small gilt chairs. Bright islands here and there showed where editors and their coteries were dressed in whatever colour they were backing as the season's winner: dove-grey for *Vogue*, fuchsia for *Harpers*, an acidic blue-green for *Women's Wear Daily*. Close to the footlights, at the end of the catwalk, sat Blalack and his People, solid and black as a beetle. Among them was

Nick. I slipped out a side exit and then in again through the main doors, and took the empty seat waiting for me next to him. The house lights dimmed, there was some music and palaver, then the first models appeared in daywear to open the show. Watching them take their haughty gallop, I tried to imagine myself slinking out there on stiletto heels with my big nose in the air, and behind me the Irish girls, all of us sashaying down the catwalk, thinking 'fuck you', the way I'd heard Helsinki tell Jinx a model always should. Talk about a show stopper! Our homely broad-boned troupe, toes-out on the runway, would have posed a threat to the very fibre of fashion. The waitresses and I would have stopped that show. And how.

And then Jinx came out in a stalking dress of black sequins. She stood, then turned slowly, and as she faced my way a very strange thing happened to me. I knew what it was to be lovely; I felt light of heart, of step, and with no brooding weight of scholarship upstairs, I felt light of mind, too: light in ways I had never imagined. I cannot explain how, but I had become part of Jinx's length and golden warmth. I knew for an instant what it was to be tall. Full to the brim with light and lightness, I stepped out with her on to the long catwalk, together we crossed a threshold into highest performance, beyond friction, and impervious to pain. She took me with her over the heads of men and across an acre of worshipping faces. It was wonderful to be so fearless and so free of common sense, free of myself, as in a dream of flying. When the whole crowd erupted into applause, I returned to my insignificant shell, still elated, knowing much, much more about temporal splendour and airy forces.

Nick was slouching a little in his chair. Like everyone else, he was watching Jinx spin radiance from herself, and the dress that fitted her like a flashing skin. When I turned

66

to Nick to share the excitement of his best girl's triumph, I found myself confronting his unguarded, sullen face, and another revelation: sooner or later, love grows old, and lovers can turn nasty.

TEN

The day arrived at last for me to set off in feverish excitement on my own adventure. My parents, resigned but not enthusiastic, wished me luck by telephone, and made it clear, whatever I might say, they thought I'd be back and signed up for teachers' training before very long. Nick and Jinx came to the pier to see me off. The night before, Jinx used my departure as an excuse to skip a party at The Hook; there was nothing Nick liked more than Tom-Tom's parties, he hated to have missed one, and he was in a bad mood. My last sight of him, he stood with his arms folded, leaning disconsolately against a wall. Jinx, who had finally stopped waving, was sitting on a bollard with her back to the water. Our ship was being tugged towards the mouth of New York harbour and I saw from afar how she was showing her legs for a press photographer who had been hanging around for days, and finally got lucky. For some time after the figures were lost to view, I saw the camera's flash popping, until it too was gone, and we passengers who had been leaning on the rail fell suddenly silent. Great cities of the world were not yet back-to-back, crossing an ocean involved elements of spiritual quest. When the land birds circling overhead started to drop back at last into the sunset, and the deep currents snatched our hull, we were struck dumb by the enormity of our undertaking. I had never been to sea before, but the moment I felt the deck creak and stretch under my feet, the memory of a voyage was shaken loose, not my own, but once or twice removed, and stored in me for safekeeping. Then it too disappeared, and I gave myself wholly to the rolling waves that were going to deliver me, reborn, on an unknown shore.

Strictly speaking it was an eventful crossing. One event, in any case, took place which they say every girl is supposed to find memorable. Common knowledge has it the first time is no good. I found it fascinating. But perhaps I knew one way or another my first time was likely to be my last, so I put a lot into making the best of it. He was an Italian, an indiscriminate race of men, on the whole, used to immediate feeding, not persistent, very short on strategy. He was hardly a man at all, to be honest; he was certainly no older than I. 'Bella, bella . . .' he whispered as he replaced my bowl of macaroni with a plate of fried fish, and I felt his damp breath on my cheek. 'Bella . . .,' said the liar again, closer to my ear. I raised my head, astonished. The first thing I saw was his nametag, 'Adriano', hovering at my shoulder. A thin face blazed overhead between a pair of ears massively outspread. My first thought was that should I, with my shnozz, stand next to him, with his ears, me in profile and he looking out, we'd be the very image of a creamer and a sugar-bowl. 'Bella . . .' he said again, the scoundrel. Was he taking me for a fool? I looked up into his eyes of mud-brown, and I knew right away what he was thinking, his intentions were as plain as the you-know-what on my face. Let the handsome stewards compete for the pretty girls, mostly American students dying to practise Italian, Adriano preferred a sure thing. The lazy boy picked me the first night out at sea because he figured I'd be easy and grateful. And he was spot on, too.

I had a cabin the size of a broom-cupboard all to myself and later that night, when a confident knock sounded on the door, I let Adriano in, and with him a pleasant waft of Parmesan cheese. A lot of what transpired then interested me, not least the lack of common sense in how men are put together, and the awkward way we humans mate

69

compared to, say, the way we dance, or swim, or compete at active sports. But it was a promising business, if much too quickly done, by any standards. Although only my brute curiosity had been satisfied, and barely, I had felt a kind of – how to put this? – a kind of clenching during the act, not just of my body; a kind of clenching, inside and out, spasmodic and just strong enough to suggest an almighty unclenching, had Adriano gone on long enough. After he left, which he did quickly, with a brisk peck of a kiss, I knelt on the tumbled bunk and leaned my forehead against the porthole to watch the little whitecaps skipping home. Later, I woke in a cold sweat, compulsively doing the ancient sums back and forth to twenty-eight, until I was too tired to go on worrying, and I left it all to destiny.

When I woke next morning, our ship was rolling and pitching like a matchbox set adrift. The few passengers up and about eyed each other's approaches from opposite ends of corridors, then ricocheted off bulkheads, smiling sheepishly while the sea made vaudeville drunks of us all. I staggered off for breakfast in the empty dining salon. To my surprise an unfamiliar agitation all my own had started to take place: would he be there? Had he told the others? How was I supposed to act? But my jug-eared Romeo was not on duty. Disappointed, and relieved, I shouldered my way out on to the deck where the wind whipped my face flat against the bone, baring my teeth and pouring into my lungs savagely so for a moment I was actually drowning in air. Adriano did not serve at lunch. I didn't bother struggling in to dinner. That night I waited. But no knock came on my door. For a long time I lay awake on my berth while the oceanic swell drew my hurt feelings forth to foreign lands, and rolled them back again.

Sometime after midnight the sea relented and turned motherly. It was very early, the breakfast gong hadn't yet sounded, when I crept out on deck into the gentle,

70

whispering light of dawn. The only other people around were a young couple; they had pulled two deckchairs close so there would be no need to reach far for each other's arms. The girl's back was to me, I guessed from her untamed waist-length hair she must be one of the beatniks from steerage. She said a few soft words. Laughing, her lover raised his head from the hollow of her throat. The rising sun lit up his ears that glowed like big bright wings. The price of making love was going to be too high for me, I knew with the first terrible blow to my heart. Tennessee Williams wrote in his play *Camino Real* that Esmeralda, the gypsy's daughter, became a virgin again at every full moon. Virginity returned to me only once, once and for all. Never would I be able to hold the lover I wanted, I saw that clearly, and never would I have one worthy of such suffering.

I'm not ashamed to be a born-again virgin. Many people these days think it's queer for a woman to stay celibate into her dotage, but in other times chastity was undertaken as a celebration of great virtues such as hope and faith and love itself. I think God or nature, or whatever you choose to call the transcendent schemer, is most of all a materialist of the utmost craft, a wheeler-dealer on a grand scale with a good head for business. For a female to offer herself to males who do not want her is bad business; to give herself to man after man and never to the one she wants is bad sex. There on the deck of the ship, with the chuckling sea all around, I vowed that, barring a miracle, lovemaking was all done for me. So you see, what Jinx has done over and over and over again for love, I swore never to do again, for the same reason.

Paris stunned me. I was so deeply impressed by its looks and its uncanny self-containment I can even now recall with uncommon clarity bridges, trees, cats in shop windows, and the faces of children I saw during the endless walks of my first weeks there. I was dazed by its beauty and sheer glamour, and for almost a year I hardly realised what a hard-hearted place it is. At bottom, when the bright lights go out, Paris is a high-buttoned puritan, passing judgements with no right of appeal on what is good, not good, what is done, not done, what is worth having, what not: on what is Parisian and on what, being not Parisian, barely deserved a second thought. At the same time, Paris embraces craze after craze – for an exotic cuisine, for a popular tune or singer, a movie or star, merely for a word or turn of phrase – and Parisians welcome any little drollery at all, as long as it passes without threatening real change. If cities could speak their minds, Paris would say: 'Piss off. I amuse myself.' In no city I can think of is a plain woman plainer than she is there. The French frame mirrors to flatter, but that only makes matters worse for a sawn-off runt with not a shred of their native chic. While I was struggling to learn the language, I was as isolated as it is possible to be, and even after I was pretty fluent, very few Parisians saw any reason to speak to me. In the end, it was all for the best. Jake was right to say we grow only when we are alone. Now I know that my lonely ordeal in Paris was a long ceremony of initiation. It was hard. But I was never going to regret it. It made a woman of me.

Nick and Jinx married a few months after I left the States as everyone who read the *Herald Tribune* or *Time* magazine was told. Tomas Blalack made a 'Home Movie' of the ceremony. It was called *Black and White Wedding*, and it was the first of his films to be sent out worldwide. I went to see it at a Paris art-cinema, where the audience was lapping it up. When Jinx appeared on screen, there was a soft intake of breath all around and for the first time since I'd left America, I felt pride. For the first time I didn't mind not being Parisian. I wanted to stand up and shout, 'See

here, you smug frogs, that beautiful girl is my best friend!'
She drifted down the aisle of the old church where they'd
been married, and Blalack played his camera on her as
gently as a brush, finding the same qualities of youth and
unchastened hope he had painted in 'Oyster Cracker III'.
He drew his camera back to show the cavernous vastness
of the place, and how the bride glowed through a curtain
of dust that must have been hanging around unchanged
since parishioners long gone had breathed their last
'amens'. Then, the angle of the shot changed, disquiet
rippled through the audience as it panned along the faces
of the guests in the pews, all Blalack's People and dressed
in black. Like children trying not very hard to be good,
most of them were stifling laughter, fidgeting, sneering.
Tom-Tom's wicked camera played along the banks of
waxy flowers that looked tinged and funereal, then back
to the only pure whiteness anywhere, the bride in her
plumage of an angel. The famous playwright escorted her
down the aisle. He wore an old-fashioned southern gent's
suit, taut over his belly and tailored beyond the point of
parody. When he delivered Jinx at the altar, he was wob-
bling noticeably on his pins. It was at that point we started
to wonder if we were being tricked. Very slowly, disturbing details started to accumulate; a woman draped in veils
sat in a pew, she was knitting something shapeless, like a
long, uneven shroud; the officiating cleric, when he asked
'Who gives this woman . . . ?' showed incisors like fangs;
everything seemed to be happening at less than half human
speed, it was drawn out and druggy; most disturbing was a
godly malevolence that filled every frame, I could almost
hear Blalack's hiccoughing giggle. What we were watching
was not a celebration, it was a travesty and a sacrifice. The
whole thing was done with sardonic brilliance. Blalack
certainly knew his business. When it was Nick's turn, he
edited with a scalpel. Nick's good looks were there, dark

73

and saturnine as I remembered, but over them played physical vanity, which is essentially an effeminate weakness, so for an instant when Nick bent to put the ring on his bride's finger, through Blalack's merciless, mustard-coloured eyes we glimpsed not a man in love and in the prime of life, but a soured and envious old maid. Poor Nick. No wonder the film did his career no good. Even less wonder that in the end, it outlived the marriage by decades.

ELEVEN

Life presents beauties with a million, million possibilities every bright morning of their youth. Each time the telephone rings, every letter through the door, let a new man walk in, and the pretty girl needs only to ask herself: 'Why not?' But as for us others, the plain ones, our possibilities, if we're to have them, must be generated from within. Nobody else delivers us the goods, and if we dare to have a dream, then we must learn to build it, page by page, or stone by stone, deed by deed.

As the months piled up in Paris, I learned the great lesson of doggedness. Friendless, and plodding at a dreary job just to subsist, when the little voice woke me, crying: 'Why? Why? Why?' I found it in myself to say, as a good mother would: 'Because you must.' Without industry and stubbornness, an ugly girl goes right down the tubes. Meanwhile, I wrote regularly to Jinx and she sent me back postcards from exotic places whenever she was on location for fashion shoots. Letter-writing came hard to Jinx. 'By the time a letter gets there, honey, everything has changed. So what's the point?' I used to enclose a note for Nick until after I'd been living in Paris for about two years and a card came from Jinx in Jamaica. 'Divorce pending', she wrote, and then went on to tell me how much fun she was having in the islands. It was not the only time I had to notice that as wholeheartedly as Jinx rushed into love, equally, when love ended, she moved on with barely a backward glance. So many fish in the sea for a beautiful young woman, I guess, and so many why-nots knocking at her door. I honestly think I was sorrier than Jinx when her marriage to Nick broke up.

Jinx was my only true friend, and she always has been. Oh, the Tchernokoff Sisters are very good to me and I would go to the ends of the earth for them. But they were twice my age when Helsinki introduced us in Paris and as soon as they became my employers, the practical distance between us was too great for real intimacy. Ditto: Glynis, my miracle of Miracle Products, my handmaiden, my very own 'girl back east', my London treasure – she is half my age, and I am her employer. When I say Jinx has been my only friend, it is not a pathetic declaration. People who have lots and lots of friends skimp in their devotion, and my feelings for Jinx have not wavered. Not really. After I left America it was to be a few years before we met again, and in the decades we have known each other, I can count on my fingers how many times we've turned up at the same time in the same city. But I have never once thought of Jinx except with deep concern and love, even if, for increasing periods, I did not think of her at all.

A few weeks after the divorce, Jinx wrote to tell me she was coming to Paris, at last. The grand old man of couture, Gregoire la Bastille had asked for her to be in his spring show, and Helsinki had made the booking. Not only was Helsinki coming along, Tomas Blalack himself had decided it was the right time for him to make his first assault on Europe. Although air travel had become commonplace, quick and convenient, they were travelling by ship. They had to. For Tomas Blalack to have taken the slightest risk with his health or safety would have been a monumental crime. A sacred responsibility lay upon him, you understand, to stay alive. The end of Blalack meant the end of human endeavour, the end of fun and games, the end of fame and fortune. The end of Tomas Blalack – as who knew better than himself?– must be the end of everything.

Blalack was a martyr to reality, a saviour of us all. Airplanes were too newfangled, too daring and dangerous for him upon whose continued existence life itself depended, and so he was understandably afraid of flying.

I went out by train to Le Havre to meet the ship when it came in. Even from a distance I recognised the changes in Jinx since I'd seen her last. Straight away I clocked the studiously unselfconscious way she hesitated at the top of the gangway, then slowly came down on to French soil, modestly, and as if she did not notice that every face in the waiting crowd on the pier was raised to her in curiosity and admiration. Not many heads need to turn or autographs be requested before even the healthiest ego is attacked by a low-grade infection, which in Jinx's case was manifested by aggravated humility. But then she had brushed past reporters and everyone, and hurried straight to where I stood, off to one side, struck suddenly shy by so much glamour.

'Oh hon, I've missed you,' she said.

I noted how slim and smooth she had become, brought to peak condition inch by inch, and then it was as if we'd never been apart. Helsinki dealt with the waiting press in good, heavily-accented French; Jinx and I rode alone together in the back of the chauffeur-driven car that Gregoire la Bastille had sent to meet her. And with a lot of prompting, to keep her on the track, we pieced together the story of her first Atlantic crossing.

Jinx was a whizz at down-home parables, and whenever I did not immediately grab the point of them, it turned out that I was being obtuse; she always knew perfectly well what she meant to say. Long narrative, however, brought out the magpie in her; she would detour for any glittering object that caught her eye. We were on the outskirts of Paris before I had the facts of her journey, more or less patiently winnowed free of musings on the marital status of good-looking sailors and long descriptions of Velvet's wardrobe. The throbbing chanteuse had been on the journey too, along with as many of Blalack's inner circle as were required to keep an eye on him. I do not intend to mislead deliberately, but over the years I have come to take Jinx's story as my own, and I see it all so clearly in my mind, sometimes I forget I was not actually there.

It was a soft, hazy evening when their ship slipped out of her berth on Manhattan Island into the thick, land-tinged water of the lower Hudson River. She was bound for Southampton first, then on to Le Havre, a crossing that in those days took between four and five days. Passengers leaned on the portside rail to watch New York's skyline dwindle until it was hardly more than a broken comb forgotten on the shore. When the first big swells hit, Jinx saw Blalack raise his eyes skywards, contemplating momentarily the possibility of a power greater than himself. The sea makes all men equal; ships, however, do no such thing. Blalack and most of his party were occupying first-class cabins. Jinx found the accommodation splendid, like Radio City Music Hall, she told me, and I had to stop her before she went off on a tangent of rococo interior decoration.

On the first morning out, she explored the ship further, and found slippery stairs that led down into steerage and the hollow of the hull. 'Oh, Marsha, it was strange down there. The paint was all bubbling and where it had flaked away were big patches of rust. Do you know, they must have built that boat out of iron. Honey, how can iron float? I was in a long passage. It would have been pitch black except there were light bulbs overhead set into these little cages. They flickered once and went out, and it scared me half to death. It wasn't my kind of place, Marsha. Not my style. I couldn't wait to get back up on deck. And I saw something down there, too. Something moved.'

'A rat?'

'No. Too fluttery. Maybe it was a bat.'
'Oh Jinx, there are no bats on boats. Ha–ha.'
'A ghost,' she said, and she meant it, too.

Blalack and Jinx sat at the top table for dinner, surrounded by the ship's officers in their uniforms. The captain was a silvered Dane or Swede, Jinx wasn't sure which, he sat between his two distinguished passengers and told Jinx funny stories about his life at sea. A little smile on her face when she remembered him as good as told me he would have changed course for Timbuctoo on the instant had she leaned over and whispered: 'would you be a darling . . . ?' Tom–Tom was enjoying himself. He smiled a lot, wide enough to give a good glimpse of his small, even teeth that were like rows of kernels on the cob. Helsinki was at the main table too, and so was Velvet. The rest of Blalack's People sat at smaller tables nearby. Some of them were new, replacements for those who had fallen out of favour since I'd left New York. At a table to one side, watching Blalack's flank, were the two I used to call 'the knife throwers'. They were brothers, the twin despair of their poor mother, alike in their arctic disregard for everyone else except Tom–Tom. Between themselves they communicated by nods and half-completed gestures; when they spoke to anyone else, it was basic: yeah, no, gimme, drink, meat, fuck. They were never far from the boss, holding him always in their squint-eyed, marksman's gaze and ready to push away anyone he did not want too near him.

Blalack rarely appeared by day when he stayed mostly inside his suite on the top deck where a few of his People kept him company. Helsinki bustled among the first-class passengers, making contacts. And Jinx spent her time alone in a shaded corner of the deck, reading magazines and gazing out to sea, imagining what a fine place a ship would be for love. Sometimes the officers came by to flirt with her, but it was not serious; they were all married. And besides, though Jinx did not say it, sailors are practical men on board, they save their extravagance for ports, and she was too dazzling and dangerous, too rich for their maritime blood. Then, two days before Southampton, they ran into very bad weather, and Jinx, like all the others, even Tom-Tom, kept to her cabin. She wasn't sick, but beauty has its dignity, remember? And she did not care to risk the comical pitching of the decks. Just as the storm had cleared quickly on my own crossing, so the wind dropped dramatically overnight, and in the morning they found themselves gently rocking under a sky of baby-boy blue. Encouraged by the fine weather, Blalack's People went ahead with plans for a last-night party.

Now, Jinx tried to rush ahead to her conclusion. But for once I wanted to know every detail of the party – what people wore, what they ate, what they heard – and I kept her at the embroidery frame like a stern governess.

'Go back, Jinx. Tell me what was Helsinki wearing?'

Helsinki wore fuchsia from the tip of her turban to the ends of her silken slippers, and she wove her way from group to group like a parasitical vine. Velvet wore blue velvet. Jinx was in apple green silk chiffon, a thousand-dollar dress Helsinki had borrowed for her from a designer who owed a favour. Aside from Blalack's People, fifteen or twenty first-class passengers nominated by Helsinki for their looks or their position had been invited to the party, which was taking place outside at the stern of the ship on a secluded deck reserved for VIPs. Jinx said it looked like a little night-club under the stars, and though I had never been to a night-club, I'd seen enough of them in gangster movies to picture the glittering women and the men in dinner-jackets as they circulated, and sized each other up. Round tables had been set up for the occasion, and stewards pressed into extra service handed around drinks, and offered trays of canapés, such as you would have found at any on-shore cocktail party of the times.

'Pigs-in-blankets, liverwurst on Ritz crackers, and Blalack's favoured cheese-dip,' Jinx said.

The knife throwers flanked the oaken door that was the only exit to the inner companionway, and kept their cold eyes on Tom-Tom. Everyone else was milling around, and a few were dancing.

The night was calm as glass, and for once Blalack did not mind music at his party; an upright piano had been rolled out on deck from the upstairs bar. The dancing stopped about an hour into the party when Velvet took possession of the instrument. Most people continued to talk and gad about, but a small group gathered around the piano to hear Velvet belt out the old ditties. Her bellicose attack trailed away into the open air; whenever her breath was choked by vibrato and ran out, she addressed the usual interjections straight at Blalack: 'God I love this song. I hope you love it too. This song means the world to me . . . .'

'Where were you, Jinx, when all this was going on?'

She frowned. 'Do you really need to hear all this, Marsha?'

Jinx was standing elbow to elbow with Blalack and leaning back on the taffrail where it curved out over the stern. Thanks to the obligatory space always kept clear around Tom-Tom, they looked like a royal couple on a dais, and there was no doubt in anyone's mind the party was being given by Blalack and was also in his own honour. Behind Blalack and Jinx the ship's wake grew and spread out importantly in the moonlight, as if it had designs on permanence. Jinx turned to smile at the captain who had come down from the bridge and was making his way towards her through the crowd. He was holding a paper rose that he'd snatched from the buttonhole of a steward.

'What was Velvet singing then? Was she singing?'

81

'Yes, Velvet was singing.'

'My mama done tole me . . .' Velvet warbled, and she smiled at Blalack. For a moment, there was one of the strange silences that settles on a noisy party sometimes, as if a wing of ominous portent were sweeping overhead. And as that moment was passing, the door flanked by the pale brother exploded, or seemed to, and something shot out of it like a bat out of hell.

'No bats on boats,' I weakly said.

Faster than its own trailing scream, the fury flew across the deck. The brothers hurled themselves forward, but they were too late. Where Tomas Blalack had been standing, was one small black shoe: its mate had gone with him over the side.

'Did he scream or cry out?' I asked, for I wondered if Tom-Tom at the very end had behaved in a commonly human manner. Jinx brushed away some tears, and shook her head. There was only shocked silence on the deck. And then came Velvet's unholy shrieks.

The captain did all the right things. They criss-crossed their wake for hours and cut the darkness with searchlights until the sun was up. But Tom-Tom had gone, with the stowaway wrapped around him like a colossal squid. They must be there to this day, somewhere at the bottom of the Atlantic, Trans Sylvia and Tomas Blalack, utterly immersed in each other.

TWELVE

Here beginneth the period of Jinx O'Malley's life which in my mind's eye rises under a word embossed in gold: *Mayhem*, or *Havoc*, or simply, *Jinx*. Since biblical times and before, beautiful women have been a natural resource, to be exported by the countries that produce them. Loose from Blalack's ambiguous and suffocating patronage, Jinx found herself able to fly wherever she wanted to go. With Helsinki Braw on her side, money was bound to keep rolling in. Jinx could travel freely, and she often travelled free; but she never travelled light. Thanks to my line of work, I've known many great beauties over the years, and a few of them were tightwads, even in their youth. Most beautiful women, however, have a greater than average need to reassure themselves while the going is good that there's always plenty more where that came from, and it makes them understandably extravagant. Jinx was no exception to the general rule.

Even when we were waitresses living on a shoestring, Jinx used to suffer from a genuine inability to leave a shop of any kind before she'd made a purchase: a packet of tacks, laces for tennis shoes, a ball of string, a tin of clam chowder, a toy, a pencil, something, anything, no matter how useless or insignificant it was. When her travels began in earnest, Jinx never flew out of a country without more luggage than she'd had flying into it. God alone knows what has become of her immense wardrobe, her rugs, bird cages, vases, furniture, bolts of cloth, and all the other stuff she toted around the globe. As she went from place to place, on location or just to cruise at leisure for a while, she often left suitcases behind, meaning to collect them later. At this moment, in the basement of my London house is a Gucci trunk full of clothes she left there nearly twenty years ago. 'I'll be back for them, sugar. As soon as I've got my act together.'

Nothing in my experience prepared me for the luxury of the suite Gregoire la Bastille had reserved for Jinx. When it comes to putting on the ritz, the Sun King's descendants take the biscuit. Take this pink hat-box I'm in for comparison; it costs a pretty penny even by the inflated standards of Beverly Hills, and it has all the patina of an operating theatre. Over here, in the land of my birth, protection from germs counts as five-star luxury. But the truth is there can be no real style without wear and tear. The rugs and chairs in Jinx's suite were worn all right, and the moment you saw them you knew by only the most noble boots and backsides of all time. The air was heavy with perfumes of golden ages. I had been surviving in relative penury up to then, and I was struck dumb; I hardly dared move away from the door. Just as surprising as the splendour of the rooms was how effortlessly the little filly out of Louisiana white-trash, my old friend Jinx, took to it. After giving the photographers waiting on the pavement outside the small sad smile Parisians expected from one they saw as Tomas Blalack's spiritual widow, she swept on easily into the sanctuary of the magnificent lobby. Before I had gathered the nerve to perch on the end of a straight-backed chair in her suite, Jinx had tossed her fur over the scrolled chaise-longue and was confidently ordering drinks up from room service.

At last I could look at her closely. I saw new planes and shadows that suggested high breeding. She seemed to have acquired extra vertebrae; her neck looked perilously long and slender, reminiscent of history's young executed queens. When Jinx reached out to the waiter for sparkling wine, I noticed how her fingernails were polished and shaped, and how they were so long, they curved slightly. Later, she told me her nails were one of the greatest burdens of her day-to-day life, and she showed me from underneath where they'd had to be patched and mended. But the way Jinx took the glass with the balls of her fingers to spare her nails was enough to show that for the time being, and probably for a long time to come, when Jinx O'Malley needed heavy lifting done, someone else was going to have to do it.

Until Helsinki Braw turned up, Jinx and I talked about old times. And she was strangely nostalgic it seemed to me, not for Nick, or for Blalack's high life, but for Schrafft's and the Irish girls, and our mildewed apartment in Manhattan. Even Flavia Jane came into her happiest reminiscences, as if they'd been the best of friends. Those early days that were still only yesterday to me, had already acquired for Jinx the soft-focus of a distant past. When Helsinki finally arrived, bursting into Jinx's suite without even a knock on the door, the first thing she did was snatch away the remains of food we'd ordered up and put it on a tray outside the door, berating Jinx all the time for not counting calories, and threatening her with a diet of lettuce leaves for weeks to come. Poor Helsinki, she was Blalack's only true mourner and for the rest of her time in Paris she hid her grief under fits of temper and scorn. I heard her angry squawking behind me all the way to the elevator. From time to time I fancied I heard her yell still ringing in the distance while I walked alone in the dark back to my place on the Left Bank.

Sometimes a memory stays only because it contains an unanswered question. For example, when I was no more than six or seven, one of my mother's friends asked if she had told me yet about menstruation, and for ages carted around in my memory every detail of an otherwise unremarkable moment, until much later, when menstruation was explained to me, and the fragment of awkward conversation along with all its trimmings could be forgotten at last. Many years after my meeting with Jinx in Paris, I still remembered how it felt to walk back alone along the quays, and how the Seine beside me shivered like a wet cat, filling the air with the prowling smell of Paris at night. In spite of the meal I'd just had with Jinx, and my pleasure in seeing my only real friend, I drew my coat close, and shivered with a foreboding I could neither explain nor forget for a long, long time; not until another night years later here in Los Angeles, when Jake and I were downstairs at the bar of this very hotel, talking. He was talking, is what I mean.

'It's not just one song the sirens sing, Marsha,' he said. 'Their repertoire is endless. And it's magical. Every sailor hears the song that's tuned to his own deepest desire: not a trace of static, no interference from any other wavelength. Believe me, a man will hear whatever he must to account for his urge to abandon ship. See that dolly wiggling into view? She could be whistling 'Dixie', for all any guy cares. Let him dream he's in with a chance, and he's deaf to everything but the song of his hot blood, you can bet on that.'

Big Jake couldn't see what he was describing was his own condition ever since he'd laid eyes on Jinx. The truth about love is like death, nobody believes it can happen to him. But as he spoke, the memory of that Paris night full of foreboding came back whole, and suddenly the question it contained was answered. For the first time I had wondered whether Jinx's great quest for love might not be hopeless. That was the question tormenting me beside the river. The siren, poor creature, sings her heart out, and she sings in vain, for every man is hearing his own music and paying not the least attention to her song. Any man who dared to love Jinx O'Malley was bound to be inclined for worship, whether that was what she wanted or not. Worship is not love, and worship was not what Jinx wanted, but her beauty and the finesse of her style had begun to demand it. She hadn't turned grand or haughty, I don't mean that; it wasn't in her to be either. But sensitive nerve-endings had been uncovered that weren't there before, and to lug, to strain, to scrub, to crouch, to grunt, practically any action designated in English by a sweaty one-syllable verb, was bound to be inimical to what she had become: quite simply, the most beautiful woman in the world.

I used to join Jinx at her hotel for a drink most days after work while she was in Paris. An anonymous admirer decided that camelias ought to be her chosen flower. Whether we were in her suite, or at the bar, masses of the waxy blooms were never far away. Even now a sniff of camelia bloom – 'bloom' is the word for camelias not blossom or flower – is enough to make me remember those days when Paris received my good friend Jinx with fanatical rapture. But Jinx did not fall for Paris the way I had. 'I've never liked men who wear brown shoes', was the best she could return the besotted Parisians.

When we slipped away on Sunday mornings to stroll through the Tuileries Gardens, whether it was a national propensity for flirtation, or that she had become so much more alluring, her effect on Frenchmen in the park was phenomenal, at least twice as great as I recalled it being on American men. Every move she made illustrated her basic almost primitive awareness of the discrepancies between desires of the male and of the female. When she stopped to admire a flowerbed, the way she licked her wicked ice-cream, when she sat on a bench in the dappled sunlight and leaned slightly my way with her head back to smile at the branches, she was sending out a challenge as unconsciously as her pulse beat. Stunning girls take to heart early on how apart the sexes really are in this life; and not a man, not one, not an old man, not a man in love, not a homosexual, didn't hesitate on the path and wonder what it would be like to have her. And the women? They looked at her too, and wondered what it would be like to be so incomparably beautiful.

Helsinki was never far away from Jinx though often she was hidden. To make a living out of exchanging favours with the rich and beautiful the way Helsinki did demands a working knowledge of the underworld. When a shady lawyer was needed, a tax-haven, an abortionist, a supplier of goods or services that were not quite kosher, Helsinki bridged the gap, always to her profit. She covered her tracks and wherever she travelled, she preferred to go alone. Tomas Blalack himself had been left standing on occasion after Helsinki leapt into a passing cab to speed up-town on her own.

As terrified as Blalack was of solitude, was Braw of goodbyes. Even at the end of a telephone conversation, she left the other dangling, sometimes still speaking into the deserted receiver. Helsinki was a pedler on the muddy roads of earth, streetwise on a planetary scale, and all she was ever known to give away for free were caveats gleaned from experience; Jinx and I used to call them 'Helsinki's look-out-fors'. 'Look out for any guy who inherits money when he's under thirty,' I overheard her tell Fawn Ellis, another top model of the '50s and early '60s, 'little rich boys got no place left to go, but straight into the gutter.' 'Look out for Parisians,' she warned Jinx, 'they can't stand anybody but each other. And they hate each other.' 'Look out for Irishmen,' I remember her telling someone, I can't remember why, 'they talk too much and they drink too much for the same reason: to forget.'

If space travel had opened up in our time, Helsinki

would have been the first to warn us to beware of Martians, they mean what they say when they say it, but not the day after – quite the way she used to say Italians were here on planet earth. 'Look out for those handsome guys you go for,' she told Jinx in Paris, 'handsome guys are all liars right up to the day they die.' I was too foolish to admire Helsinki in those days, and too young to like her. Can you believe it? The egregious old bawd was the agent of my good fortune and responsible for a great change in my life.

I went to la Bastille's *maison de couture* a couple of times to meet Jinx after her fittings, and once to see the show. From the moment you crossed the threshold of the classy building, you were drawn into an uninterrupted contemplation of authenticity and style. Every inch of the place, right down to the taps in the Ladies Room, had been overseen by la Bastille himself – within the holy precinct he was called '*le Maître*' – and if one of the *vendeuses* wore a pair of shoes *le Maître* did not like, or painted her nails a colour on his black-list, she had to make an immediate change even if it meant going home to do it, and losing a day's pay. The refinement of the joint made me perverse; while I hardly dared move for fear of being clumsy, a rampaging sprite within me was dying to spit over the railings of the balcony, or stub fags out on the carpet that was a pale colour I would have called light blue; la Bastille's *vendeuses,* the least of whom outclassed dear old Miss Kaloczek in hauteur, called it 'la Bastille grey'. Two dozen seamstresses worked all day by electric light in the basement, and Jinx told me the attic where he had his studio was in a perpetual ferment of hysteria. On the public floors, however, was the cultivated serenity of a world where there were no glaring ambitions or chores, or bills that couldn't be paid.

La Bastille was one of the greatest names in the history of French couture, he had been around for ages by the time

Jinx was invited to be in his show, and still only models of
the greatest distinction and beauty were allowed to be seen
in his clothes. The man was unabashedly a snob as only a
Frenchman can be, but he was no fool. He knew the kind
of international high society he relied on for his clientele
had been as mortally war-damaged as any blitzed city, and
was virtually kaput. Only the myth of a leisured class
endured, but Gregoire la Bastille was part of that myth, and
he had no intention of going under. Finally, as gracefully
as ever, he bowed to necessity and opened his gilded doors
to those who thought they could buy the elegance of
another age, and had the wherewithal to give it a try. In
the past, only women of title and breeding had been invited
into the salon of Gregoire la Bastille, by the early 1960s,
however, when less provident couturiers had started going
under, la Bastille was managing to hold his own, though
to do so he had to rely on women who had actually in their
time been seen to sweat. The wives of dollar millionaires,
the mistresses of Central American politicians, a few movie
stars and others whose credentials did not bear close scru-
tiny, kept le Maître afloat.

Worse yet, the press expected to be invited to his
fashion-shows, and so he had to hire dubious middlemen
to keep the peace with the scribbling harridans, whom he
despised with all his fastidious soul. Helsinki Braw was one
whose services he required. It was she who brought him
Jinx, and it was she who arranged for the most famous
movie star since talkies began, the titian-haired firecracker,
Dereena Foyle, to wear his creations to all her openings
and to use them in her films, in exchange for a free
wardrobe. It was also Helsinki who suggested he change
the title of his black organza ballgown from 'Soir de Paris'
to 'Un Hommage a Tom-Tom' and fit it on Jinx instead
of his previous favourite, the redhead, Fawn Ellis. As
Helsinki predicted, the crowd went wild. I was surprised

90

that Fawn hardly grumbled at all when la Bastille's master-piece was stripped off her back and given to Jinx. I'd yet to learn, you see, that young beauties do not bitch the way plain women do. Only when beauties are growing old and their looks are fading, do they turn into aggressive, unchari-table ill-tempered bullies.

Jinx wangled me an invitation to the party la Bastille gave after his final show. It was in the main salon, a fair replica of the Hall of Mirrors. What struck me right away was the dulcet murmur of a continental crowd, compared to the din of New York parties. There was a band playing, not very loud, at the far end of the big, rectangular room. Foxtrots, waltzes and Latin Americana were at that time right on the verge of being swept off the floor, forever, they were already starting to sound square, but *le maître* and his guests didn't know, or care, and when a foxtrot was struck up, a few of the braver ones began to dance. La Bastille himself was not dancing, of course: wasn't his whole career devoted to the control and chastening of bouncing flesh? Instead, he made his traditional promenade through the crowd seeking out his mannequins, one by one, and giving each three kisses of thanks: right cheek, left, right again. He was a very tall man, his noble head floated high above the others as if it were being carried on a pike, then dropped from view here and there for a kiss, kiss, kiss at the lower levels. From behind a convenient palm I watched his progress, and I saw Jinx whirl by in the arms of an exiled king. Fawn Ellis was dancing with a fat English press baron whose wife watched thoughtfully, figuring maintenance, I guess, and her share of the settle-ment when the house in the country was put up for sale.

Many of the international eminences came from such high levels of a hidden world they were not familiar to me by sight. The most famous face in the room, as far as I could tell, belonged to Dereena Foyle. Dereena Foyle is now no more than a late-night footnote on the old-movie channel, I know, but in those days she was still a big star, and those of us in our early twenties had grown up with the image of her temperamental beauty representing mature, abandoned sexiness. When I was a child, I'd had a Dereena Foyle paper doll, her wardrobe of sarongs and clinging off-the-shoulder dresses had to be cut out painstakingly with blunt scissors and fitted carefully on her cardboard body, to prevent it fraying at the edges. Male movie stars had often turned up at The Hook to play stooge to Blalack, but I had never seen a world-class female movie star before la Bastille's party, and if Dereena Foyle was one to go by, any stooges in their vicinity were expected to be all their own. A group of distinguished men in dinner-jackets danced around her like chorus boys, while she stood still at the centre of the ring, not very tall, but commanding. Her disproportionately big head rose out of a drift of snowy furs, despite the warmth of the evening. Early in her career her hair had been almost as coppery as Fawn's, but it had deepened in time to a colour natural only for foxes and varieties of tropical wood.

Helsinki Braw was suddenly striding across the dance floor, the potted palm did not exist to shield me from her predatory eye, and to my alarm I realised she was making straight for me. Flanking her were two of the most peculiar and striking women I had ever seen. They could have been thirty-one or sixty, I was too young at the time to estimate ages over thirty. Only long-time Parisiennes could present themselves as they were doing, not a single item they wore jumped to the eye or made itself more memorable than the ensemble: the skill of keeping a silk scarf just so, of choosing jewellery that is neither flashy nor inappropriately demure, the seamless chic of women in Paris, is passed down from mother to daughter and generally it is unmistakable. But those two had hand-painted their faces on flat-white, and they were as exotic and odd and inscrutable as geishas. When Helsinki introduced the stunning pair to me as Olga and Nina, the Tchernokoff Sisters, each extended a hand that was strong and surprisingly warm to be related to their visages of chilly porcelain.

The Tchernokoff Sisters are of White Russian origin, or so they claim. They are probably not Russians at all. They are probably not sisters, not Tchernokoffs, not Olga, not Nina; and certainly they were never raven-haired: not naturally. Who knows what is hidden behind the masks they put on every day? Or perhaps they never take them off, and they sleep in their mouths like small petunias, and their eyebrows of minute ink-strokes. When I came to love them both, it was for their lies as much as anything else. They were such dashing liars. They still are. Only a few weeks before I left London on the quest which is engaging me now, a note arrived from the Sisters, long since retired in the south of France, to ask me – or command me – thereafter to address letters to 'The Princesses Tchernokoff'. They said they were reinstating their neglected title.

'Royalty, even when losing control of its bodily functions and going a little ga-ga, remains welcome at good tables,' wrote Olga. Olga has always done their writing, with a silver Dunhill fountain-pen, while Nina stands behind her and dictates. Are they princesses? Probably not. But my letter by return was addressed to Their Royal Highnesses, and so they will remain in my book for as long as we all shall live.

You have to marvel at Helsinki's shrewdness: she knew very well when she introduced me to the Tchernokoff Sisters, she was introducing me to my future. 'You owe me one, shrimp,' she said, and then off she went, bracelets clashing on her windmill arms, to see what other deals were waiting to be made.

The next day Jinx left Paris. She rang me at the language

school where I was working, to say goodbye. During an after-hours breakout with Fawn Ellis and a couple of the other models, she'd met a tall dark Frenchman – 'Isn't it funny how they're all called Jean-Pierre?' – who had invited her to go sailing in Cannes, so she wasn't accompanying Helsinki straight back home after all. Jinx hadn't changed. People don't change, not at their core. Somewhere is a Flavia Jane, for instance, proud of her persuasions, prickly and essentially a picklepuss. As for me, I continue to keep my most prominent feature to the grindstone, and whatever the future holds, I shall be stalwart. And Jinx?

'He's the cutest thing,' she said. 'I think it could be love.' The only small difference I noticed was that for the first time she said 'thing' instead of 'thang'.

THIRTEEN

Tchernokoffs' beauty treatments were recognised as the best in the world by an exclusive brand of rich matrons who used to decide such matters and broadcast them by word of mouth in the days before publicists and ad agencies took over. In the same way fathers of high society once upon a time shipped their sons for initiation to de luxe brothels, mothers who were able took their debutante daughters to the Sisters Tchernokoff in Paris for their first grown-up haircuts and facials. During the German Occupation, the Sisters moved their business to Lisbon where, according to the rumour among their staff, they were spies: for the good guys, it was generally agreed. As soon as Paris was liberated, the Sisters returned with cash enough to reopen their *salon de beauté* on the rue du Faubourg St Honoré. Like la Bastille and other survivors of the pre-war period, they soon discovered their former clientele quite simply was no more. By the time I joined them in the last months of the 1950s, they were doing good business mainly out of women belonging to the households of Greek shipowners, and Texans, and South Americans. Occasionally, a shrouded client arrived from a middle-eastern harem, the boom in that region was just gathering steam; there were no Japanese on our books, they too were yet to come in force, but a few of the more mature Hollywood movie stars turned up by way of a secluded entrance at the back where the famous and infamous slipped in unseen by lurking gossips.

On arrival a client was whisked immediately into one of the six treatment suites, no more than cubicles really, each

95

named for the colour of its fittings, and all arranged in such a way that when two women whose bills were going to be paid by the same man happened to turn up at the same time, they did not have to meet. Elderly Frenchmen and the few surviving British aristocrats who could afford it, continued to send their young mistresses to the Tchernokoffs with instructions for them to be given the same skin-tone and hair-colour as their wives.

'They're old men, my dear,' Olga explained to me, 'and at their age they don't want to master anything new, only a springy version of what they already know.'

For a long time, the Sisters had refused to expand their range or put their excellent beauty products on the open market, and any woman who wanted the Tchernokoffs' famous treatments had to come to the salon in person, where she paid the earth for sessions lasting up to eight hours. Cosmeticians employed by the Sisters, manicurists, colourists, and so on, were without exception women. Only the four hair stylists were high-spirited, youthful men.

'To have one's hair cut', Nina said, as she was showing me around on my first morning, 'is an act of submission and the Tchernokoff Sisters do not subscribe to such a perversity between women.'

I was invited practically on sight to join the salon as an English-speaking receptionist, interpreter, amanuensis, and language teacher for the other employees. By then, I'd been in Paris long enough to see what happened to others at the shabby language school where I worked, how season after season accumulated until they found themselves mired abroad, neither real Parisians nor able ever to return to homelands that no longer existed, except in their memories. Already I'd begun to be aware – not of stirrings in myself, no indeed – of the creeping lethargy all too evident in older expatriates who were further down the road that leads to exile and spiritual exhaustion. The truth is, my soul had been dwindling in Paris; I was being mesmerised by day-to-day life there and would soon forget the point of the future. The confidence of beautiful women that something or someone is bound to come along was denied an overnosed little creature like me, but I was still too young to despair, and when the Sisters asked me to work for them, I leapt at the chance to make something of myself.

I wore a uniform designed by Olga's old friend, Coco Chanel. Although the suit was untrimmed and drab blue, I had never before been as smartly dressed. There was no other conk like mine on the Tchernokoffs' staff, and nobody so indisputably plain, but there were no real beauties employed there either. Even the junior manicurist, who was a very pretty girl, scraped her hair back to look as unattractive as possible.

'Our clients do not want us to make them beautiful only in order to compete with a junior manicurist,' said Nina, as usual a jump ahead of what I'd just been thinking.

'You see, dear,' said Olga, 'Nobody who buys a Rolls Royce would be pleased to discover the salesman driving one too.'

From my first day, the Sisters watched me closely, and gradually it dawned on me that for some reason they had plans for me. Not that I understood for a long, long time I had stumbled into what was going to be my life's work. On the contrary, after I'd been in the salon for nearly a year, carrying out mainly secretarial duties, for the first time Olga had me called into a cubicle where a treatment was going on, and if anyone had asked me after what I saw in there, I would have replied never, never could I devote myself to the service of the beauty business. It was the eau de nil cubicle, reserved for redheads because the colour put a damper on the high orange in their hair. On the table lay the actress Dereena Foyle, one muscular leg was extended and being painted with hot wax by an apprentice while

97

Nina stood over her, watching like a hawk. The air smelled of singed hairs, a curling-iron contraption lay smoking to one side, and I caught the stinging whiff of hydrogen peroxide. Dereena Foyle's right arm was hanging free and her hand gripped the neck of a bottle of vodka on the floor beside the table. Otherwise, she was wrapped entirely in pale green sheets, even her face was covered except for a patch about an inch square on her chin that Olga was studying through a high-powered magnifying glass suspended from a bracket on the ceiling.

'Ah, Mar-see-ah,' said Olga when I came in. They always pronounced my name so it sounded like 'mousier'. 'Mar-see-ah, my dear. Come, what do you make of this?' It was a good thing Dereena Foyle's eyes were covered so she could not see the look on my face when I peered through the enlarging glass. What lay under my eye was a dank pitted field with no sign of life past or present, except a nest of petrified scarlet thread worms, and a few dark stalks of what looked like blasted vegetable growth. If it was a test of my potential in the hands-on cosmetic trade, I failed miserably. On the spot I knew I'd never make a beautician, and not in a million years bring myself to touch strange skins past their prime; the Sisters must have seen it too. But they did not mind at all. If anything, from that day, their interest in me increased.

Thanks to the Sisters I found a better place to live than the Left-Bank hotel I'd been calling home. It was my first real flat, two rooms under the silvered roof of a building near Etoile. They paid a fair wage so I could go to restaurants sometimes, and to movies. I even went once on holiday to Spain, alone to be sure. Except when Jinx came to Paris, which she did twice a year for la Bastille's shows, I hardly had a friend, and I had no social life. I don't recall missing either, not really; only a little at holidays and on clear summery nights when all-Paris went out to play. I enjoyed the Sisters more every day, my job was growing broader, and I was squirreling away all sorts of information about beauty. Life was under way.

One Friday evening in late summer, when the others had hurried off for dinner dates and weekends with their lovers, I sat alone in a corner of the stockroom that served as our staff common room. I was at the big dressing-table we all used for coffee and occasional card games. In the triple-mirror I studied my reflection, nose after nose after nose of it. My all too defensive little mug looked out and out and out endlessly from under fly-away hair. Suddenly, in the mirror I saw the Sisters watching me.

'Could you make me beautiful?' I asked, half joking and half in hope.

'No,' Nina said. She pulled up one of the bridge chairs we all used in the staff room and sat next to me, holding my gaze in the central glass. 'Nobody can make you beautiful, Mar-see-ah. You are too sceptical, too analytical. You're too damn smart, you silly girl.' Olga stepped up behind me, her white face hovered over my head like a ghostly visitation.

'When a woman believes we can make her beautiful, or make her young again, well, then we can. For a little while. But you? Dear child, you lack all wish to be deceived. And always remember, that is what our art depends upon: a woman's wish to be deceived.'

'No preparation in the world, or treatment, will do our clients any more real good than they could do themselves with a little steam from the kettle and some vaseline,' Nina said. 'But they need to be deceived, wish it, will it. Now, Mar-see-ah, I want you to ask yourself why?' Nina put her elbows on the table and leaned so close to our images in the glass I could have counted the stiff black hairs of her lashes. 'They need to be deceived, in order to practise little deceptions of their own. Olga and I, we let that deception occur. We are illusionists.'

'But that's a confidence trick,' I said. 'Where I come from we call that getting money for old rope.'

'Fiddlesticks!' said Nina. 'What we do harms nobody, Mar-see-ah, poor cabbage. And to do no harm to those who want to be deceived is not so easy as you think.'

'Of course, they have to pay as much as they can,' Olga explained. 'Payment is part of the treatment. If they didn't pay for what we give them, how would they believe it had any value? And if they did not believe, then how could they make others believe?'

'You're saying, in a way, it's the thought that counts.'

'I like that,' Nina said. 'Yes, I like that. The thought that counts. Sure. For head-doctors too, those pissy-key-atrists, for them too it's the thought that counts.'

'. . . And philosophers, Nina, dear.'

'. . . And magicians, Olga.'

I smiled and shook my head; I was still not so all-fired sure. 'Don't be so thick and rational, Mar-see-ah,' Nina told me in the mirror. 'When the magician pulls a dove out of his big hat, yes, it's a trick,' she said, and asked: 'but does the dove know that?'

Over the next months, over the years to come, right up until I went to London to set up Miracle Products for them, the Sisters used to corner me from time to time, usually on Friday in the common room, and give me a few more of their trade secrets. 'These boiling, oiling, waxing things we do here, these pastes, our lotions, and our colours, they are very, very powerful,' Olga said one rainy autumn Friday. 'For example, you have seen Miss Dereena Foyle from Hollywood . . . ?'

'Soon-to-be-forgotten *femme fatale*,' said Nina as she pottered on the shelves, rearranging jars of fuller's earth. 'She is not as young in any way as she believes herself to be, it's true. But what is belief, dear Mar-see-ah? Belief is not what we know. Belief is what we prefer to think. Now, when we are done with Dereena Foyle she prefers to think herself young again, and for all intents and purposes, she *is* young again. But the transformation, you may notice, requires increasingly radical and astringent treatment.'

Nina pulled up a bridge chair and joined us at the table.

'The truth becomes more and more assertive, you see, as we age. Even the Tchernokoffs can go on just so long against real time.'

'And those pores!' Olga cried. 'Oh la Foyle's poor pores! Time's hammer-blows are landing on that face, Mar-see-ah. Vodka is burning craters on that face. And it's a big face, too . . . .'

'Not, God knows, to house intelligence or courtesy,' said Nina.

The sisters often sent me to their laboratory. It was in a grim area on the road to Orly, but I liked the feel of the place, and preferred it to the cubicles of the salon. Over the years I understood more every day of how the business worked. Sometimes I tried out the products in secret, and painted the colours thick on my own ugly phizz. Only once, they caught me redhanded, removing traces of a dark base coat and rouge at the mirror.

'No! Ah no!' Nina cried, and slapped my hand lightly. 'No, no, no, no. Haven't you seen yet, little hard-head? These concoctions and decoctions and distillations we make, these pastes and rouges and fards, they dangerously alter perception. Don't you see what we are dealing with here? These are drugs. No, no, no!'

'Mar-see-ah, dear,' Olga said, 'you have a future in this business, we knew the moment we saw you. But you must keep off the stuff yourself. Can you imagine drug addicts would trust a dealer who sampled heavily? They would think, quite correctly, that he cut what he sold in order first and foremost to satisfy his own craving.'

Something in my expression amused Nina. Only her

101

voice and eyes laughed, you understand; the sisters never cracked their faces. 'Olga, darling, she's thinking about us. The impertinent girl is thinking about these masks of ours. Don't you see, child, we designed our face years ago. We drew it first on paper, then on ourselves. Behind this unchanging invention, we can be any age, any mood, either sex. Or none. This is our gimmick. This is our mystery.' Olga leaned over and stroked my arm.

'It's hard for you Americans to understand how persuasive an ingredient is mystery,' she said.

That was the first time I asked the Sisters why they did not advertise their products and sell them on a wider scale. They looked at each other, and I sensed a silent exchange between them. But they did not answer me.

'Apropos,' said Nina, turning away, 'Dereena Foyle has failed to pay for her last three treatments.'

'Beauty is as beauty does,' I said.

'Beauty is . . . ' said Olga.

' . . . As beauty was,' said Nina.

FOURTEEN

I slipped into the position I liked best, backstage, watching the audience watch the production. The Sisters Tchernokoff remained at the front of the house, and I never presumed to any new responsibility before they handed it over to me willingly. My growing influence in the salon, particularly over its general management, was not due to a putsch or treacherous machinations; the Sisters themselves, in the traditional style of childless dynasts, were grooming a likely urchin, me, for succession. They controlled my steady rise, and I needed to prove myself every step of the way.

A busy decade was going on for Jinx, too. Early in the 1960s, at an event organised by one of the oil companies, keen to sweeten its image, an international panel of photographers and designers voted her 'The Most Beautiful Woman in the World'. Not only did the title gain Jinx phenomenal publicity, she started being paid large sums to attach her name to all sorts of products, from motor cars to bathing suits. For a year or so you would have said the whole world belonged to its most beautiful woman; her cards arrived from the most far-flung cities of the globe, and no glossy magazine went to press without a Jinx O'Malley beauty regimen, obviously disseminated from Helsinki's office – 'Look out for late nights. Drink lots of water. Think "beautiful". . . .' – a Jinx O'Malley diet, Jinx O'Malley at home (wherever that was!), or something Jinx O'Malley had been heard to say: 'Warren/Jack/Frank/Flex and I are just good friends . . . .' Jinx O'Malley dolls appeared in the shops, equipped with little lacy negligées, wigs, wig-stands, and miniature hair curlers. They still come up for sale occasionally, believe it or not; I recently saw one listed in London at an auction of period toys.

Hardly had the fuss over the world's most beautiful woman begun to subside, than she was elected by the board of Capran Cosmetics to be their 'Capran Girl of the Year', it must have been 1964 or '65. Capran had recently branched out into western Europe. Nina considered their creams cheap and greasy, their colours overwrought, their packaging beneath contempt, but I wasn't so sure we didn't have lessons to learn from the American giant, and I had a feeling Olga agreed with me, though she always kept her own counsel when Nina was fulminating. Capran's advertising and what a few decades on would be called their 'corporate image' were levelled straight at single women between eighteen and twenty-five in the lower-middle to middle income brackets, the questing unwed, in other words, a market as capricious and fickle as it is enormous. I managed to get my hands on market research that bore out what I'd suspected: most of Capran's customers were unfaithful to their products within months of marriage. Jinx's contract to embody and glorify the fantasies of universal unmarried womanhood was worth what now would be around a million dollars for the year. Helsinki must have been licking her chops over the commission.

Jinx rang me more than ever in this period of her growing fame. During one call I asked her about the famous movie star, Flex Baker, with whom the gossip columns were linking her name.

'He's sweet,' she said, 'and Helsinki's fixed it for us to see a lot of each other. But there's nothing between us. Don't tell anyone,' she whispered over the trans-Atlantic line, 'he doesn't like girls.'

'At midnight', I said, 'Prince Charming turns into a fruit . . . .'

'Oh honey,' Jinx cried. 'I'm so lonely! I miss you.'

A substantial machine had been built on Jinx's beauty by that time, not just hairdressers and cosmeticians, but a secretary, a masseur, and a 'personal assistant' assigned by Helsinki.

'How can you be lonely with all those people around?'

'Honey, I don't even know what to tell my personal assistant to do. Personal things are what I like to do for myself.'

During Jinx's final month as the Capran Girl, something occurred to keep her lovely face in newspapers and on television everywhere: General Juan Reyes, inflamed by her beauty, mounted a kidnap attempt on her. For months after his failed plot came to light, it was meat and drink to leader-writers and stand-up comics all over the world, except of course in his own homeland, which had neither, newspapers not cabaret, scarcely any meat, and only raw rum to drink. 'El Generale', also known as 'Juan the Disemboweller', ruled the Central American flyspeck, Una Recolta. *Paris-Match* printed a long interview with an anonymous political exile who said the bachelor-dictator kept a large room in his palace filled with pictures of Jinx O'Malley, some of them framed in silver and gold on a candlelit altar. Whenever he needed solace from the pressures of his public life, he used to lock himself up in there, alone. The previous year, when his mother had died, he spent so long in meditation at the shrine of his American blonde, the little nation was in an aggravated and explosive state of its customary military emergency by the time he finally emerged. Somehow, El Generale got wind that Jinx was to be on location for a Capran photoshoot in the Florida Keys, only a short ride by speed boat from Una Recolta. Probably, logically, I'd stake my life on it,

Helsinki Braw was the source of his tip-off.

Wild with desire to meet the woman of his dreams, and maddened to learn she was so near, Reyes sent a hand-picked bunch of his personal guard to grab her. But it was a dark and moonless night, their English was awful, and because of one damned thing or the other, they snatched the wrong victim. Sometimes there's nothing much between comic opera and great tragedy: a sneeze, a fatal blink, a banana skin, and either on the instant becomes the other. When the thugs' speedboat landed in the small hours on the coast of their homeland, where El Generale was pacing the sands impatiently, they unrolled their victim from the rug they'd used as camouflage, and only then saw that the tall blonde they'd gone to so much trouble to procure for the big man was not Jinx, but a young photographer's assistant called Phil, wearing his hair in a style not yet familiar to Una Recoltans.

What happened to the kidnappers is anyone's guess. According to one left-wing Parisian paper I read, the American government had a cynical alliance with Una Recolta, and it was decided on a high level to forget the incident in the interests of averting a small Trojan War. Besides, Phil had been sent home first class, loaded with Una Recoltan artifacts, and no real harm had been done. Things were allowed to blow over as fast as possible, but Jinx was the talk of international society for a while, and of course her stock soared. Two months after the botched attempt, the very day 'El Generale' had himself declared 'El Presidente', he was blown up by guerrillas while driving through town in his big white Cadillac. Presumably his shrine to Jinx was dismantled by the new leader, and the whole incident subsided into lore and legend surrounding the most beautiful woman of her time.

Jinx was so unimpressed by El Generale's attempt on her person I had to piece the story together for myself out of magazines and newspapers. Bigger news, as she saw it, was that she had met a man on Key West, and married him. To be frank, the whole notion of marriage puzzles me, and always has. I can just about understand it as a business deal: to establish a family, and purvey a cure for loneliness. But whenever I see a couple side by side in that peculiarly encrusted marital silence, I have to wonder why those two came to believe they could not live without each other: or, more to the point, why they ever thought they could live with each other? And how many couples actually shoot two lives' allowance of romance into a single searing look, and know at first sight they have to tie the knot or die of longing? That was certainly the way Jinx believed marriages were made.

'I like being married,' she wrote. 'I always feel good when I'm married.'

And she enclosed a picture of the new husband so I could see for myself how gorgeous he was. What I saw was a dark, handsome fellow who was terribly aware of the camera. He could have been Niccolo de Lisi's younger brother. In his eyes was the same future spite and weak-willed aspirations Blalack had discovered in Nick, and shown the world in *Black and White Wedding*. Jinx's husband-number-three had no steady job, he was a poet if I recall correctly, and there was nothing to stop him upping stakes to follow his beautiful wife to Hollywood, where Helsinki had fixed for her to be in a movie. His name escapes me now. By the time Jinx and I saw each other again, the marriage was all over.

We did not meet again face to face until the 1960s, when the Tchernokoffs sent me to London where they wanted me to assess the renascence of taste and wealth that was supposed to be happening there. I do not recall precisely what year it was: 1967 or '68? Properly speaking, the 'swinging sixties' didn't get underway until well on in the decade; they then endured into the 1970s, before they stumbled, weakened, and were eventually bought out lock stock and barrel by the 1980s. Also, it's not quite accurate of me to say the Sisters 'sent' me to London. In fact, they allowed me to go. They must have seen I was approaching a time when urges a woman may not admit or care to acknowledge start pushing her into deeper water. In a nutshell, although I was not yet ready to inherit their little empire, they could see I was fretful, and had begun to long beyond sense or comprehension for something of my own making.

FIFTEEN

The previous epoch had not been youthful at all, not much
fun. Teenagers were invented in the 1950s, its true, but
teenage didn't actually begin until fourteen or fifteen, it
was heavily chaperoned, and all finished within four years.
Then along came the late 1960s and early '70s, and even
those of us on the brink of our final vows of adulthood
were given a stay of execution. Not only did youth start
bossing its own show, but nobody had to grow up after all;
we could hang on to youth, be younger than we had ever
been, younger than anyone had ever been. It was an offer
I was happy to refuse. The banked fires of middle age were
right up my street, and suited me just fine. London suited
me, too, more than Parisian chic or New York's
razzmatazz. From the moment I arrived, it was bliss to
speak my native tongue and to hear it all around me. The
world at large considers the English to be cold and indif-
ferent; I found them, and still find them, merely rather shy.
True enough, there was an explosion locally of glittery
juvenility, I felt it as soon as I got off the train at Victoria
Station, but London has always been essentially a place for
growns-ups, and the loud noises the kids were making
caused barely a twitch in the muscle of the city. A thor-
oughly enjoyable week of clear summer weather, not too
hot, had gone by when I received word from my office in
Paris that Jinx was passing through London, and dying to
see me.

Like most of our meetings over the years, it took place
in an hotel. The moment I saw Jinx at the door to her suite,

in her microscopic skirt with legs travelling for ever in pale tights, I knew she was one of those who had skipped eagerly into the 'swinging sixties' and found a good time waiting with his electric guitar under his arm and a neatly-rolled joint between his teeth. But it was ever the same when Jinx and I met, even after years had passed, within moments small changes were swallowed by the warmth of our greeting, and any alterations had barely a chance to register before they melted into her immutable beauty.

The air of the room behind her drifted with smoke that smelled of burning leaves. On the bed was a young man, asleep. 'We met on the plane,' Jinx said. 'He's a Libran.'

The boy twitched, muttered in his sleep, and turned his closed face my way. A beaded band held his dark hair back and kept it from tumbling over his forehead.

'Your lovelife, my girl, is starting to be like a game of Chinese Rumours,' I said, slipping easily into the old affectionate chiding. 'Your ideal image is being distorted bit by bit through repetition. You'd better watch your step, Jinx O'Malley, or you won't know the real thing when it finally turns up.'

'Oh Marsha, honey,' she said, 'I miss how you make me laugh. I miss the funny way you see things. Don't you worry, sugar, when love comes along, I always know it.'

London was the first stop on a promotional tour for a movie Jinx had – 'decorated' is the word, I guess. Her only line in it was: 'He's all yours, Ivan'. Spy films were popular that season, and girls who appeared in the genre enjoyed a flurry of publicity before sinking, bikinis and all, without trace. From the moment Jinx arrived at Heathrow in a blaze of flash-bulbs, she was at the centre of the very phenomenon I was supposed to be observing for the Sisters, so it was convenient for me to tag along. I wasn't all that old myself at the time, after all. And I tried, I tried, and I tried to have fun, the way Jinx was doing. Going by the principle that brings

110

a sinner to her knees on the chance her posture will attract genuine salvation, I laughed pointlessly along with everyone else; at parties I tried once or twice to shimmy by myself, lifting my arms to a phantom partner the way the dolly-birds were doing. But without their audience of fascinated men, I wound down quickly, and slumped in a corner of the room like a forgotten old toy. Even the most accomplished actors have trouble faking a party scene, and soon I slipped away to my sedate hotel, a book, and a nightcap.

The time I spent with Jinx in London blends into one hectic fabric from which a few images and words jump out at me. I can still see Jinx gyrating, pelvis to pelvis, with a procession of good-looking men. She was incomparably beautiful, willow-slim, thanks to pills she and the other girls swallowed like candy; her long hair was ironed straight to the waist, and swayed like a yard of precious silk. To watch her in those days made it seem almost possible she possessed faith and force enough to go on dancing for ever. The redhead, Fawn Ellis, was around too, in the merry throes of another divorce, her second or third. Jinx told me Fawn's ex-to-be owned an airline I think, or racehorses; probably both. Fawn nobbled me at a party once. I don't imagine she recognised me or knew who I was; she just needed someone to listen to her for a few minutes. 'I don't believe in religion,' she shouted over the music. 'Religion is responsible for so much suffering and wars, and stuff. But I believe in a, you know, a higher something. There's gotta be a higher something, like God, I just know it, because He's been so good to me.' Her pretty face was squeezed by thought. A lumpy cigarette burnt between her fingers; she offered it to me. I puffed on it, coughed, and immediately felt very sleepy. 'I hate churches, you know,' Fawn said. 'You will not ever see me in a church.'

'If that's the case, I guess I won't bother going to one,' I replied, and found myself laughing.

'I'm a particle of cosmic flow,' Fawn said. And as suddenly as she had arrived, she tripped away to dance with a fat man wearing big cufflinks.

I saw Helsinki Braw once at the *vernissage* of a popular young artist. 'Elemental' the exhibition was called; it was composed of frames mounted, empty, on the walls. Local celebrities packed the gallery, and reporters were sprinkled around, scribbling in the notebooks they still used back then. Suddenly Helsinki was soaring through the crowd, her turban higher than ever, earrings longer, voice more ready to blister paint. Her bangles slid and clattered, though less easily than they had, because her arms, like the rest of her, were growing stout. Cagily, I fielded her questions about the Sisters. Then she noticed Jinx talking to a reporter and hurried away from me, back into the dense mass of people. 'Look out for the press,' she cried over her shoulder, 'the bastards are getting younger and meaner; they're not romantics like they used to be. All they want these days is dirt . . . .'

On days when Jinx had nothing to do, we went out to the shops together; she to buy, me to see what was going on, and to take notes for the Sisters. Boutiques had replaced department stores for stylish shopping and were very much in vogue, opening as fast as pretty umbrellas on every high street. Speaking of umbrellas, I remember when Jinx bought a spectacular umbrella in an arcade that was like a middle-eastern bazaar, right down to the reek of incense, only fearfully expensive. Big money was being spent. The price and variety of cosmetics on sale in there astonished me, and so did the way youngsters were snapping it all up. I watched a girl who looked like a student nurse, or perhaps herself a shopgirl, spend in a few minutes what must have been a considerable chunk of her week's salary on a thick mascara that was bound to clot, and two white lipsticks destined to be out of fashion in a week. When I emerged empty-handed,

Jinx was waiting where we had agreed to meet outside, eager to show me her new umbrella; it was Italian, silk, and pink. It had cost what would now be around one hundred and fifty pounds sterling.

'Lord Jinx! Nine-tenths of the people on this planet are not even aware there is in existence such a thing as an umbrella costing as much as that!'

'I keep forgetting pounds aren't the same as dollars,' she said, and flagged down a passing cab to take us to the trattoria where we, and half the young celebrities of London, were booked for an overpriced lunch.

In the past, Jinx's extravagance had been in proportion to what was in her pocket. Even so, she often used to run out of cash, and I had to tide her over until the end of the week when, without fail, she counted out to the penny what she owed me, straight into my hand. But in London I realised that money had flown into the abstract for Jinx. It had become like merit or a kind heart, something to have without being able to see it, and to be spent endlessly, no need to wait for change. The real money, the paper and metal stuff we waitresses swept off the tables, was finite; when you had it you could run out of it. But it was beyond Jinx's comprehension anyone could ever run out of unreal money as symbolised by cheques and a few years later by credit cards. A good thing Jinx had Helsinki Braw looking after her finances, that's what I told myself when she frowned as we were leaving the restaurant and told me she must have left her new pink silk umbrella in the back of the taxi.

In London I went with Jinx to one of her photo sessions and I saw for the first time the way a woman can be brought to a pitch of desirous excitement simply by being looked at. Most attractive girls have the knack of readjusting themselves, their very bodies, I mean their flesh and bone, to suit fashion after fashion; but the way Jinx was able to change from moment to moment was unnerving to behold. Like a predatory witch, she transformed herself before my eyes, and pushed herself through every embodiment of flirtation, from luscious promise to promise, to sexy threat, to submission, and back to innocence again. With mounting speed, in a kind of desperation, she burnt through all nuances of the female repertoire, seeking the ultimate seductive pose, the one to end them all.

I think it must do a woman's spirit incalculable harm to strain and qualify herself that way for the camera's hissing eye, in time to rhythmic music beating in the background, and the vicious tenor of crooning boys. The photographer circled and advanced, pimping for his Nikon, and urging her on.

'Do it, baby. Do it, Jinx. Do it for me. Yes, oh yes. Give me pouting. Give me knowing. Give me menace. Oh yeah, oh yeah. I like that. I like the way you do it. Oh, baby don't you do it good?'

Finally, she stood on the edge of exhaustion, looking back over her shoulder. The desire for love overwhelmed all other expressions on her beautiful face, and the foreboding I'd felt in Paris came back again, for on some level, hidden even to myself, I had to see that the Siren's case was as hopeless as my own.

'Youth has no culture!' cried Nina, when I made my report on what I'd seen in London. 'Culture is what youth inherits from previous generations. Holy heaven, Mar-see-ah, what else is youth's inheritance if it is not the culture of the aged? Except for sport and acts of brute procreation, no advantage whatsoever attaches to being young.'

'Nina, what Mar-see-ah is telling us is quite simple. By "youth culture" she simply means that these days, youth has money to burn,' Olga said, and I was happy to let her do the explaining. 'Let the kiddies burn their money elsewhere,' Nina replied. 'We do not want it here.'

'No, no, of course not. I agree,' I said. 'Not here, but . . .' And I told them how in London I had seen face-paints in wild colours, some even containing flecks of metallic pigment, and each requiring a special cream, too, for removing it at night from eyes, throat, mouth. I told them about brushes shaped for cheek or chin or lips that once had been only for professionals but now were being mass-produced, along with instructions on their use. Sophistication formerly only for the richest and most beautiful of women was on offer across the counter. From a clandestine affair of spells and potions passed down the distaff side, beauty had grown into very big business and our exclusive scale of operation had nearly had its day. Even though women in menopausal blues continued to shell out whatever the market would bear for a decoction of nuns' urine or placental residue, that did not mean a profitable company could afford to sneeze at the free spenders of the new youth culture.

'All I'm suggesting, mesdames, is that the time has come to branch out. Women know more about beauty these days, and with knowledge come needs. The trick is to find a need, or even better to create one, and fill that need over and over again.'

To my surprise, Nina laughed. 'What you have just said – find a need or make a need, fill it, then do it again – means you think we ought to apply the dynamics of lovemaking to the mass market.'

'Well, is that a crime?'

'In some societies, yes, I believe it is,' said Olga. 'But even if it is not a crime in Paris, it would be unspeakably vulgar for the Tchernokoffs.'

If it sounds as if the Sisters and I were coming to a parting of the ways, blame memory for hanging on to conversations of high pitch. The truth is, the Sisters and I had never got on better than we did during the year after my return from London. My uncouth yapping was the voice of their future, and they knew it, only they were not ready to tell me so. Nina used to bait me quite coolly and then, as soon as I broke surface spluttering and holding forth, indulgent pride soon took up residence behind her impassive face. Looking back, of course, I see that under the Sisters' protective colouring they were not getting any younger, and they had already decided between themselves to see me right before they called it quits.

One Friday evening the Sisters came into the staff room where they found me, as they had years before, dabbing at my face.

'Don't worry,' I said. 'It's only a touch of powder. I know too much. That's what you told me, right? I'm safe from our terrible drugs. Thank you, Olga. Thank you, Nina. And don't worry about me. The cosmetic has not been made to persuade Marsha Leah Feldstein that she could, or should be beautiful.'

'But yes! Oh, yes. But yes,' they cried in the French manner that means you're all wrong.

'There is the most ruinous cosmetic . . . ' said Nina.

'Most addictive of them . . . ' said Olga.

'It's glorious, but it fades in no time and leaves behind insatiable desire for more, more, more . . . '

No need for me to ask what this fatal beauty aid was. Hadn't Jinx O'Malley for nearly twenty years been letting me in on the secrets a virgin never knows? I hadn't been friend to the most beautiful woman in the world without learning a thing or two.

'Oh,' I laughed, 'I'm not afraid of love.'

'You damn well ought to be,' said Nina.

116

SIXTEEN

A streaky blonde with the utterly incurious gaze peculiar to native southern Californians, has just arrived from room-service bearing the single-malt whisky I ordered twenty minutes ago. I was smoking one of my occasional cigarettes when she came in, and she fairly twitched with disapproval. If the girl weren't an hotel employee she would no doubt have come right out and ticked me off for polluting her air space. Next time I write to Nina, I'll tell her how American youth has started claiming air as their very own real-estate. That's how much the youth culture she derided long ago fancies itself these days. As if the whole of history convulsed and heaved to bring forth this single batch of kiddies beyond the touch of time. They claim the earth, too, call it their inheritance and expect it to be handed down like granny's Limoges tea-set, never used. 'Don't they see that it is the earth that will one day inherit them?' I can almost hear Nina reply.

'And hold them in her larder for eternity,' Olga would tack on in her sad way.

Even though it's late afternoon here in jolly Los Angeles, the hour when civilised people stop for a drink, I had the feeling the local gal from room-service did not much approve of my solitary whisky, either. This is America, and here one does not choose, as one does in Europe, to have a drink, or not to have a drink: here one is a drunk, or not a drunk – there is no manoeuvring space when it comes to morals in the United States. Where outside Islam is it so hard to be good, and so easy to be bad?

117

'America was established by puritans,' was how Jake put the idea to me. He'd only met Jinx a few days before, we were waiting for her as usual. He was excited and talking, talking, talking.'Puritanical ways were endorsed by the majority,' Jake said. 'So we got the prigs and the proles in charge here, and between them they kept all the queer ducks out of public life. The most original and daring minds had nowhere to go in these great United States but out into garden sheds where, for lack of anything better to do, they invented the motor car. What the oddballs should have been doing, of course, and would have been, too, if they'd had the chance, was pouring all their humour and vitality and tolerance into our society at large. If eccentricity and charm had ruled the roost, this would now be a better world. Instead America has been dominated by solemn idealists, who believe themselves to be missionaries in their own land, and who can't see what chumps they are, or how much harm they do. Thanks pretty much entirely to America's crude idealism, the planet will never lack an underworld.'

Oh, Jake. After I'd been back from London for a couple of years, when the Sisters Tchernokoff suggested it was time for me to make another reconnaissance, this time in America, it still surprises me there was not a shiver of premonition in my heart. True enough, I am no predestinarian, it's not in my nature to believe in the unavoidable collision of lover with beloved, assassin with victim, or falling apple with superior bounce. There never was a palpable hit without an infinite number of unknown misses. Existence is subject to luck and to accident, existence probably *is* luck and accident, but no elegant interventions of fate are sent to help us make plans for the future, no disembodied warnings. Great beauties like Jinx and the flibbertigibbet Fawn Ellis may have had reason to imagine themselves touched by individual destiny, but, hell's bells,

118

I only need to look in a mirror to know myself as one of the multitudinous ordinary run. Life is a down-to-earth business, full stop. But, tell me why, why, why it should be, that even now when I look back on the days before I left Paris for my first westward journey, in spite of knowing better, I scour my memory for omens?

I flew from Paris to America. It was my first flight, and less strange than I had imagined. Except for a constant niggling awareness that the human body is no more built for permanence than a light bulb, being on a plane turned out to be not all that different from travelling by train. Only once I looked down through unbreathable spaces as the fluff under us parted for a moment, and when I saw how the ocean lapped its setting in the crust of the planet, I felt a flash of what must be the eagles' joy of flying. Otherwise, all that can be said for air travel is it gets you there fast. And, of course, there are an infinite number of much more pressing matters for us business people than to lounge on the mighty breast of mother Atlantic letting time pass unimportantly in contemplation of the nature of existence, while fathoms deep below us lie the drifts from which humanity wriggled free. Oh yes, and down there too are Blalack's bones to think about, perhaps with bottle tops, carelessly jettisoned by Italian stewards, that were his eyes. Oh dear. Digression is half the fun, but we business people must not digress. There are always more important things for a sensible business person to do. Or so they would have us believe.

There was I, back in the early years of my gruelling middle age, touring the great cities of my homeland as I had been sent to do by the Sisters, for business. And incidentally wondering why, as soon as the weather is warm, do the old gals of the New World change into sleeveless blouses and dresses? Being so determined to hoodwink age, you'd think they would know the Gauguin

119

principle: an urban woman's upper arm is the first thing to go. They are a real phenomenon, those sharp-shanked, leathery, over-the-hill, big-city glamourpusses of my homeland, flashing their twiggy appendages. In the most expensive department stores of Chicago, Dallas, Miami, I observed them snapping up anti-ageing creams as if there were no tomorrow. Geriatric anorexics, every one of whom has seen better days and who, right to the end, will mistake the tally on their bathroom scales for divine judgement. How they struggle and beat their puny fists against old Father Time's great hairy swelling chest as he carries them kicking and screaming into the desert where homely little women like me have spent a lifetime.

'Relax and enjoy, it, girls,' I wanted to say. And, 'Welcome to the harem of unused women. Welcome, old birds, one and all. Why fight it? From here on in, a lifetime membership is guaranteed.'

For the past many years Jinx had been more or less based in Los Angeles. Although she was modelling less, and much less to be seen in magazines, she still travelled widely to locations for bit parts in movies, and Helsinki was keeping her at work in tv commercials. Jinx preferred the west-coast climate to New York. And she no longer had any reason to return to Paris. La Bastille had finally slid gracefully under in the mid-sixties, in spite of a perfume he'd launched in hopes of saving his house. Perfumes, tights, ready-to-wear, and popular accessories had saved comparable couturiers for a while. But unwisely, and against the advice of Helsinki Braw, he'd called his scent 'Quoique'. Most English-speaking women had no idea how to pronounce 'Quoique', and those who did, preferred not to. 'Quoique,' 'Quoique,' 'Quoique': it made them feel flat-footed, I guess. Without the American market, he was doomed.

I flew into Los Angeles from Dallas and Jinx came to

the airport to meet me. Seeing her in the arrival lounge was like being struck momentarily by double vision or a ringing in my ears. I actually had to shake my head hard as she was running forward to enfold me in a cloud of just a little too much 'Arpège'. Men milling around us were magnetised as usual, and to the eyes of other women her high gloss must have been more enviable than ever; it was so professional and expensive. Two young businessmen near me by the luggage carousel pulled their gaze away from her, and I saw them wink at each other. You understand, I had been watching men react to Jinx for a long time, and I could not remember ever before seeing a man who did not prefer to keep to himself what he was thinking when he looked at her. I stood back a step. It was as if I confronted a painting of my old friend, not a masterpiece that showed the freshness of a soul, as 'Oyster Cracker III' had done, but a more commercial piece, slick and glorifying of her skin.

She led me to a flashy, open car in the parking lot. When she kicked off her high-heeled slippers so she could drive it barefoot, I laughed, and felt myself settle back into our old friendship. Jinx was an excellent driver, she nipped into every opening, her hair crackling like little whips in the wind. Men looked over in surprise that turned into pained anguish when the beautiful woman raced her powerful machine past and left them standing. As we drove, Jinx talked mostly about all the men she'd known since we last met; she spoke with a curious detachment, almost cynical, and not like her old self at all. She said she was unattached at the moment; she called it 'a dry patch'. We were on our way to an apartment Fawn Ellis kept in Beverly Hills, she let Jinx use it when she was abroad at one of her other homes. I planned to stay there with Jinx for ten days before I went back to New York and then to Paris.

'I guess you're going to tell me I ought to find a place

of my own, honey,' she said. 'But once a girl has a place and fixes it up so it's really nice, she's going to get the kind of man who moves in on her. I've had enough of that, thank you very much. That's not what I want right now in my life. I want somebody who helps me for a change, instead of helping himself.'

I looked out at the traffic, nearly bumper to bumper.

'Millions of men, Jinx,' I said. 'Not a knight on a white horse in the bunch.'

'Oh, honey,' she said. But she didn't smile. 'You're a hoot, Marsha.'

Fawn's place was one of a stack of huge glass-fronted specimen cases set at crazy angles to each other on a hill. Inside were bare architraves, bricks and unstained wood, too chill and stark to be Jinx's taste, but there were big embroidered cushions on the floor, and silk roses in vases, which I knew were all her own. On glass shelves against one wall were Fawn's crystals, and her library: *In Search of the Miraculous*, *Siddartha*, *Little Women*, and *Gone With the Wind*. 'Oyster Cracker III' was propped up against a candelabra on top of the white piano. When I glanced at it, I felt a shiver of unease; I looked away quickly, and didn't look again. Jinx was stirring saccarine into her coffee.

'I love sweet things,' she said. 'How come everything we like is bad for us, Marsha, can you tell me that?'

'I guess because we can never get enough of it,' I replied, 'and because whenever we get what we like, it's never as good as we thought it would be.'

She nodded solemnly, as if I'd said something profound.

It was a Tuesday, 22 November, the day after my arrival in Los Angeles. It was 1972. I was feeling pretty good in myself. I woke very early and strolled out through the sliding doors of the living-room on to the roof of the garage that lay just below, so its roof doubled as a sundeck. From

122

the apartment on the terrace above a woman's laugh rang out, too bright and caustic, like the water in the communal pool glinting several levels below; it sounded equally de-natured by chemicals. Then a spry man in white ran down the wooden staircase that zigzagged between terraces. He moved headlong, like an escapee. A few minutes later, from the same apartment emerged a frail old woman with blazing orange hair, wearing a dressing-gown. She slipped stealth-ily downstairs and stopped at the back door that led into Fawn's surgical little kitchen. From where she stood she could not see me, but I watched her look around furtively before she pulled four empty wine bottles, one after the other, out of a bag on her arm, and dumped them into Fawn's rubbish bin. Then she beat it back to her own apartment as fast as she could. When Jinx finally woke, I told her what I'd seen. 'She's that pathetic old movie star,' Jinx said. 'The one with the funny name.'

Jinx had a small part in a television situation comedy. When she drove to the studio, I taxied to Rodeo Drive to have a look at the buying habits of the local rich folks. I could have been intimidated, believe me, but I chose instead to view with icy contempt the mostly European riffraff pushing their overpriced goods in the last commercial outpost of the western world. In my report later I wrote to the Sisters that never before anywhere had I seen a clientele so ardently in search of magic as the highly-strung babes of Rodeo Drive.

'At least when I'm shopping, I don't eat,' I overheard one skinny million-dollar tootsie telling another.

The Tchernokoffs would have done very well out of a salon in that locale.

'But you'd rather sell door-to-door in Calcutta than have to live here. And to be honest, so would I.'

At one o'clock I was in the commissary to have lunch with Jinx. At one forty-five she arrived at last. Everyone in the commissary looked up when she entered. Jinx was having a good day. Good days come to all women less and less with age, for they are not really of the spirit; they require a sprightly system of hormones to spread the message. Nevertheless, on her good days, Jinx was as naturally alluring as ever, and seeing her you could almost believe she sustained every gorgeous molecule in place, even against time, by force of her own will. On days like that, Jinx was as impervious to the admiration of common men as a priestess of ancient times who had spent the night before making love to a god. Jinx was having a very good day, indeed. Her hair lay in strands of bright light, and those O'Malley bones were seen, like spiders' webs and suspension bridges, to ally form perfectly with function. She waved and brought her tray over to my small table near a window. One moment, she was telling me about the costume she'd been fitted for — tight skirt, tailored blouse, high heels — and the next moment, there he was, was he, looking down at her, not me. Of course. One look, and America's great man of letters was a gone goose. He stammered and shivered, and hovered over our table in the commissary. Finally, he fell into the seat beside her, gibbering a little. All it took was a smile and a single slow flutter of her green eyes to bring Jacob Orben panting to his knees. O Jacob of my anxious nights, would you have been less stunned, or more, if you had known that the way Jinx smiled at you was not because it delighted her to bring down such a great man as Jacob Orben? On the contrary, the smile she gave you was the tolerant smile beauties reserve for nobodies. Jinx had not the least idea who you were.

I knew Jake immediately from his pictures on dustcovers. Had I not read Jake Orben's novels as fast as they had appeared, ever since I was a girl in Teaneck, New Jersey? He was taller than I had imagined, more lanky and

124

loose-jointed, and there was a beguiling touch of dilapidation about him. He glanced at me with those uncannily balanced eyes.

'So this is the great cosmetic,' I thought, 'this is love.'

And then all thought was blown away in such a sweep of boldness and despair as tommies must have felt going over the top. I heard shells whistling and felt the hot wind on my face.

Jinx went off to her sit-com. Jake stayed in his seat, and we were alone together, both deafened momentarily by the pounding of our hearts.

'Beauty like that is truth,' he said after a while. 'What other truth can there be? Beauty like that must reflect a glorious and all-knowing mind . . . must . . . does . . . inside, skinside . . . seeing her, a man's eye is seeing deeper than it knew it could. I feel I've been waiting all my life to look into the light of her beauty.'

Jesus Christ. I ask you. Here's a man who has read everything: a man of letters. Had Keats taught him nothing about the fatal weakness of men's eyes? Not to mention all the brawny Greek heroes brought down not by the sword but by a pretty face. Why, the list of chumps goes back past Ahab and Samson, to Adam and the very foundation of myth and allegory. Don't those big guys ever learn?

The next morning a package arrived by messenger at Fawn's place. It contained a first edition of Jake's masterpiece, *The Zeitel Codicil*. Perplexed, Jinx handed it to me. On the flyleaf in Jake's hand was the inscription: 'For Jinx, who is sprung of Circe's isle . . . .' Oy! Had the shlemiel thought what that made *him*? I told Jinx how rare a man Jake was, how respected in many circles, and gifted, and sensitive, and widely published all over the world.

'For crying out loud, Jinx,' I said, actually in pain, 'why not have a grown-up for a change?'

She fell thoughtful, and then she asked: 'Is he married?'

'Not at the moment,' I replied.

I spent most of the day on a bench near the two fake mastodons suspended inexorably over their bubbling pit. The smell of tar even now brings back a shade of agonised wonder and makes my eyes tear. Back home in the late afternoon I found Jinx asleep in the hammock on Fawn's sundeck. *The Zeitel Codicil* was beside her. When I took the book into my hands, it fell open where an emery board marked her place. She'd managed thirty-five pages out of four hundred, for Jinx it was a brave attempt, and it meant that even though she did not love the book, she was interested in its author. My heart took up its battle station.

SEVENTEEN

When I was on holiday in Spain, I went alone to the
bullfights once. During my final week in Los Angeles I saw
myself dressed in a little suit of lights, fighting the beast, but
to no applause. A homely undersized torrero does not draw
the crowds, and the stands were empty—there was nobody
to see my courage. 'Egg-head squires living doll . . .' said the
headline of a local gossip rag. Ole! With a swirl of the cape,
I led the sharp horn past, it barely grazed me. On their third
night out together Jinx did not return to her own bed. And
when she appeared next day to tell me in a tone of mild
surprise that she thought Jake was 'nice', I awarded myself
the ears and tail. And nobody knew, not even Jinx, how hard I
had fought to stand there, arched and tense, but able to smile.

I planned to spend some time with my family before I
returned to Paris. The night before my departure, Jake
turned up with a pair of tickets for him and Jinx to see a
visiting *King Lear*. I overruled all objections, and insisted
that they go; I swore to Jinx I did not mind being home
on my own, which it happens was the truth. In fact, making
Jinx go out that night to sit through *King Lear* was the only
cruel trick I ever played on her. A better friend, a better
person, would have insisted on company for her last night
in town, and so spared Jinx what must have been the
excrutiating experience of sitting through Shakespeare's
great tragedy with a man who expected her to find it a
revelation, and to talk about it afterwards. This is as bitchy
as I will ever be about Jinx, by the by. And, remember, I
was suffering horribly at the time.

127

'Am I going to like *King Lear*, honey?' she asked me, when Jake was out of earshot. What could I say but: 'No'.

Hardly had I settled into a comfortable wallow of self-pity, glass in hand, than there came a rap-rap-rapping at Fawn's front door. Dereena Foyle brushed past me and through the hall straight into the living-room, where she turned in frantic circles. Her dressing-gown was ragged around the hem, and there were stains on its deep trailing sleeves.

'I'm all out,' she said in a sloppy, rubbery voice.

'Out of what?'

'What've you got?' she replied. When she threw herself down on Fawn's big sofa, her robe flew open to the knee, and out poked the skinny mottled legs of a hard-drinking woman. She wore slippers with pompoms and high thin heels.

'I'll have a drink,' she said. 'Vodka, ice and soda in a tall glass.'

Mascara had bled down either side of her nose, a cute young giggler's nose that did an ageing face no favours. Tomato-red lipstick flowed into hairline tributaries around her mouth. The carmine smear on her top front teeth was a sure sign of a woman whose heyday was in the 1940s and early '50s. She had let herself have it with the base-coat and blusher; her makeup said 'Take that!' and beat her face into a parody of youth.

'Don't call me a dreamer.' I could have sworn that was what she said. But then she repeated quite firmly, 'I say, I say, don't call me Dereena. Don't ever call me Dereena.' She took a great swallow of her drink.

'Miss Foyle?' I asked.

Tears and mascara suddenly poured down the ravaged skinscape I'd peered at in horror years before through the Tchernokoffs' glass.

128

'Rita,' she said. 'My real name is Rita Cramm. Poor Rita Cramm. Nobody ever loved her. They took one look at her, those lousy bastards, and kee-rist, she was gorgeous back then. And they said "ooooooh nooooo!" We've got a Rita already. There's only room for one. And the bitch was a redhead, too.'

Another swig of vodka. As quickly as tears had come they were sucked back, but the dry dark beds of their passing stayed on her powdered cheeks.

'Cramm has no class,' she said, angry. 'And Rita had to go. I was so young, so young and tender. What could I do? So it was bye-bye Rita Cramm, I hardly knew you.'

She went to put her glass on the table between us, and just made it; some liquid splashed the carpet.

'Errol Flynn . . . Errol Flynn . . .,' she said thickly.

When she winked at me broadly, the upper lashes of her left eye snagged on the lower. She peeled both lashes off with two fingers, and dropped them in the ashtray. Her lopsided face was weepy again.

'Dead. Dead. Poor Errol-in-like-Flynn. Dead as the doornail he in some ways resembled.'

A lethal fog swirled behind her eyes, they spun like little catherine wheels.

'How about that drink?' she said.

I reached over for her glass on the table and handed it back to her.

'Thank you, kind sir,' she said, and immediately nodded off, glass in hand.

At the precise instant the liquid lapped over the side of her glass, just as I was reaching to rescue it, a sixth sense woke her. She sat up, and took a big swallow.

'Poor Rita Cramm . . . dead . . . murdered by the bitch, Dereena Foyle.' Enough was starting to be enough of Dereena Foyle, née Cramm. I would have let her pass out where she sat on Fawn's sofa, were it not for the cigarettes.

They were appearing from everywhere. Three of them burnt in a row on the lip of the ash-tray from which arose the stink of smouldering false eyelashes. Small burns spattered the front of her dressing-gown.

Persuading Dereena Foyle it was time to get up and go was not easy. If she hadn't somehow taken it into her head that we were on our way to a cantina in Tijuana, I don't think I could ever have started her into motion. She leaned on me heavily and together we hobbled up to her place in the darkness.

'Ay-ay-ay caballeros . . .' she piped in chorus with the cicadas. Although every light was burning, it was cheerless in her apartment, and dirty. Decay hung in the air, not as a smell, but as a presence, as if some long-ago living thing had been sealed up to die and desiccate under the floor-boards. The rooms were laid out like Fawn's below, but I did not dare escort her to the master-bedroom, as it entailed a tricky flight of stairs. I could feel how calcified were the bones that leaned on me, and friable under dry skin; they would have crumbled like biscuits in a paper bag if she'd fallen on to the terracotta tiles of her hall. Somehow I dragged her into the living-room. It was littered with clothes and greasy plates and bottles, and it stank in there of stale tobacco mixed with the dying perfume of old facecreams. Over the piano was a portrait in oils of Dereena Foyle in her prime; she looked imperious, magnificent, a savage queen. Obviously, the man who painted it had adored her slavishly.

Pushing and pulling, I finally got her to an overstuffed sofa that was covered in small burn marks. When she fell back on to the cushions, her robe flew open from neck to waist, and before she drew it together, I saw the dreadful extent of a natural catastrophe.

'Don't wanna be alone, lover,' she said.

And she passed out cold.

130

Sleep is not absolutely required for nightmares. I stayed out on the sundeck, or moondeck as it was that night, wide awake until Jinx came home the next morning. Before I went inside to join her for coffee, I decided, out of the blue, that while I was in New York, I was going to see about having a nose job.

There are periods in life when dangling strings are tied into pretty little bows, and for a while hardly anything that happens is without significance. We draw significant coincidences to us in times of self-obsession, that's why self-important people find them everywhere. 'I just know mind control works,' I overheard Fawn Ellis telling Jinx once – they'd been discussing the horrors of driving in Manhattan – 'because ever since I started EST, I always get a parking space.'

Before my flight left for New York, as I was feeling unusually self-obsessed, I browsed the bookstall at LAX, not very hopefully looking for a paperback to take my mind off myself. The book I pulled out of the shelves, according to the blurb on the back, was 'a dark tale of illicit passions, madness and despair . . . .' On the cover was the picture of a woman in a long, hooped skirt and a blouse cut very low to show a lot of bosom. She was standing on a windswept hill, looking out wistfully from under her bonnet at a field of daffodils. *The Unshaded Heart* was the title, sub-titled: A Life of Dorothy Wordsworth. And the author? Flavia Jane Garvey.

EIGHTEEEN

My childhood home was smaller than I remembered it, a banal observation, I know, nevertheless astounding the first time it happens. At the door was my mother, smaller, a flash of welcome in her eyes turning on the instant to accusation and caution. On the one hand, I'd been distant and disobedient, and not a very good daughter. On the other hand, so little had been expected of me, I had not done too badly: a letter a month over the years, regular gifts from Paris, and a flourishing, if mysterious, career – a lot more than anyone had predicted would be accomplished by marshy Marsha Leah. Things were not merely smaller at home, they were also crystal clear, miniaturised and sparkling, as if seen through a great immaculate space. My father had shrunk faster than everything else, faster even than the clothes he wore, or his favourite easy chair. When he lifted his arm to wave at me, his wrist-watch slipped and disappeared under the sleeve of his shirt. He smiled, and for the first time since I had known him, he looked fearless, like a youth on some reckless adventure.

'Your father is not a well man,' mother said over a glass of iced tea in the kitchen. 'Do you understand what I'm telling you, Marsha?' Silently, there flowed between my mother and me the ancient and complex sympathy of two women preparing to lose a man they both have reason to mourn.

Death cast a quilt over the household, so even pangs of unrequited love were muffled and easier to take. Hot weather came early and added to the lassitude of illness.

For a few days I read or dozed in a chair near my father's chair. Sometimes I looked up to see his eyes suddenly clear, recognising me for a moment before he sailed away again under the spreading Feldstein nose down his private channels of recollection.

A thick letter from the Tchernokoffs had been waiting for me at home in Teaneck. It contained introductions to people in New York, and errands they asked me, please, to run for them. The Sisters' shopping-list for Aztec-patterned bedsheets from Bloomingdale's, tins of Hershey chocolate sauce, and outsize bathcaps from a speciality shop on Madison Avenue, gave me an intriguing peek into the domestic lives behind their showmanship and their attic masks. My mother was occupied with preparations for the impending funeral, and plans for her surviving years, which she intended to spend in a retirement community near Phoenix, Arizona. She did not mind at all, or seem to notice, that I went back and forth to New York frequently during my visit. Of course, I did not tell her, or anyone, when I made an appointment to see Doctor Emanuel Yipp, the Park Avenue plastic surgeon. He had been recommended by a Capran sales representative I'd met in Hollywood and pumped for all sorts of information.

'Should I have a nose job?' I'd asked the Sisters once, as if I didn't know what they were bound to answer.

'Don't you dare!' Olga cried. 'It is a disfiguring operation. And only think how long it takes to recover, lying around like a toucan with big black and yellow eyes!'

'What good would a nose job do you?' Nina said. 'No surgeon can correct a shadow on the wall. If in all these years you haven't been able to believe yourself beautiful with that great shnozz of yours, then it's much too late to believe yourself beautiful at all.'

'Nina means a girl must learn to believe she's pretty early

133

on, while she is impressionable,' Olga said, and added gently, 'especially if she happens to be rather plain.'

'Nose jobs!' Nina said, and snorted. Her own nose, by the way, was slightly flat with nostrils shaped like tiny keyholes. ' That's what our skills are coming to, you see? That is what they will soon be calling beauty. Starve and carve and lay on pigment with a trowel. One day soon, you just wait and see, they'll turn girls out to a pattern, shrink them all to one size, and paint them by numbers. Little dolly faces everywhere.'

The Sisters, especially Nina, were going to be disappointed when I appeared with my nose radically changed. But their wrath wouldn't last, and it was a risk I had to take. It was not in hope of becoming beautiful and stealing Jake from Jinx I was ready to submit myself to the knife; I had no dreams on that score. But I needed desperately to exert control over the tide of emotions that was threatening to sweep me away. All would be lost if I could not get hold of myself again. I had to assert some kind of mastery over the shape of things to come. And frontal lobotomies not being on offer to the general public, a nose job seemed the next best thing.

The moment Yipp came bounding out from behind his desk to meet me at the door, my doubts began about the operation. Ebullience is not a quality to trust, it is nearly always half bull, never very bright upstairs, and ruthless. Ebullience is an asset only for quiz show compères, and I was not pleased to find it in a man who was threatening me with a knife. When he said, 'May I call you Marsha?', it was all I could do to stop myself saying: 'Call me a cab, instead.' But Yipp was the type of enthusiast who turns nasty at the hint of impediment, a true utopian of the American heartland, I mean, who will slaughter as many as it takes to make things neat and tidy. No, I did not like Yipp's ebullience. I did not like the perfect whites of his eyes, or the smooth apple-polish of his cheeks, or his pin-striped suit. I did not like the gold chain and fob hanging from the pocket of his waistcoat; I did not like his waistcoat. And least of all did I like the fleshy little hand he put out for mine. The pink half-moons of his cuticles filled me with disgust. And I hated the smile on his small, soft, oily mouth when he looked straight at my nose. He was more deeply interested in my face than a man had ever been, and his surgical gaze started making me feel sick.

'Let me speak honestly, Miss Feldstein,' he said, a classic prelude to bad news. As if I needed him to tell me how nature does not bless us all equally. Hadn't I figured that out for myself thirty years earlier? 'The shame for you is that one day soon, Marsha,' he went on, 'there will be no correction to, let's call it nature's mismanagement, too great for us to undertake. Oh yes, Marsha, with a spot of judicious juggling of genes and hormones, backed up by the newest surgical techniques, we'll even be able to help people who lack stature, by which I mean the height-deprived like yourself, Marsha. It will only be a matter of catching the shorties young enough, possibly *in utero*.' Now he became unctuous and smug, he tipped back in his chair and folded his hatefully clean hands over his belly. 'We can shift a gal's fatty tissue from here to there, we can do that already, Marsha, or dispose of it altogether. We can enlarge her lips, lift her eyelids, trim her buttocks, tuck her tummy, reduce or augment her breasts. We can do all this, and more.' He brought his gaze down from heavenward and looked me straight in the nose. 'Rhinoplasty is only a start,' he said.

A whiff of his cheery aftershave hit me and I started feeling a little sicker. On his desk was a framed photograph of a pretty woman in twinset and pearls with her arms around a homely little girl of six or seven: Yipp's women. I studied the picture to avoid looking into his too-bright eyes.

'Only think, Marsha, one day there will no longer exist a gal unhappy with the way she looks, or one who makes others sad to see her.'

He glanced over towards the photograph as he spoke; the homely kid was nearly ripe for rehabilitating. Obviously daddy had designs on her.

'Cinderella will always go to the ball,' he said.

Yipp spoke a few words into an intercom on his desk and his pretty, perfectly-proportioned assistant entered with a big black book containing photographs of what was available in the proboscis department. Dozens of disembodied noses lay between us on the desk, frontal and in profile. My nausea and my doubts were growing moment by moment. And when I recognised one nose among the others, it did the trick.

'Oh!' I cried. I sat up straight. I pointed at the nose I knew.

'Excellent choice, Marsha,' said Yipp. 'And very popular, too. I must do, oh, fifty or sixty Jinx O'Malleys every year. She used to be the most beautiful woman in the world, you know. Officially. If the O'Malley nose is the one you want to have, just say the word.'

But I was on my feet and out of there so fast, Yipp didn't know what hit him. As sure as my father's house and money would be passed down to my mother, the Feldstein nose was my inheritance. I'd been mad to think I could leave a chunk of it in the bucket under Yipp's workbench. Lose the flag of my own small nation? Not on your life, Dr Yipp. Entire in its essence, the Feldstein nose was stuck to my very being. And whatever I was in for in this life, it was bound to be right there with me. Even a considerable distance ahead.

The next morning my father took a sudden turn. A turn away. A turn to the wall. And that night he went into hospital. Two hours before the dawn of a day that was going to be unremarkable except for his absence, he sent his last sigh out into the world's great breathing space. When I rang Jinx to tell her, she wept a little in sympathy.

'You know, honey, there really is much more to life than death . . .'

'How are you?' I asked quickly before she threatened the return of my father's poor soul by way of a Navajo spirit guide. The pause on her end of the line was long enough for me to guess what she was about to say.

'Jake and I are getting married,' she said.

'That's good news, Jinx,' I replied.

My eyes filled with tears, as they hadn't even at my father's funeral.

'I hope so, honey,' she said. 'Because you're the one who told me to do it.'

A few weeks later, on the plane to Paris I finally got around to opening the newspaper there had been no time to read earlier. On an inside page was the announcement of Dereena Foyle's death. She had perished in a fire in her bedroom; faulty wiring was blamed. A list of every movie she had made with their dates in brackets showed that Dereena Foyle snuffed it fifteen years earlier as far as Hollywood was concerned. I folded the paper, sat back and closed my eyes.

'That ought to be enough of dying for a while,' I thought.

NINETEEN

I was barely back in harness before the Tchernokoff Sisters called me into their inner office and announced their plans to retire.

'We're ready,' said Nina.

'More to the point,' said Olga, 'so are you.'

They were closing the salon as soon as they could. Already every last member of their staff, right down to the daily cleaners, had been found new positions. They had seen right away I hadn't the mystique or charisma to take on their name, and without them up front, the whole operation was bound to fold in a matter of weeks. But they were going to give me a considerable sum of money, at the mention of the sum they exchanged one of their secretive looks, so I imagined there was plenty more where that came from, and they were turning over to me all the formulae for their preparations, to market under any name I chose except, please, not their own.

'Miracle Products,' I said right off. They had not caught me altogether unawares. I too had been making plans, though they were half daydreams, about what I'd do if my big chance came along. Had I not brought back a case full of reports and samples and directives from my travels?

'We're giving you honest money, dear Mar-see-ah,' said Olga, 'from a lifetime of selling illusions. Can you accept that? Can you remember and keep remembering there is no villainy in selling illusions? Not as long as the illusionist keeps affection for the suckers.'

'Questionable . . .' I began, and to my delight Nina rose happily for me one last time.

'Ha! A lucky thing you have no children, Mar-see-ah. You would not tell the poor things any fairy-tales, I guess? Or allow them to trust in Father Christmas? No poetry for your unfortunate babies, no fun, no metaphor. You'd drop them right into the shit. Fill them up with the so-called facts of life, and age, and death, without the shield of fantasies. As if the scrubbed face of brute knowing were more worthy or urgent to survival than imagination. Oh Mar-see-ah, I pity your poor little kiddies!'

I laughed. And suddenly we three were embracing, awkwardly, but with a warmth and emotion that took us by surprise, and made us shy for a moment.

Olga asked me where I wanted to set up my Miracle business. And as soon as I replied, London, out came the champagne. They were not pretending their investment in me was altruistic: they were going to be my partners.

'Silent partners ,' said Nina, in English, and we laughed again.

They expected me to make enough out of their investment to keep them in their retirement, and that meant I was going to have to turn some slick profit quickly out of what they were giving me. If the least hint of commercialism had to attach to the good name Tchernokoff, they'd rather it was in London, and not on their home ground.

Should I ever indulge in autobiography, details of my wheeling and dealing during the following year would fascinate other business people, I'm sure. So far in my life, for most of my life, I have been, above all, a businesswoman. Not that I sneer at magic, but I call it by other names: applied psychology, for example, chemistry, intuition, entertainment. I would not call myself an artist, either: I'm no Flavia Jane Garvey of the base-coat and blusher division. What artist worth the salt would choose

139

material as perishable and wilful as human skin? A business-woman, pure and simple, a self-made woman, too, is what I have been. I'm not ashamed of it. It has been interesting and more than necessary. What else can a plain Jane be in this life? She makes herself; or she's a slave.

By autumn of my first year as a boss, I had kissed Paris goodbye with few regrets, and severed links with France, except for regular reports to the Sisters in Antibes. I set up laboratories of my own in England, relying on the French chemists, as we still do, only for the original Tchernokoff recipes. Who are 'we'? 'We' are what 'I' became as Miracle Products grew, not into a label-proud monolith like Capran Cosmetics, but as I had long ago envisioned, a broad-based family of differing products under the aegis of Miracle. Our 'Genesis' line, for exam-ple, including 'Balm of Gilead for Tired Skin', 'Goshen Exfoliating Creme', and 'Galilee Rehydrating Masque' are all based on the original Tchernokoff formulae, and quite astronomically priced. High prices don't in the least discourage the post-menopausal crowd. On the contrary, the more the old dears spend on Miracle Products, the happier they are, and happiness gives them a little spe-cious glow. The 'Young Miracle' line is much cheaper. 'Don't wait until it *takes* a miracle . . . ' runs the copy line for moisturisers and face-packs. The kids lap up our cartoon colours, the lipsticks are called 'Loudmouth', and in the United States especially, twelve and thirteen year olds climb all over each other to get at the stuff. Against received knowledge, we change the packaging of 'Young Miracle' at regular intervals; last season the bottles and tubes were shaped like babies' dummies, outsized. Two years ago we brought out a revolutionary new group of products; they're called 'Black Miracle', featuring 'Zambezee Eye Colours' and a line of plum and orange lipsticks called 'Mouth of the Nile'. I could go on and on, I'm afraid. And not long after I'd moved to London, our distribution and sales departments were in full swing out of a suite of offices in Knightsbridge.

Choosing employees is a very special talent, and I am as proud of having recognised on sight the acumen behind my sturdy girl Glynis's wary little face as I am of any major coup in the market-place. Like all highly organised individuals, Glynis is very secretive, all the more reason her fidelity to me has made her an ally without equal. Until the company grew to such a point we needed a personnel department, I used to boast that we at Miracle had never sacked anyone. This is not to say I haven't sometimes hired scamps and scalawags; of course I have. But only when they were needed for the job: in our legal department, for instance, and to write press releases. Admittedly, it is very hard work keeping an English staff on its toes. Although the English drink like northerners and show all the eccentricities that are bred only on small islands, I soon discovered them on the whole to be basically as indolent as South Sea natives; day-dreamers too, though, like most great romantics, courageous in the crunch. Money excites Americans, pay them a lot and they'll work hard, but the British find money soothing, the more they earn, the less they do. In fact, they perform best under pressure, and never better than when they are at war. Inspiring an English staff to keep a constant beleaguered mentality so they stay spry, is a full-time job for any boss. There is no cure for a broken heart. But hard work makes time pass, and in due course my heart cobbled itself together again.

From the offhand response of the Sisters to the flood of reports I sent them during my early days, it was soon clear they preferred not to know details of what I was doing for our mutual prosperity. Every spring I fly out to Antibes for a few days with them, but mostly we sip white wine in their lovely garden while they tell me scurrilous tales about neighbours I have never met. The Sisters remain upright even now and their faces are unchanged; only their hair lost all colour suddenly about ten years ago; when I came back to see them after the usual interval, it had turned as white as the skin of their faces. One April, when Miracle Products was nearly three years old, and already doing well, I sat with them on their terrace that was drenched in perfumes beyond the skill of chemists to recreate.

'And your friend, the beautiful Jinx O'Malley?' Olga asked.

Night had fallen the way it does there, swift and glimmering as an axe. A chorus of small creatures had taken up their nocturnal theme, and behind us the Mediterranean whispered: '*Mañana, mañana, mañana ...* ' Hidden in the dark like that, it was easier to tell them what little I knew about Jinx and Jake.

Not long after their marriage I had to fly out to the Coast to set up a franchise for our products in a boutique on Rodeo Drive. Jinx and Jake had both been working on *Reflected Glory*, and I had seen them a few times, usually on the set. On her side I was surprised to detect a kind of irritability when she spoke to him.

'But I wouldn't do that, Jake!' she complained several times about the part he'd written for her. As for Jake, he seemed completely nonplussed. He couldn't understand she was not speaking as his heroine, but as herself: she meant that she, Jinx O'Malley, would not keep a diary full of feelings, or fall in love with a man in a wheelchair, or wear pearls with a grey twinset, or do practically anything her husband expected of his creation. Since then, Jinx had sent me occasional postcards, and sometimes she telephoned at odd hours. Her marriage fell into the same category as my nose; we both knew it was there, but to discuss it directly would have been tasteless. 'How's Jake?' was as much as I trusted myself to ask, and it got so I could

142

mouth her reply: 'Oh, he's okay, honey.' I told the Sisters that six months or so before I'd come to see them, I had noticed that the return address on Jinx's letter was Fawn's place in Hollywood, not Boston where, I knew, Jake was lecturing at Harvard. Finally, I had to ask her during one of her late-night calls, why she wasn't with him.

'And she said . . . ?' Olga prompted me in the dark.

'She said the talking got her down. "Words, words, words!" she said. And she said she hated the cold weather of New England. She said she thought Jake had not really meant to marry her at all, only his idea of her. And he had never really known her.'

'And you said then, Mar-see-ah?' Olga asked.

'I said was she actually telling me on a trans-Atlantic telephone that her husband didn't understand her?'

'And . . .?'

'She laughed,' I told the Sisters. 'And then she said, "I'm just so bored, honey, I could die." You see how it is. Jake bores her . . . .'

My voice betrayed me, and they heard what was unspoken. I shut up. We sat in silence for a few minutes.

'Dear Mar-see-ah, you are not unlucky, you know,' Olga said at last. 'Unrequited love stays bright.'

'And sharp, sharp, sharp,' said Nina.

'Unrequited love, dear girl,' said Olga, 'is the love that lasts a lifetime.'

Not long after that meeting with the Sisters I had to fly back to Los Angeles to straighten out a mess one of my sales representatives out there had got us into. I stayed in this very hotel, where I now am. Jake was in LA too. Their separation was underway. They were not living together, but Jake nursed fading hopes for a reconciliation, and they saw each other regularly. He did not know, of course, about her affair with the young English guitarist or he would have pushed

143

the divorce through as fast as possible. Jake was ready to fight a man of his own weight, you understand, but no lion like Jake Orben was going to stoop to compete for any woman, not even his own wife, with a skinny strummer of cigar boxes who dressed in velveteen and called himself Ziggles. I saw quite a bit of Jake on that trip and kept him company while he waited for Jinx. And I connived secretly to fly back east with him. He was carrying the first draft of *In Light of Venus* to have it transcribed by his 'girl back east'. Words were solid things in those days that could be lost in transit, and he kept the manuscript in a briefcase on his knees. I myself was burdened with bittersweet excitement just to sit close to him in mid-air. I had even let myself imagine that the ticket agent, the stewardess, and our fellow passengers mistook me for something more in the tall man's life than his estranged wife's oldest friend.

By that time in my working life, I'd already begun travelling first class. I had assumed Jake flew that way too, and there was a flurry of surreptitious dealing at the airport so he would not know I'd had to have myself downgraded (ha! ha!) to be with him.

'I always fly economy, on principle,' he said, as we were boarding. 'I owe it to the slum kid I was. Besides, there's too much gallivanting around the globe these days. Too much dirty laundry being shipped across oceans. Too many illnesses exchanged with too little time for immunities to be acquired. Discomfort makes a guy think: "Is this trip really necessary?" I tell you, Marsha, the day I travel first class is the day I lose proper respect for my destination.' He stretched his long legs into the aisle, pulled them back to let a woman with a baby pass. Whenever he moved I caught the layered, leafy whiff of a northern man, born to live in cold climates. We brushed arms; our hearts had never been so close. At least, he had restraint enough not to mention Jinx until after our second round of drinks.

'The first time I set eyes on Jinx, I felt I was meeting destiny. I keep looking back, trying to recognise omens. There was an inevitability about my meeting her. Ah well. I don't know if you can understand this, Marsha, but love makes us superstitious.'

He waved away the plastic meal, and closed his eyes. 'I don't mind being a sucker for love,' he said, 'but I will not be a martyr.'

And those were practically the last words Jacob Orben ever addressed to me. He fell asleep at my side. And I, awake, envied all those who were free to show happiness in each other's company. We parted at Logan Airport, he to deliver his manuscript, and I to make a very awkward connection home to London. The final look I had of Jake Orben, he was in the comical flap of an intellectual in a hurry, loping away from me, towards a taxi.

Before their divorce was cool, an article appeared in the London *Times* to announce the marriage of America's premier novelist, Jacob Orben, to – what was her name? It sounded like a processed cheese-spread. Oh yes, I remember: it was Priscilla. He married Priscilla Thingamybob, his forty-year-old 'girl back east'. Not a bad looker either, to judge from the newspaper photograph. Jinx happened to call from Los Angeles that night. I asked her if she knew about Jake's marriage. No, but she wasn't surprised.

'Smart old guys like Jake always end up with their secretaries, honey,' she said. 'The dumb old guys marry their nurses.'

TWENTY

If I were lifted into space, then dropped spinning back to earth, I'd know without needing to open my eyes if I had landed in London. There would be the familiar dampness in the air, and the smell of wet wool over a subtle base note of tidal river mud. There would be the cawing of crows, even in the heart of town, and street noise of a lower pitch than in any other city I have known well. The pace of pedestrians is slower too than in Paris or New York. My first home in London was a maisonette in a Georgian crescent that backed on to a communal garden the size of a small park. What remained of the New Yorker in me took a little time getting used to a neighbourhood neither on its way up nor its way down, and after living so many years in Paris, it was a while before I learned to greet my neighbours when we passed, not to treat them with utter indifference. At the same time, you know, it would not do in London to be too gabby or invite folks in for drinks before a year or two had passed and we had the measure of each other. I parcelled my rubbish in sacks as a good Londoner should, and I toyed with the idea of keeping a cat.

Upstairs were two small bedrooms, each with a bathroom, and downstairs a big living-room cum dining-room, and a small open kitchen. Off the kitchen was a conservatory just big enough to hold a wrought-iron table and a chair. There had been no room for plants in my Paris place, and when I was a girl in New York, it was Jinx who installed pot-plants on the sill, and usually remembered to water

146

them. She preferred cut flowers and silk roses. To my surprise, I discovered my green thumb in London. Women take to gardening late in life, after they've lost their looks. You'll find crones are rarely far from green and growing things. I'm sure there must be a correlation between maternal and horticultural skills, and only at the end of our childbearing years, when the fierce nurturing passion has subsided at last, as embers to the flame, can it be turned to vegetable life. While we're on the topic, it's probably a good thing that beauties like Jinx so often remain childless; evidence is for the most part they'd make bad mothers. A beauty is too flirtatious to raise healthy sons, and even after her looks are fading, the legend of her power over men will live on to break a daughter's heart.

The year after Jinx's divorce from Jake she spent a week with me on her way to a photo shoot in Greece. Of all our encounters it was the least satisfactory or cordial. When I met her at the airport I found she had not warned me that the English rock musician, Ziggles, was going to be staying with us, too. I had heard much about Ziggles, of course, but I had not met him before. He had Niccolo's colouring, and the same provocative swing to his shoulders. Ziggles was also about the same age Nick had been when he and Jinx were married. I suppose I have to grant he was good-looking. But his thin nose was pinched and white over the bridge, as if it had been lifted with revulsion, and dropped in place quickly by its maker. Shall I be honest? I loathed him on sight. And it was mutual. Within the first moments of our meeting, Ziggles and I became a pair of warring creepy-crawlies, ready to do slow, slimy battle to the finish. The hand he gave me was slippy, we couldn't let go of each other fast enough, and even though all he said was 'Hullo' when Jinx introduced us, I as good as heard the words, 'I'll bugger you, you ugly grub', replete with the gong sounds of his northern accent.

147

Fortunately, Ziggles was another short episode in her life. When she left for Greece, he went up to Liverpool, he said it was for a 'gig'. I heard them talk about meeting each other again back at 'the place' in Los Angeles, and with my own eyes I saw her give him his plane ticket, along with an envelope containing money, you can bet. I guess he never turned up in LA. His idiotic name was dropped from her cards and conversations during the years ahead; it was as if yet another man in her life had never existed at all, and I had no occasion ever to tell Jinx that the day Ziggles left my flat for the north, a Parker pen and sixty pounds of loose cash went missing from my desk.

He was always near Jinx and me in London, listening, casting triumphant glances my way while he was giving her orders: for tea, for a drink, for restaurant reservations, for sex, implied by a nod towards their upstairs bedroom, for bits and pieces out of their luggage, for replacements of brushes, boots and other items he said he'd left in LA. Once or twice there were shameless demands for money. Fortunately, I could make myself very busy at the office, so I did not need to be much at home. Every time I looked at Ziggles, or saw Jinx look at him with her green eyes fully charged, I had to remember that this gloating wide-boy with only the dubious assets of youth and good looks was the successor to Jacob Orben. When we were together, Ziggles put a strain on our old intimacy; never had so much been unspoken between Jinx and me. It was going to take some time in the years ahead for the damage he did to be absorbed into the overall texture of our friendship. But eventually memory swallows its bitter pills, and sometimes past misconceptions are reversable. Now, for example, I realise that when Jinx ran his errands, gave him food and love and money, what I took at the time for her contemptible weakness, God forgive me, was actually the confusion that accompanies a sickness of the soul.

Coincidence has occurred just often enough in my life to persuade me it must be accident, or why would it not happen more? Accident, and the not very adventurous way most lives are lived, in patterns that are repetitious, restricted, and bound to overlap. One evening, Jinx and I were sitting with Ziggles in my living-room, enacting a parody of the happy threesome we used to be with Nick. Jinx was sewing a button on something, and talking softly to me, while Nick read his paper, a feat he could accomplish only when his snakeskin boots were up on my upholstery; at all other times, the man was illiterate. He cast the paper aside, and switched the television on very loud, as he usually did when Jinx and I were talking. It happened to be a season in the 1970s when American tv cop shows were being imported into England, one after the other, like salted peanuts, and Ziggles had landed us in the middle of a pilot for a new series. It was set in Los Angeles and featured a local male cop who was a vegetarian and a surfer, teamed with a smart-alec brunette carnivore, a female originally from Manhattan. The show was called 'Nolan and Klein', and any fool could tell within seconds that its main tension lay in guessing when the mismatched couple were going to throw in the sponge, and go to bed together.

'Nolan, get off my case,' said LAPD'S Beatrice to her Benedict. 'I hear the Loo-tenant coming . . . .'

Whereupon the door to the station room flew open and in marched a big man, florid, and thick with drinker's bloat. Around his mouth was the wobble of self-indulgent envy that Blalack had forecast so cruelly. However, unlike most eyes that grow weaker with time, Nick's eyes, though a little puffy, had turned bright blue. This hotel puts a glossy magazine in every room, and only last night I came across a page in it advertising tinted contact lenses for 'people who have stars in their eyes'; I now know Nick had chosen what

149

in the trade is called 'Paul Newman Blue'. At the time, however, the unfamiliar penetrating colour made me wonder if it really was Niccolo de Lisi prancing around on the screen, or an older look-alike. It was a moment before Jinx cried: 'My ex-husband!' As if there had been only one.

So strong is the nursing instinct in many females, along with its curiously sadistic component, they cannot resist the flagging hellraiser who is still on the hunt, though barely. They itch to feed him gruel and change his nappies when he finally caves in and pays the price for his excesses. Nick filled that bill, and in spite of evident ravages, he qualified easily as a secondary love-interest for the series. Ziggles was leaning forward, watching the loo-tenant make a meal of his big scene. Poor Nick. To be subjected to the hostile appraisal of an ex-wife's future live-in lover is surely a hazard of public life no actor anticipates. I'd have given a lot to have improved the script, or turned Nick into less of a ham, or to have returned him for a few minutes to the vigour of stallion youth.

'Hasn't he got old,' Jinx whispered, almost in awe.

Neither she nor I tried to stop Ziggles when he reached over to switch off the picture.

'The guy's a drunk,' he said, 'and an old faggot.'

Jinx was still looking good at this time. She was fuller than before, ripe, yet singularly unbruised. Only a hint of shadow lay under her eyes, and at each side of her mouth was a tiny semicircle, like a fingernail print. Fortyish was too old for fashion's cameras, true enough, but the most discriminating lens of the age was still happy to be at her service. She had stopped off in England, on her way to Greece for a photo session with Henri Dimanché. The octogenarian recluse broke his long retreat and wrote to Helsinki, asking her to send Jinx O'Malley to his studio on the Island of Mykonos. The book of photographs called *Jinx and other Gifts of Nature*, which resulted from this collaboration, is still to be found in libraries, and sometimes on second-hand bookstalls. No further evidence than the glorious photographs it contains is required of my friend's continuing beauty at that time. Interspersed with the flowers, fruits, and landscapes which the old man preferred to human subjects at that late point in his great career, are the best photographs ever taken of Jinx. I have always thought that photography is to painting among the arts as motor-car racing to mountain-climbing among the sports: a dubious hybrid of man and machine, with an advantage to the machine. But I must admit, as Blalack in his time had painted Jinx in all her glowing hopes, so Dimanché, a couple of decades on, discovered in her face traces almost ancient, for which she herself had no vocabulary, and which I was too pigheaded at the time to recognise as tragedy.

On the cover of *Jinx and Other Gifts* is a photograph of a plump dewy rose, mawkish at first sight, not what you expect from Dimanché, until your eye is drawn to a little shadow where stem meets blossom, and with a shock you recognise a first petal about to fall.

'The holy moment in nature is the one on the turn,' Dimanché writes in his foreword. 'What comes before is sublime; what follows is decay. It is the time for a miracle.'

Of course, I only saw Dimanché's book long after Jinx and I had parted again. But when she had first arrived with Ziggles in London, and I saw her coming through the doors out of immigration, pretty much those very words had flown into my mind: 'Time for a miracle.'

TWENTY-ONE

Three years after I'd seen the last of Ziggles, and my favourite Parker pen, and sixty quid, I happened to be present when Jinx met her next and, so far as I know, her final husband, little old Mo Gittleman. In the wake of the ghastly Zig-Zag, Jinx and I were less in contact than we had ever been. For months at a time, I didn't know where she was, or what she was doing. Then in the spring of 1977, it must have been, or '78, I had to go in person to New York City to promote the concept of an in-store boutique at Bloomingdale's, to be called 'English Miracle', where we could start selling our products to the man-hungry females of Manhattan. It was one of Bloomie's buyers who mentioned that Capran Cosmetics was holding their annual Gala that very night in the Plaza Hotel ballroom, to celebrate the announcement of the new Capran Girl. By that time, the Capran Gala had been blown up into a world-class publicity stunt; bookies put money on the contestants, and the whole shebang was watched by tv viewers everywhere. The buyer told me former Capran Girls were going to be included in the event, which was staged as a formal dinner, a cabaret, and, of course, the beauty contest.

'Do you know if Jinx O'Malley will be there?' I asked. She nodded.

'My mom used to say if she looked like Jinx O'Malley she'd leave my dad and marry King Farouk. Whoever he was.'

It took only a couple of telephone calls, and there was Jinx on the end of the line.

'Oh honey, I just always feel so good to hear your voice,' she said, and time rolled back its dreadful canopy.

We met that afternoon before the show. It so happened I was staying at the Plaza, and I invited her up for a drink in my room. She said if I didn't mind, she'd rather meet me at the bar, not to drink, I soon discovered: she had only mineral water. But the place was full of men. As usual, every one of them turned to stare when Jinx walked in, you bet they did. Jinx preserved was as splendid as Jinx in her prime, only it was the splendour of brilliant artifice, like those clockwork maidens of legend, made to the specifications of the Caliph, then given a semblance of life by sorcerers. Silicone hemispheres rose like little moons over her summer dress; tiny scars at the corners of her eyes, practically invisible under eye-shadow, showed us who were in the know about such things where her lids had been stretched and tightened. I recognised the gallic highlights imported for her hair, and I knew skilled backcombing hid where loose skin had been taken in behind her ears. She was a rare and stunning example of the cosmetic arts. But the fact of the matter is, in spite of all we at Miracle do, and the Yipps, and others, to outfox men, when healthy males are in peak form, they possess a nearly infallible divining rod that lets them know if even the most dazzling female is running dry. Only inexperienced boys, neuropaths, psychopaths, and greedy opportunists do not sense, or do not care, when a woman is at the end of her natural resources. Oh yes, and old codgers like Mo Gittleman, of course, whose vision is veiled and backwards. After the men in the Plaza's bar had looked at Jinx, and looked again, all but one or two of them turned away.

We hugged; we talked. But Jinx was not all there. Whenever the door opened to let in another man, she rattled with false intelligence, and laughed too loud. Although she tried her best to meet me intimately, exclusively,

153

the way we had always met each other, since the very first day, I could sense her recoiling in spite of herself from memories engendered by any encounter with an old friend. To make it up to me, she gave me a ticket for the Capran 'do' that night. To make it up to her, I said I'd be there.

We were in a patch of the late middle twentieth century when space travel was hip again. The theme for the night was 'Capran's Astro Beauty Gala', and the Plaza's ballroom had been turned into a honky-tonk version of an inter-galactic departure lounge. Globes of changing colours hung at varying levels over the drum-shaped tables and moulded chairs, where we three hundred or so invited guests were to be served a late supper after the show. I took my place at a reserved table for two below the stage. Jinx was going to join me as soon as she was free. Helsinki Braw sat a few tables away, but she did not find it convenient to notice me. Rhinestones sparkled on her turban, and her arms churned, while the man who accompanied her, as well as any man could accompany a glittering mass like Helsinki Braw, watched her with evident amusement. From the way she was smirking and booming at him, I took him for a rich client. The beard he wore made his head look like a pomegranate: round, bald, ruddy, with a frill at its base. For such a little fellow he was singularly undaunted by Helsinki. I thought I liked him, though I didn't pay him much attention at the time.

Frail aluminium stools were ranked at the back of the stage, where Jinx and four or five other old Capran Girls were already in place. Mercifully, drinks were served before the lights dimmed and the tv cameras started to roll. First of all, the four Capran Girl candidates came out, and did their party turns in formal gowns; the compère gazed solemnly into one pulsing cleavage after the other, and asked about their aims in life, and their greatest hopes. Tziganya, the Polish six-footer, was keen on world peace,

154

and so was Ellen Mae, a sweet-faced brunette with hair like melting chocolate. She also said she hoped for happiness, poor kid. The blonde wanted world peace too, as I recall. A magnificent West Indian beauty was in the running. She was obviously a token to current chic, didn't stand a chance, as Capran made no cosmetics for her skin tone. When she said her fondest hope was to be the Capran Girl, I wanted to jump up and cheer, until she spoiled it by giggling, no, no, no, she was only kidding; what she really wanted was world peace. There were the usual sub-Broadway musical numbers, and the compère exchanged bad jokes with visiting minor celebrities while the contestants were backstage changing into bikinis. After their final walk-around, as the judges were deliberating, the old Capran Girls were supposed to be called forward one by one, for their rehearsed interviews. I had observed that Helsinki's companion was mesmerised by Jinx, his eyes had not left her once, not even when the younger girls were parading, all but naked on high heels. Jinx looked silky and long-legged; from the distance, you would have said she was unchanged from years before, and she was the image of poise. But I knew how much Jinx had always dreaded speaking in public, and as her moment approached to step forward I felt myself chilled by sympathetic stage nerves, like a mother at the school play.

The contestants, in their bikinis, had draped themselves strategically around the stage to wait for the winner to be announced. Jinx was just coming forward to the microphone. The glass trembled a little in my hand and I said a silent prayer on her behalf. Suddenly, there was a confused scrambling at the entrance to the ballroom. Men and women could be heard shouting, running hard nearby in the hotel. The doors at the back of the hall burst open and six or seven silhouettes came jumping and yelling in the dim light down the central aisle between the tables. Behind this simian cluster was another just like it. Everything was happening so quickly, people on the far side of the room could not have known what was going on until the gang swarmed up onstage. Only then did we all see that every last one of the invaders was a woman.

Pages have been written about the Capran Riot. I hate to say it, but there wasn't very much to it in the end. Females of every shape and size, most of them dressed in army surplus khaki, milled around the stage. A voice screamed: 'Beauty contests demean women . . .' A big girl in overalls waved a sign hand-lettered to read: 'WE ARE NOT SEX OBJECTS'. In the midst of the fracas, the Capran contestants tore strips of silver fabric off the back-drop to wrap around their half-naked bodies, and the fully-clothed, older Capran Girls, uncertain about what to do, looked around for someone to tell them if this was a joke, or a change in the running order of the show; or what? The compère, in a panic, struggled with a short, squat girl who was trying to get his microphone away from him; he ad-libbed wittily: 'Fuck off, you slimebag . . .' before the mike went dead. The audience was rising to its feet, mostly jeering. It was barely a minute or two before uniforms poured on stage and started to drive the women back the way they had come. One figure broke loose from the mêlée, jumped down, and landed right in front of me. She was fuzzy-haired, beetle-browed, dishevelled, big-breasted, and chunky on strong legs. She was all over resistance, let me tell you. No petticoats for bandages on that chiquita. 'Join us, sister,' she cried practically into my eyes, before they dragged her off.

The show limped to an anticlimax, and at its conclusion, after Ellen Mae was named the new Capran Girl, most of the audience hurried backstage, where all was confusion. Corks were popping, flashbulbs too, and every available telephone was busy. One of the old Capran Girls, a pale woman with angry dark eyes guarding the ruins of a once great face, held a snarl of leads attached to a pack of leaping, yapping mongrel dogs. The woman and her animals added a note of monstrous irascibility to the hullabaloo. No stunt to come out of the wildest dreams of highly paid publicists could have done for Capran what the gatecrashers had done. In the midst of the excited mob stood Helsinki Braw, quiet for once. She was looking thoughtfully at Jinx who was off to one side, smiling vaguely into the air. And I knew Helsinki was thinking, exactly as I was, that Jinx and the other Capran Girls, old and young, in their glossy perfection and stabbing heels, with their lacquered hair, and their wicked mandarin nails, looked suddenly quaint and going rapidly out of date. In that moment was born in my mind the concept of a whole new line in cosmetics. We'd call it 'Natural Miracle'.

Helsinki's short bald man was hanging around back-stage. Before I slipped away I saw La Braw take him by the arm and lead him over to Jinx, and I heard her introduce him as Mo Gittleman.

Only four months after the Capran Riot, the telephone rang one night, late enough to alarm me, and the operator asked if I would accept a collect-call from Jinx O'Malley in Goa, India. As Jinx never came to terms with time differences, our talks over the years blend into sleepy reminiscence, like a running dream.

But the call that night was unique, and jumps out from the others. For a start, she asked if I could wire her money, something Jinx had never before done; she needed a return ticket to New York. Two weeks earlier she had gone out to Goa for a holiday. I already knew that: I'd received a postcard from her – 'This is paradise' scribbled on the back, the front showed a fringe of palms beside an eye-blue sea. Over the crackling line, Jinx told me she had been travelling with a 'gorgeous' American, another pop musician, I think she said. Or a hairdresser. They had slept the days away in each other's arms on the beach, and played all night. They'd stayed in a thatched hut that was part of an enclave of hippies. 'A lizard lived on the blades of the bahama fan, honey, so we never switched it on. But our door opened on to the ocean, and there was always a breeze. I wish it would have lasted forever, Marsha. But he was a Gemini. When will I learn, honey?'

Our telephone line flickered in and out, and at best the connection was fuzzy. From what I could make out, Jinx had awakened one hard, bright day, and found the mattress cold beside her. Between observation and realisation is always a gap that contains the last gasp of the status quo, a pause no longer than it takes to think: 'What's going on here?' and then: 'Let this not be'. But he was gone all right. He'd taken her gold watch too, from next to the bed, her money, her passport, all her travellers' cheques, and her return ticket. 'What do you think about that, Marsha? Doesn't that just make you wonder?' Jinx asked me, without a trace of anger or fear; as a child seeing death for the first time, bemused, not yet realising it gets us all in the end.

Of course I wired her the money immediately. And within a few days she had reimbursed me. Then, five months later, on a damp December day in London, I read in *Time* magazine that Jinx O'Malley had married the millionaire financier, Mo Gittleman. Obviously she did not love him. It was a matter of attraction, yes, and who can say what genetic imperative? Jinx was breeding stock for a long-legged race and never, not in a million years, could she have fallen for a man shorter than herself.

TWENTY-TWO

The closer my memory comes to within striking distance of this antiseptic pink tank in la-la land, the more trouble it is keeping to the straight and narrow. Naughty scavenger, memory, circles back over stuff not quite picked clean or gone, all but a bone or two, into the vanishing currents. Apropos, I wonder how Tomas Blalack is doing down there, commingling with his unhappiest creation? It was generally held to be a great loss that Blalack died when he did, but in my opinion it was a very artful ending, indeed. Had he lived to be one hundred I doubt he could have done anything better for his reputation as a genius than to die violently and young; anyone desiring fame, as Blalack did, would be well advised to do the same. Death in full flood, as it were, kickstarts the business of being remembered and reinforces it with regrets, before a man's energy has dribbled away and he's started to be forgotten in his own lifetime. Besides, when a celebrated man dies young, he leaves plenty of survivors who knew him, even just a little, or merely crossed his path, and who work to keep his memory alive because that way some of his fame rubs off on them. Practically every surviving member of Blalack's People, for example, who was the least bit literate, wrote a book about having known him. With the help of a ghost-writer – how apposite! – even Velvet managed to sustain a line or two of thought long enough to produce *Tom-Tom and Me*, a bestseller for a few months. It was published the year before she threw herself off the Staten Island ferry, and drowned. I myself haven't been above boasting a little, if only to Glynis, about how close I stood once or twice to the great Tomas Blalack.

The next time I came across Tom-Tom's portrait of Jinx after many years, it was hanging on the wall at the head of the Gittlemans' immense dining-table. As I studied it, the powerful shade of Tomas Blalack at the top of his form was grinning behind me, and I saw more clearly than ever before why Jinx had never liked 'Oyster Cracker III', or treated it with respect. When Tom-Tom gave her the painting to carry with her all the years of her life, it had been no unusual act of courtesy, after all; only another of his heartless tricks. How perfectly lovely had she been! How firm, how dewy, how deluded! No destiny had ever been invented or imagined, not even by an author of paperback romances, to justify the wealth of expectation that radiated from her young and beautiful face. The portrait, so bright and deft, looked out of place in the gloomy opulence of the Gittlemans' Park Avenue apartment as, I'm bound to say, did Jinx herself.

Mo and Jinx had been married only a few months at that time. I had flown to New York to attend meetings on the potential of vending machines for lipsticks and mascaras to be installed in ladies' rooms: 'Penny Miracle', was the working name of the project. When I turned up on their doorstep, Mo was patently relieved to find that his wife's oldest friend was short and plain, not a rackety high-life glamour-girl from her modelling days.

He was friendly and expansive, particularly after Jinx told him I was in business, too.

'In business as in life, Marsha, when you're on your way up, never look down. Keep your eye on the apogees.'

'And on the way down, Mr Gittleman?' I asked, made playful by his pontificating. 'Do the apogees slide past again? Can I grab hold of one as I'm falling and hang on for dear life?'

'Ah no, my dear. Kiss all the watersheds and apogees goodbye, once and for all. You will not come at them again, not even from the opposite direction. The downward slide does not take place on the same slope as the upward trudge, nor in the same dimension. Believe me, dear Marsha, in business as in all else, when one falls back to the beginning again, the trip thither is made by a different route from the trip thence, and a good deal faster, too. Please,' he said, 'you should do me an honour, and call me Mo.'

Because Mo sprinkled his conversation with archaisms there were many, I know, who suspected a bogus side to him; but the fact is he was utterly self-educated, and even into his mid-sixties, as he must have been then, he retained a zest for language and literature that professionally educated men of his age had long ago lost or forgotten. While Jinx was giving half-hearted instructions to the kitchen staff about our dinner, he showed me his polyglot's library. Mo dreamed in Polish, he said, he thought about daily life and business in Yiddish, and for what he called his 'soul's delight', he read in English and Russian. Although he'd left the mundane furnishings of his homes to his first wife, Ida, who had gone to her rest after nearly forty years of marriage, in his study was a locked glass cabinet that contained his own treasures, all of them rare, and some of them priceless. When he knew me a little better, he let me hold the Fabergé egg in my own hand, though he kept his eye on it, and his relief was evident when I returned it to him.

The Gittlemans had few friends apparently, and not much of a social life. That first night, and most of them afterwards, I stayed for dinner and was the only guest at the big table. We ate from ornate china with heavy cutlery. Mo and I made conversation and sometimes, awkwardly, he tried to draw Jinx into it. 'You tell her, Marsha. You tell my wonderful bride to take this place in hand and

161

refurbish it any way she wishes. Let her be the gem that designs its own setting.' Jinx meanwhile toyed with her food, and I could barely taste what was on my plate, so keenly did I feel how her soul was shrinking under her ugly little husband's begging eyes.

'I'll bet Mo murdered his first wife,' she said to me when we were alone in her sitting-room upstairs, after Mo had gone back to his study. Inadvertently, I glanced through the open door at her wide bed covered in antique laces. Warning bells rang in my mind: bad sex breeds violence, you know. On subsequent visits I used to join Mo for a whisky in his study before dinner or on my way to see Jinx upstairs, and I soon noticed how it was enough for him merely to hear her name, and he lost all composure. 'Jinx . . .' I'd begin, and his eyes teared like the eyes of an old man recollecting unattainable delights, or else, nearly as often, they narrowed and through their slits showed a poisonous underside to the trembling mass of his devotion.

'Perhaps in time . . .' I started to say to Jinx once, when she was unhappy and complaining listlessly about her marriage. But how to explain to a beauty the long, hard lesson of patience that we uglies begin to learn early in our lives? Give time a chance and it will blunt to a tolerable degree pain that at the start seems unendurable. Why, at this rate, boys and girls, even hopeless love that has been strumming my ribcage with its claws since the day I met Jacob Orben, will someday soon subside into just another geriatric twinge.

'What's happening to me?' Jinx cried with more evident distress than I had ever seen before in her.

When she threw back her head and swept her hair away from her temples in an uncharacteristically histrionic gesture, the delicate tracery of her last face-lift gleamed in the lamplight. I wanted to help her, to console her, to share

162

what little I'd acquired of wisdom. But Mo's foot was on the stairs, and I felt her shudder. And what could I have said in any case? She fell to temptation when she married for money; her innermost self was betrayed and in despair.

And Mo was a charming man, you understand. Not a bad man at all, except where his wife was concerned. I got on with him best of all Jinx's husbands, better by far than I'd got on with Jake, whom I loved. Of them all, Mo alone saw me as an independent figure, and I think he liked me, too. At least, in the beginning. We talked easily, and I told him all sorts of things about my daily working life, a topic for which Jinx had not the least interest or curiosity.

'I don't like these newfangled shopping malls that are springing up,' I complained to him once, over a whisky in his study. 'They're purpose-built and pretentious.'

'Like cathedrals, Marsha?' he asked. And then he winked and said: 'Only in malls, nobody lives over the store.'

You see? Mo and I entertained each other. 'Mighty Mo', that's what they called him in the *Wall Street Journal*. But when it came to love 'Mighty Mo' was a mighty mouse, a wreck, a fall-guy, and likely to turn bad. I myself could have lived with him in contented friendship. But as a husband for Jinx he was a perfect dud, except that he happened to be as rich as many a small nation. The upkeep of ageing beauty is no undertaking for a poor man.

For my first two weeks in New York I dropped in every day after work to see Jinx, and I think she was glad to see me. It was a little like visiting a sick-room where the patient's thoughts were turning increasingly inwards, in search of the old sustaining faith that mocked her from Blalack's portrait every time she sat at table. Often when I arrived in Jinx's rooms the television was on, and she was staring at it, but not seeing. All her responses had slowed down, as if she were afraid to startle sleeping memories and cause herself pain. Mind you, she dragged herself out to shop every day. I know she did, because there wasn't a time I visited I didn't notice something new, a scarf, a bowl, a vase, a fur, a jewel, that had not been there the day before. The copper-coloured maid, Esperanza, kept Jinx's clothes and possessions in good order, and had no other job. Often when I arrived long after all but the kitchen staff had gone off duty I heard Esperanza singing softly, still at work in Jinx's bedroom or dressing-room. Clothes and knick-knacks flowed steadily into her suite of rooms that was like a lush delta at the far end of the upstairs hall. Mo liked her to spend his money, I often heard him urge her to spend more, but her extravagance lacked its former exuberance. She could rarely be bothered to show me new things she'd bought, or the lavish gifts her husband gave her constantly. They lay where they fell, sometimes still in their wrapping paper, until Esperanza got around to putting them away.

Glorious Glynis was in charge of the office during my extended trip to New York and I reckoned I could spend another week at least before returning to London. Although I was at a loss for ways to help Jinx actively, or how to reanimate her gentle spirit, I flattered myself my very presence was doing her good. Then, I arrived late one afternoon at the Gittlemans' to find that in just a few hours everything had changed. From the landing outside Jinx's door I heard her bright, soft laugh as I remembered it from long ago. My first thought was that at last she had come back to herself, and her marriage to Mo might after all make her relatively happy. Wasn't I a fool not to realise these two possibilities were incompatible? Jinx restored would lack an atom of even rude tolerance for a loveless union. When I stepped inside her room, I saw we were not to be alone.

I hadn't seen Fawn in donkey's years, not since she had been a pretty young fashion-plate, and it took a moment to recognise pretty little Fawn Ellis all grown up into The

164

Great Mother of Corn who sat in a modified lotus position on one of Jinx's two facing sofas. She was dressed in a long linen cowl; a curious necklace – it looked like a chunk of coal – swung low on a leather thong between her breasts. Her hair was streaked silvery grey and she wore it hanging down her back the way only mad women do over a certain age, or women who live off the land. In her hands was a Victorian paperweight Jinx kept on the coffee table; she was peering at it intently, as if the tiny cornflowers inside the dome held a runic message.

'Learning', Fawn was saying to Jinx as I entered, 'is a fabulous personal growth experience.'

Jinx blew me a little kiss of welcome, and kept her hand raised to prevent me from interrupting.

'It's hard at first, Jinx, but once you've learned about your own beingness and confronted your beingness, you never look back. I confronted beingness and see? How calm I am.' She put the paperweight down and held out her hand so Jinx could be impressed by its steadiness. 'Since I confronted beingness I don't do drugs. I don't drink. I've quit smoking.' Fawn looked up, recognised me, and with a martyred smile, she gestured me to take a seat next to Jinx on the sofa across from hers. 'There's beingness in us all,' she continued. 'There's beingness in everything. There has to be. Or it couldn't be. There's beingness in fireflies and ants and fishes,' she said. The look she threw my way was openly challenging, but I had no quarrel with what I'd heard her saying up to then. I've stood on a deck at night and seen the ocean striped and churning; it's sure as hell not nothingness being coddled out there. It's a something-ness, all right, an 'isness' and if Fawn Ellis wanted to call it 'beingness', why not? I only hoped she'd shut up soon and Jinx would offer me a drink. But she, unstoppable, was telling Jinx how this beingness of hers lived on, she meant eternally, forever switching vehicles for return trips to earth. Jinx, who had suspected something of the sort for a long time, smiled and actually clapped her hand softly. Fawn continued: 'Our lives never end,' she said. 'It's really neat. We come back and back and back over and over. And as long as we go to, like, higher levels of consciousness every time, we come back in a better shape than the one we left.' That was when I started to feel uncomfortable. The beingness of fishes and fireflies was acceptable. Beingness was a doddle. But consciousness? Consciousness was a whole other ball game.

'Whoa. Hold on there,' I said, and I leaned back as if drawing in the reins of a horse.

'Our lives never really end, Jinx,' Fawn cantered on, ignoring me. 'We come back over and over to lead, like, better lives than before. Dig?' I looked longingly at the little bar in the corner of Jinx's sitting-room. 'We're aiming for the Ultimate State of Beingness.' said Fawn. 'Some people achieve it, too. Like, Jesus? He was really a Buddhist, you know. And Buddha? He learned lots of things from Christian monks. Not many people know that. A wonderful guy in Tibet told me about it. This guy, like, he'd made it to Ultimate State of Beingness, too. And the Ultimate State of Perfect Love.'

Jinx's eyes flickered with a deep emerald flame. She was contemplating endless mortal stabs at love until she got it right. I pushed myself off the sofa and poured myself a stiff whisky.

When I returned to the sofa Fawn was telling Jinx in detail about her 'endless search for wisdom'. And Fawn had found wisdom, too. You better believe she had. And how. Fakirs, gurus, psychics, shamans, healers, spiritualists, trance mediums, clairvoyants, clairaudients, readers of crystal balls, the I Ching, bones, stones, entrails and tarot cards, sensitives of every type, witches and warlocks, and a couple of aliens from outer space: they had all brought out their wares the moment they saw the rich, ageing American on the horizon. Wisdom had been absolutely everywhere Fawn appeared. She couldn't get away from it. In Peru she made contact with Quetzacoatl, he had appeared in all his plumage through the medium of a village magician to tell her she was on the right track. In Alaska she had been lightly mauled by a bear spirit, which the local soothsayer said was a sign of favour. In Tibet she'd met a fellow traveller in the mystic realms, formerly a policeman in Detroit, who was more highly evolved even than herself; and she'd knelt at his feet, drinking in wisdom.

'We could tell each other's thoughts without a word. We'd been husband and wife in another life. Know what I mean?'

'Oh yes, oh yes,' cried Jinx.

'See, the air around is just full of beingnesses,' said Fawn, 'passing from one level to another. Entering and re-entering consciousness to reap their reward. Or if they're not careful . . .' and I swear, as she paused she looked right at my nose, '. . . their punishment.'

Morosely I sucked at my drink.

'You and I', said Fawn to Jinx, 'are real old souls. I always know another old soul. Old souls give off, like, this old-soul aura, you know? Many consciousnesses ago, in another beingness, I was a priestess for the cat-headed gods of Egypt.'

'Mouseshit!' I cried. It just burst out of me. They both turned. I tried to smile appeasingly. 'I was just thinking that ancient Egypt must have been a very boring place,' I said 'entirely inhabited by priestesses and princesses who couldn't wait to call it quits, and come back as models and movie stars.'

Jinx said sadly, and as if I weren't sitting right there: 'Marsha is a sceptic.' And that did the trick.

'The hell she is,' I exploded. 'Marsha isn't sceptical at

167

all. Marsha has no doubts. Marsha knows it's mouseshit!'

'Marsha is an aggressive sceptic,' said Fawn to Jinx. 'Aggressive sceptics make these ripples in the ether, see? And then beingnesses can't make it through to consciousnesses. See what I mean? Beingnesses cannot penetrate the static of aggressive scepticism. That's how come sceptics only know what they want to know.'

'Without sceptics, Fawn,' I said, trying hard to control my anger, 'we'd all still believe the earth was flat.'

'The earth', said Fawn Ellis, '*is* flat. I have that on the highest authority. But you sceptics can't see it because you're blinded by so-called facts; you, with your so-called educations, from your so-called universities. And I'm sorry to tell you, Marsha,' she finished in scorn and triumph, 'your aura has turned dark brown.'

Jinx walked with me as usual to the elevator, but she turned away before the doors had closed, so eager was she to get back to Fawn who had started rabbiting about a mountain she'd bought in Utah, where ley-lines met, and where she was going to set up her very own alternative theology. 'Good night, honey,' Jinx said before she left: she could as well have said, 'adieu'. Riding down to street level from the Gittlemans' apartment, I had never felt myself so alone. And as things turned out I was not going to see her again or receive more than a few postcards from her until nearly fifteen years had gone by. Until only the day before yesterday, to be exact.

I stayed away from Park Avenue for a few days. But on the morning of my flight home to England, I woke feeling contrite. I bought Jinx a silk rose, a pink one, to show how abject was my apology for being sulky, and I walked over to deliver it in person. The instant Esperanza opened the door, I knew something was very wrong. Believe me, there was nothing other-worldly about my premonition; no telepathic messages winged their way to me; no feathered brave or Egyptian royal chose that moment in the Gittlemans' hall to renew our acquaintance from a past existence and prepare me for bad news. But all cataclysms above ground, and that includes human dramas too, must commit themselves to the atmosphere. There is nothing weird about that, is there? It's a common sense, isn't it? And as soon as I stepped over the Gittlemans' threshold, even before I saw that Esperanza's normally cheery face was puffy and her eyes were red, I felt the molecules around me quaking in the after-effects of shock. Without a word she led me quickly past the door to Mo's study, past the stairway up to Jinx's rooms, and straight to the arch that opened into the dining-room. Mo was alone, seated at the head of the table, facing me. The windows were still shuttered, he must have been sitting there all night, and the chandelier was lit. Its cold light glittered on a heap of sparkling objects in front of him. When he saw me, he scooped up a handful of the precious things, I recognised them as gifts he had given Jinx. He held them out.

'She took nothing,' he said.

Behind him was 'Oyster Cracker III'. Leaving her beautiful image behind was no kindness: Mo looked where I was looking, and when he turned back to me, his eyes were full of tears. He dropped his head into his hands. I made a step towards him. A woman in emotional pain wants to be held and stroked, but it's hard to guess which way a wounded man will jump. Ought I to touch Mo? He might think such a move on my part was condescending, or worse, opportunistic. Should I go to the sideboard and pour him a glass of port? Perhaps a better thing would be to ask cook to brew tea. If I spoke consolingly, would it relieve him, or humiliate him further in his pain?

'Do you want me to stay with you for a while, Mo?' I asked at last, thinking I would ring Glynis, change my

169

reservation and postpone my departure for a day or two. He did not look up for a long time, I wasn't sure he'd heard. Should I ask again? I hesitated. When he raised his head at last, his broad face was closed and cold, tilted up like a warrior's shield.

'No, Marsha,' he said. 'I want you to go.'

It was only that night when I was already homeward bound for London, it struck me he had meant for ever.

The last I heard of Mo Gittleman was about eight years ago. He was living in Palm Beach. According to the grapevine, he needed round-the-clock professional nursing after several serious strokes. His newish wife, a blonde, and not quite half his age, did nothing all day according to the gossips, but spend his money, and wait.

TWENTY-THREE

The next fifteen years or so comprised the bright fullness of my life, though looking back I see them not bright or full, but creamy, smooth, and as even as a pot of Miracle's 'Beatitude Crème de Jour'. Naturally, there were the highs and lows of every day, most of them to do with business. I have been very, very busy. Too busy to think. Too busy to rest. Too busy to reminisce. Too busy to miss my oldest friend, or to do more than wonder from time to time how she was getting on; and of course I wished her well. When I finally returned from my prolonged stay in New York, I threw myself into production of the cosmetic line anticipated in the wake of the Capran Riot. With 'join us, sister' still echoing in my memory, we prepared to launch 'Natural Miracle', which turned out to be one of the great success stories of the beauty business, selling even more widely than I'd expected to a market that I knew from the start was bound to grow straight through the 1980s, into the '90s, and probably beyond the end of this century.

'Boys,' I told my English chemists back in the days of 'Natural Miracle's' inception, 'pretty soon it will no longer be enough for women to think they look good and they smell good when they buy our products; most of our clients are going to want to think they are *being* good by using cosmetics, and doing a good thing. So first off, let's plan to be more basic and abrasive with our cleansers; let's put a little grit in them so they make themselves felt. And back off the lurid goo, too, chaps. Colours of our new line must imitate blushing flowers of the field. I want them dulcet, subtle, merely a tinted camouflage, no more full disguise. Mark my words, gentlemen, the sexes will very soon be quarrelsome enough without any help from war-paint. And by the way, exotica has had its day. Exotica smacks of imperialism, paternalism, and an old order. So no more ylang-ylang, no orchid, no jasmine, no sandalwood, vetiver, or musk; above all, not a whisper of patchouli. Oh yes, lay off the cinnamon, vanilla and cloves, as soon as women start clamouring for equal rights, culinary perfumes have to be on their way out. Make all the lotions, unguents, liquids and creams of this new line smell of moss, damp leaves, honey, herbs, grasses, apples, pears, and other wholesome fruits. I won't say no to a tang of fish-oil, even a drop of perspiration. Above all our 'Natural Miracle' must give no offence to sky or earth. We will package it – biodegradably, is the buzz-word, I believe. Maybe someday in the future, we'll come up with something to recycle. And any man here who dares test any 'Natural Miracle' product on a white rat or a rabbit, I myself with these two hands will tear out his liver and feed it to the maggots. God bless them.'

Of course, it was a couple of years before the line was ready to launch, but I knew what I was doing. Obviously, I did. Haven't I done well? What am I going to do now?

Out of courtesy I flew to Antibes to consult the Sisters before we started work on 'Natural Miracle'. By that time their confidence in my judgement, to say nothing of their ennui regarding business, whether it was affected or not, meant our meetings had become little more than a formality and a pleasure. We dealt rapidly with the project: they barely listened, and gave an automatic approval, before we moved on to matters that interested them entirely. First off, they told me the gossip about their titled neighbours, one of whom had recently committed suicide; Nina called it 'a crime of terminal boredom.' Most of the others were committing adultery: 'Or trying to,' said Olga, 'given their average age.' When it was my turn, I told them about Jinx, and how she had swallowed Fawn's mystical moon-pap.

'Mar-see-ah, don't you know', said Olga, 'that anywhere, and in every generation you will find women once famous for their looks who must try in all sorts of ways to fill the emptiness after beauty has left them? Sometimes you see the old girls slinking around big city slums with their pockets full of scraps, on the hunt for stray cats, dogs, rats, mice; any creature at all that will be grateful for their interest and make them feel the way men used to do. Ex-beauties develop great angers, too. Anger mimics other passions, you know; and it can hide grief. And then there are some, perhaps they were more egocentric and silly to begin with, who make a cult out of wishful thinking.'

Nina laughed her short laugh.

'Even wishful thinking is thinking, after a fashion,' she said, 'and to think at all, for the first time, so late in life, has come as such a revelation to someone like your Fawn, she badly overestimates the importance of her thoughts.'

Olga poured more wine. We were on the terrace at the cool side of their house, overlooking the sea. A breeze that had been blowing all day was settling down for the night; within me was a stealthy, growing calm that is the beginning of forgetting. We were silent for a while.

'How many times have you heard people say that beauty is in the eye of the beholder?' said Olga, raising her glass and looking through the wine in it to the sinking rays of the sun. 'But nobody says how gullible is the beholder's eye. How prejudiced. And racist. And timid.'

'And predictable,' said Nina. 'And banal. And nostalgic. And self-defensive.'

'Especially among men,' Olga said, and she sighed,

'what enters by a man's eye circumnavigates the higher processes of his brain.'

'And sinks straight to his groin,' said Nina.

For five years after Jinx went off to wallow in a bed of magnetic force-fields and play around with ley-lines, only two cards arrived from her, and there were no more telephone calls. The first card arrived a year after she had walked off into the sunset. It came from the 'Fawn Ellis's Church of Magical Confluence', at an address in Utah. On the front was a rough print of a pentagram encircled by a lot of cabalistic squiggles; on the back Jinx had written: 'Evolving my beingnesses. Fawn says I used to be an ancient Greek. Why don't you join us?' But the next card, less than two years later, came from Phoenix, Arizona, and it was obvious she had broken with Fawn's church by that time, for she wrote: 'On the road again, honey. We plan a romantic Christmas in the sun.' The other half of 'we' was a man; I didn't need a crystal ball to tell me.

It was three years, nearly four, and I heard no more from Jinx, nor even the mention of her name. Nor, I must say, did I think of her very often. Not until I bumped into Helsinki Braw at a fashion trade show in London. When I saw her pushing through the crowd and making straight for me, I felt the customary flicker of alarm. She was the size of a destroyer by that time, dressed overall in diamanté. Chins flowed; her great arms flailed; bracelets flashed from their moorings fast in fat. But I said to myself that I was nearly fifty years old, damn it. And when she asked, 'How about a quick one?', I replied, 'I guess I can spare a minute or two, Helsinki.'

There was a bar at the back of the hall where we found a table. She ordered a large pink gin, I had a whisky. Of course, I asked her straight away about Jinx. Helsinki herself hadn't seen Jinx any more recently than I. But Fawn

Ellis had passed through New York recently, where Helsinki helped her promote her book, *Depth Perception: A Guide to the Cosmos*.

'We got it to the top of *The New York Times*' bestseller list,' said Helsinki, and a grin pushed her jowls aside. 'I tell you, nobody has any standards any more,' she added happily.

Fawn told Helsinki that Jinx's soul was after all not so old as she had hoped, and the labyrinths of cosmology had turned out to be too complex for her to grasp, in the end.

'Fawn said the last she saw of Jinx, she was heading south with some dude from Tibet in a Ford camper,' Helsinki told me. She drained her glass and signalled massively for another. 'Maybe the guy was the Dalai Lama. But I can tell you one thing for sure, Fawn didn't look very happy about it.'

I had barely finished my whisky before Helsinki polished off her second gin, downing it like water. An English designer I vaguely recognised was waving at her from the other side of the hall: she had work to do and deals to make. With a gargantuan effort, she pushed back her chair. As a reminder that I still owed her a favour, she offered nothing towards our drinks.

'Look out for Englishmen,' she said, as she gathered herself together to leave. 'They're tricky, but you only have to wait long enough and your limey teasucker', she called over her huge shoulder, 'will outsmart himself, every time.'

The 1980s turned out to be an exceedingly earthbound decade, and very greedy. Greed is by definition short on foresight; anyone with a half a brain could have guessed that bad times, they were a-coming, and a price was going to be paid for all the getting and the spending, sooner rather than later. Miracle Products was dug in tight enough to

175

come through, but it wouldn't be very long before a lot of our big-spending customers started to feel the pinch. We were ready. Not long after the mid-80s we put together a line of inexpensive cosmetics for the newly poor, packaged austerely to suit cut-back chic, but more highly perfumed than, say, 'Natural Miracle', to sweeten the blow of a down-market slide. 'Benedictus Beauty Aids' was the original name our advertising department came up with for the new products, until Glynis argued effectively that 'Benedictus' in a cosmetic context could put off the Catholics, and 'aids' in any context had begun to put off everyone. I gave her a bonus, and we called the new line 'Kind Looks'. It was also Glynis, my angular, homely, crypto-sensualist, who foresaw that the incoming style for non-penetrative sex was bound to bring mouths back into prominence. On her recommendation, we rationalised the eye-colours that had done so well for us in the 1970s and the early '80s, and we went into lip gloss in a big, big way.

There seem to me to be two constants in this existence: the first is that everything is constantly changing, and the other is that all but very, very little soon starts changing for the worse. The time always arrives, for instance, when lovers are less lovable – which is as good as saying, of course, that they become intolerable – when friendships start to change, when ambitions that only yesterday were all-consuming begin to offer no satisfaction or purpose. Very, very slowly, cracks develop in the best of things, until what only yesterday seemed so sure, so right, so comfortable, is today in shambles. There must be an instant when the bug bites and the fatal process enters the system, but we are too behind ourselves and out of touch with the present to recognise it. Being so childishly hopeful that anything can ever be again the way it used to be, we fight what is occurring and refuse to face it or adapt when the inevitable rot sets in. A few years ago, I found myself waking up increasingly ill pleased with the morning, clammy, sweating, dreams all forgotten but their smells. I felt myself to be turning into a coffin encasing memories and other small, dying parts. For a while, instead of allowing the change, and seeing what new thing could be made of it, I tried not to acknowledge it. But I have no skill for self-deception, and nothing worked. The pursuit of profit was suddenly a bore; whisky made my head ache; when I went to the theatre, which I had always previously considered one of the chief joys of life in London, I saw the actors acting, but not the play. And then, on 10 March 1989, a bleak Monday in that interminable month, I opened my newspaper over breakfast tea, and there in the middle pages was the announcement of Jacob Orben's death. He had been aboard a train on his way to deliver a lecture at Princeton University when his heart upped and attacked him fatally.

Ah. Love that turns to water under bridges. Love that's spilt 'twixt cup and lip. I missed you, Jake. For a long time I thought that missing you was all I had ever felt, or ever would. And you missed me too, Jacob Orben. You never knew you were missing me, of course, but that's irrelevant. Does a patient miss his operation because he sleeps through it? Oh yes, you missed me, beloved. *C'était moi*, all the time. But never mind. What's done is done; there is no more. You missed me then. Then was then. Now is now. I know it's now. This must be now. I'm in Los Angeles, and it's always nothing but now in Los Angeles.

TWENTY-FOUR

For years Glynis had been after me to take a holiday, a real holiday, not just to Antibes where I was bound to talk beauty with the Sisters, but to the kind of tropical island where Jinx had spent so many long, leisurely, sexy weeks of her youth. My dear Glynis, plain as a raindrop, she too has burning yearnings locked in her hopeful chest. And she is still young enough, I guess, to dream that sun and sea and sand have a mystical power to heal us and transform us into whatever we want to be, during a fortnight away from the grind. I should have known better. I did know better. But my gloom was in deep, I wasn't in fighting form, and I finally let myself be persuaded.

Within a few days of arrival on the island, I'd had more than enough of it. The tropical spectrum got me down — red, orange, magenta, azure, sour green — I ached for colours more cunning and complex than those kiddies pull first out of the box; I longed for the honest textures of the north, thick high-piles that stay in place and aren't constantly dragged away from underfoot. I missed the pearly sunsets of England, and how they are gently nudged into reverse at dawn, so neither day nor night ends with a crash, or strictly speaking, ends at all. An instant after the sun plummets below the horizon out there in the hot spots, dry air becomes moist, cool sea water almost boils against the skin, and colours brightest at noon turn blackest under the moon, so each hibiscus punches a hole in the foliage as deep as the space between stars. Maybe the way those tropical nights take our most basic perceptions and turn

178

them upside down is supposed to be sexy: I wouldn't know
– all that mushy stuff, which in its time was not beyond
me, was certainly way behind me when I hit Tobago. I felt
altogether alien and unbalanced; a stooped, worried, big-
nosed trespasser. Except that I knew it would be bound to
distress Glynis, whom I had left in charge of the shop, I'd
have been perfectly happy to cut my vacation short.

One afternoon, when the end of the penitential holiday
was at last in sight, I gave up trying to read on the beach
– decent reading light, by the by, is yet another argument
for staying home – and after a short, sandy nap, I woke up
feeling parched. An iced vodka would have gone down a
treat, no pineapple, if you please, and no paper parasol. I
beg you, barman, put my drink in a glass, and shove your
half-a-coconut with eyelets drilled for straws. A few days
earlier, during one of my dutiful trudges on the beach, I
had noticed a seaside bar with a few ragged umbrellas set
up outside. It had a generally run-down air more appealing
to me than the bandbox tropicana of my hotel. I put my
book, *Jude The Obscure*, as it happens, into my bag, and
kicked off my sandals so I could walk down on the wet
sand, where the ocean followed clucking behind me, busily
mopping up my footprints. 'Kisses' was carved on a
wooden sign hanging over the entrance to the thatched
hut. I knew enough about tropical paradises by that time
to be pretty certain the joint was probably favoured by local
expatriates: not a soul was sitting outside under the umbrellas, and expats to hot places never court sun or open
air as tourists do. As for natives, bars on the beach rarely
appeal to them; they prefer formica and neon watering-
holes in town to anything beside their constant, cruel
companion.

Sure enough, no sooner through the swinging doors into
the cool darkness, than the customers along the bar turned
to give me the look expats reserve for tourists from their

homelands. Gorillas in a zoo survey clamorous humans with exactly the same superiority and malign indifference. Sun and salt from outside, gin from within, turn both sexes into timeless artifacts of leather and bone, and the seven or eight people at the bar could have been in their forties, or their seventies. There were a few round tables on the dirt floor of the hut, and I chose one near the door. The instant I sat down, a child as black as oiled ebony appeared from the wings. He had the knowing eyes of children everywhere who hang out with heavy drinkers. When I ordered a vodka with soda on the side, and plenty of ice, a very slight tremor of approval worked its way down the line of barflies, who immediately turned their backs on me to study their own reflections in the mildewed mirror that ran the length of the bar. Every last one of them was an alcoholic, you can bet on it, and not of the convivial variety either, but sunk in misery, and fed up to the eye-teeth with each other's company . For the first time since I'd landed on the island, I felt relaxed and quite at home.

The bar-wise child was ready with a second drink before I signalled. But when I had finished that one, and was looking around for the bill so I could leave before darkness fell, the scamp had disappeared. He knew if you keep a boozing customer dry long enough at that point, one-for-the-road will probably be in order, and after that, the sky's the limit. But he hadn't reckoned on my own cynical acuity, forged in the old days at Schrafft's. Smiling to remember Miss Kaloczek, of all people in such surroundings, I went to the bar and hoisted myself up on a stool so I could pay directly at the cash-register. It was an ancient filigreed contraption; the keys most often used were worn down, like vowels on a foreign correspondent's old-fashioned typewriter. An impassive black barman took my money, and when he moved off to serve the expats another round, I saw that the wall next to the cash-register was plastered with postcards, dingy from time and cigarette smoke, most of them curling at the edges. Some were message-side out, scrawls from old 'regulars' summoned to the mainland for funerals, I fancied, or gone to find out why their remittance cheques were slow in arriving. The cards showing their glossy sides were of New York, San Francisco, Toronto, a few from London, and other far-flung cities. High up and apart from everything else was a yellowing calendar. It advertised a shampoo popular in America when I was a girl. I noticed that the pad of months was intact, not a page had been torn from it. And then it struck me, like a bolt of lightning on a sunny day, that the beautiful girl whose hair streamed in a moonlit ocean over the numerals, 1958, was Jinx O'Malley.

I tried to buy the calander, but I was too voluble and eager, and the barman became suspicious. He dug in his heels, and finally I had to give up. Behind me when I left, the expats were already buzzing. It doesn't take much to raise a crop of gossip in the tropics, I'd given them enough for seasons to come: the ugly little grockle from back home who tried to take their gorgeous mascot away from them. Before they were done, the incident would be embroidered into the attempted theft of a holy image out of the church, and I would go down in their lives of fret and boredom as a dealer in shady icons. Which, now I come to think of it, is not far off the mark.

Back home at last, and nothing much had changed, not essentially, only its nature was different. My restlessness – I suppose I have to call it a depression – was no longer sharp-edged; it was pulpy, sticky, clinging, like one of those nasty tropical fruits that falls apart in your hand, and if you manage to raise it to your mouth, turns out to have more smell than flavour. But let me not make too big a thing of this. It wouldn't do to exaggerate what was, after all, not much more than my time of life, and therefore bound to pass: what time of life does not? Patience is all anyone needs to get through the worst of anything, and I am well equipped for patience: with a nose as overbearing as this one, I'd fall flat on my face if I tried to go at things by leaps and bounds. As befits my appearance, I am a painstaking snuffler. Or so I have always believed. For a while, the way forward was unclear again, that was all there was to my malaise. No big deal. What had to be done next, and next, and next again, was not the problem; Glynis wrote it all into the diary on my desk. But why I should meet with this manager or that buyer, why I had to go out to the lab in Lincoln and put a rocket up our chemists, why I needed to lunch with a gorgon of the press; why any of what my diary required me to do should be of the slightest importance, Glynis could not tell me. She looked perplexed when I asked, and referred me to accounts.

Late one night, a little in my cups, I allowed myself a moan in my regular letter to the Sisters.

'Whenever you cannot go forward, dear girl, allow yourself to go back,' came their reply by return. 'It's all one.'

TWENTY-FIVE

The indomitable little wood where Jinx and I had sealed our friendship an age ago was shedding dry leaves over a litter of tins, wrappers, cigarette butts, rags, condoms, and other interior garbage from Manhattan slums. Our old bench was still there, carved with recent obscenities, and greasy with motor-car refuse that is slowly burying all the cities of the world. I swiped at the splintery wood with a tissue, sat down, sighed, closed my eyes. What I wanted to do was more than simply remember: I wanted to squeeze myself into the very seed of the moment and backtrack right through the core of time itself to that very place the autumn day I sat there with Jinx O'Malley. I wanted to hear again with these old ears the homely sounds of bygone days; to smell again with this grotesque snout New York's burnt sugar and yellow mustard, back before junk-food was poison; to taste the apple as it tasted; to re-*be* Marsha Leah Feldstein, young, and open her eyes with wonder on a friend's breathtaking beauty. For a flicker, I nearly did it. I swear to you, I nearly grabbed the past and held it fast in my heroic little fist. But Manhattan has become a game played at speed, millions of pieces in motion chasing quicksilver, side to side, up and down, no time to concentrate or meditate before the next move. Where is the backwater in New York? In what leafy square does history hold its own against the inconsequence of the game? What's grasped there now slips through the fingers. Yesterday's 'in' is 'out'. And the only place it's smart to be is perpetually on the lip of oblivion. Drop out; drop dead in Noo Yawk, Noo Yawk.

Mind you, the old town ain't so young as she used to was; neither is the nation of which, for Americans of my generation, New York will always be the true capital. Since Jinx and I were girls, the city's losers have accumulated into a grumbling multitude, and the air around me was charged with howls and screeches of New Yorkers crying foul.

Suddenly, a young policeman was scowling down at me. He was prematurely grave, and his voice was scolding when he said: 'This is no place for a nice lady on her own.' I came within a breath of asking the boy what place he thought there was, anywhere, for a nice lady on her own? But 'Contempt' is what they call frivolity in law, and it's a punishable offence, I understand. Peaceably, I moved along, no axe to grind with New York's finest. Besides, I saw from my watch that I had to hurry if I wanted to be on time for my appointment with Helsinki Braw. When I'd called her from London the week before, she said she would be delighted to help me find out where Jinx was; we both knew, so she didn't bother mentioning, if she succeeded, it would count as another favour I owed her.

'Say Jinx is dead, do you want to know where she's buried?' Helsinki asked, and brayed down the long-distance line.

But I knew Jinx was alive; I would have known equally had she been dead. Not to make a song and dance out of our spiritual kinship—a factor of our friendship that had been dangerously strained by Fawn Ellis—everyone knows that obituary writers like any other reporters are on the look-out for a scoop. The death of one who was once the most beautiful woman in the world would have sent them scurrying for facts, and then to their photo-libraries for old cheesecake snaps of her to publish, as they had for poor Dereena Foyle, and do for every other ageing pin-up who bites the dust. Alive and no longer photogenic, a famous beauty is forgotten. But her death will not escape the attention of the buzzards. In short, if Jinx were dead, I would have read about it in the papers.

Even in bygone days Helsinki invited nobody to her office; Blalack himself had never been there. I realised why as soon as I saw the place. She had rooms on the top floor of a mid-town hotel called the Rossmoor. Built in the 1930s for the carriage trade, the building had been allowed to go to seed in postwar decades, crazed for modernity. When I walked into the lobby, a few unshaven greybeards dozing on the battered sofas looked up, then away again, and a crosstown wind through the open door at my back swept quarter-inch cigarette stubs into corners. Helsinki obviously didn't give a toss that the place was filthy and dilapidated: its mid-town address looked good on letterheads, and the rent must have been low. Anyhow, she made all her important contacts in restaurants and at parties, so nobody whose good opinion mattered ever needed to see her offices. I found myself wondering tetchily if I was being allowed a rare glimpse into Helsinki's hidden life as a sign of trust, or of contempt? But it's hard to stay up on a high horse for very long when you're not as spry as you used to be, and the point was hardly worth worrying about. Besides, there are countless occasions when trust and contempt are practically indistinguishable, and serve the same purpose.

The elevator was like the cage for an old slattern's budgie; it smelled of stale face-powder and animal droppings, and it moved reluctantly with lots of grumbling to the top floor. At the far end of the dark hall I found the door with 'Helsinki Braw & Associates' in flaking gold letters on its glass panel. When I knocked, a querulous, trembling voice told me to come in. Inside, was a small attic room in an extreme state of dusty clutter. Beyond it, behind another half-glass door, lay a second room, which had to be Helsinki's inner sanctum where she waited for business. The white-haired woman who looked up from a set of account books was well past retirement age. A strand of hair was free from the chignon on top of her head, she had been winding it around and around the tip of her nose where the cartilage was shapely and firm. A good nose is the last thing to go. So, alas, is a bad one. My guess was she must be a superannuated bookkeeper whom Helsinki got cheap, and who lived in perpetual terror of tax inspectors. Apparently, she was close to panic at the sight of me; her eyes swirled like blue oysters behind her bifocals. I smiled quickly, and explained I had come to keep an appointment with the boss.

A decade had gone by since I'd last met Helsinki, and when she swivelled around in her chair to greet me, I knew why she'd had me up to her offices. Obviously, she didn't get around much any more: she was of a size to sink a battleship. Swathed in ice-blue satin, her summit crowned with a turban of the same fabric, it made your teeth chatter to look at her. It wasn't flab causing the chair to groan under her; it was well-packed, high-class avoirdupois, belonging to a woman who had made the running and intended never to run again, not for a bus, not for a man, not for her living. Helsinki Braw had arrived. She gestured me to the visitor's chair, the desk between us was dwarfed to nursery furniture by her bulk. Helsinki Braw wasn't going anywhere. Then she made a commanding sound, and a very ugly girl with a big nose appeared from somewhere behind her with a vodka on ice in a wine glass for me. For Helsinki, five inches of gin straight up in a tumbler: any less would have vanished like a match struck in the Arctic wastes.

Helsinki and I clinked conspiratorially, though what she and I had to conspire about is anybody's guess, and we sipped. The ugly girl returned to the outer office, but not before she'd given me a look of curiosity bordering on insolence. Had I been equally beady-eyed when I was her age? Perhaps she too lived with a beautiful flatmate who set the race of men into a tizzy. Perhaps such asymmetrical friendships as mine with Jinx went back through generations, all the way to the courts of ancient Egypt that nuts like Fawn Ellis pillage for their antecedents.

'So,' said Helsinki, after a while, 'you're looking for Jinx, are you?' Her face had retreated into chins, the eyes were still bright, though sunken; only her aquiline nose stood its ground, dignity somewhat undermined by a constant tinny whistling through the nostrils. 'Can I ask you a question? You and Jinx, were you dikes?' I was surprised. It was the first time I had taken into account there were those so deficient in imagination as to attribute a sexual basis to my friendship with Jinx. Furthermore, it amazed me a cunning old trout like Helsinki couldn't see that Jinx and I between us had none of the political convictions necessary to make a go of being lesbians in the mid-twentieth century. And besides, hadn't she noticed how devoted Jinx was to classic coupling?

'No, Helsinki,' I said, 'we were not like that.'

Her face suddenly blazed beet red, there was a distant rumbling deep inside her, and she started giving off a lot of heat. A dreadful picture of the ugly girl, the white-haired woman and me manhandling Helsinki's helpless bulk into the lift and down to the street flashed through my mind. Anxiously, I looked around for water. But the eruption was nothing special, it seemed. She signalled me not to worry, and after a little while the high colour faded, the choking stopped, and from somewhere around her gigantic body appeared an absurdly dainty handkerchief; she dabbed at her face with it, and then at her eyes. Finally, she drained her drink. The ugly girl appeared instantly to refill her glass, and to top up my own.

'He always used to say with you two it wasn't sexual.

187

He used to say it was symbiosis,' Helsinki continued, and lovelight gleamed in her eyes, while her mind floated momentarily over its vast residence. 'He always used to say you were the brains . . . '

'And Jinx', I finished for her, 'was the beauty.'

She shook her head, turban, earrings, and all.

'No. He used to call her "the room to let". "Beautiful women," he used to say, "use 'em and lose 'em. They're all rooms to let." '

The departure of flesh from Helsinki's internal organs must have thrown her sex into confusion; when she leaned towards me, I noticed she had grown a grey moustache and sideboards. 'Well, what the hell, right? It all goes in the end. And when it goes, it goes *en vitesse*. Leaves them brain-damaged, you know, *les pauvres cons*. The fact is, kiddo, your beautiful people lack a full component of grey matter. You know what happens to brains if you don't use them when you're young? They atrophy. Golf balls, that's what your glamour girls and boys have rattling around between their ears. Most of them wouldn't know how to spot a train coming. And even if they could put two and two together, or recite the Gettysburg Address in Latin, who'd give a damn? Expectations of the flesh, that's what any man feels when a good-looker walks by, and I don't care how big a shot he is. You wanna know the funniest part, Marsha? The funniest part is that no beautiful woman in the whole history of the world, not even Jinx O'Malley, has ever lived up to the fantasy in a man's mind, or in the minds of women too, when they see her. Poor bitches. They're all disappointments about to happen,' Helsinki said. 'And sooner or later they know it.'

Her voice, which had been booming as ever to start, began to recede and strain through the wall of flesh that held it. She had finished her drink again. I went myself to the rickety sideboard and poured her another. The small nod Helsinki gave me when she took the glass was as close as I'd known her to come to a thank you.

'So what do you want to find Jinx for?' she asked.

'Because she's my friend,' I replied, as if there were not more to it, more than I myself understood.

Helsinki looked at me curiously for a moment. 'Beauty,' she said, I swear she did, 'never finds a friend.'

'Oh dear, we make too much out of beauty, Helsinki,' I replied.

She leaned forward, one lid dropped in a sly avian wink, and she said: 'Look at who's made the most out of it?'

While Helsinki rooted among the papers on her desk, she told me she herself had not seen Jinx in six years, not since she'd turned up in New York asking Helsinki to find her some work.

'How did Jinx look?' I asked.

Helsinki peered at me, amusement made her eyes glint like coals in a snowman's face.

'For her age? I've seen worse.'

'Did she ask about me?'

'Yeah,' Helsinki said. 'But not how you looked.'

The job Helsinki found for Jinx on that occasion was, as far a she knew, the last work Jinx did. It was to model tights and support-stockings for a catalogue to be sent to retirement communities all over America.

'Legs last longest,' Helsinki said.

Triumphantly, she came up with a scrap of paper on which was the final address she'd had for Jinx; it was in Hollywood, and as far as Helsinki had been able to discover, Jinx still lived there.

She managed to heave herself out of her chair and accompany me to the door of the inner office, walking with a cowhand's wide-open gait, arms pushed almost akimbo by flesh above, toes turned in against the massive separation of her thighs.

'That's two you owe me,' she said.

But we both knew there was no time left for calling in favours: her heart must any day explode from its effort to supply remote areas of the continent dependent upon it. As I was leaving, I heard her call out behind me: 'Look out for yourself, Marsha.'

TWENTY-SIX

This morning I went down and collected a fat envelope from Glynis in London. When I told the pretty girl at the desk I was going to leave tomorrow and asked her to see to it, please, my bill was ready early in the morning, she gave me a smile of featherbrained docility that is going to be her downfall. She came from open cow-country, I imagine, to make it big in Hollywood. Famous people pop up in this pink pot-pourri and the little drip, who is not nearly cute enough and certainly no latter-day Jinx O'Malley, imagines she'll catch the eye of a star or a director: as if stars had eyes for anything but the mirror, and directors had eyes for anyone but stars. I wish I could wave a wand and send her straight back home to a cosy future with the boy next door. It amazes me how all the classic cornball stories persist in the hinterlands of America. There must be Romeos and Juliets out there in the tundra of the Great Plains, and farm-boys studying by lamplight, who actually dream of being president. Obviously there are still plenty of pretty little misses who think they 'oughta be in pitchers', and who still don't know a wolf from grandmama.

Business reports I threw to one side, and then I glanced through the clippings from London papers Glynis always sends me when I'm abroad. One article she had circled in red concerned a plastic surgeon in America who has developed an anti-wrinkle treatment derived from the deadly botulin toxin. The poison relaxes muscles that have grown tense, probably for good reason, and the wrinkles slide

191

away. Four injections are required to iron out the forehead, only two for crow's feet, and the effect lasts six months before it has to be repeated. White lead, belladonna, now botulin toxin; it's not the first time we've tried to use a substance containing death itself to immunise ourselves against age. Who are we fooling? We can't fool time, it always roars back with a vengeance, wrinkling everything in front of it. We don't even fool others, who know the real thing when they see it. We only fool ourselves. Glynis enclosed a second, longer article cut out of a glossy magazine, about one of the new so-called 'supermodels', a nineteen year old, who for the time being earns more in an hour than many able-bodied residents of the planet earn in a year. According to the journalist, movie-star looks have had their day and the new fashion in beauty 'is raw, real, and irregular'. But the model featured is skinny and uncommonly good-looking, albeit a little fierce of demeanour and in rather the dominatrix mould. She happens to have one green eye, one brown, and also to be stone bald. In the main photograph Glynis has written in biro across the shining dome of her head: 'Would you call this tempting pate, Miss F.?' Near enough funny to make me smile. But if I'm being honest, I have to admit there was a time long ago when I would have plucked every hair on my head with red hot tweezers if I'd thought the pain and mutilation would make me beautiful and desired by men.

The same sanctimonious idiots who say beauty is in the eye of the beholder are the ones to tell you that what you have never had, you cannot miss. Well, they could not be more wrong. I never had a shape to catch the eyes of a man, and when I was young, believe me, I missed it like hell. However, I start to suspect that time has a soft spot after all for those of us who were ugly and unhappy in our youth; what turns out to be true enough, I now realise, is that what you have never had, you cannot lose. The sacrifices growing old demands from the likes of me are nothing compared to the price good-looking women have to pay. No amount of accumulating ticks and tocks will make me tall and slender, for instance; but the years in due course will shrink the girls up on the catwalk, until the day must come when their entrances too will go unnoticed. Bet on it. While a beauty in due course must catch sight of herself on every reflective surface and watch how she is being dismantled, inch by inch, plain little creatures like me slip from the scene with grace denied us when we were young. Time gets everything there is in the end, but we can surrender our humble goods voluntarily and privately; we are spared the pretty woman's unseemly tug-of-war in public against Big Daddy. I have been in service to passing beauty for very many years. Too long? Too long. Now that time has evened out the discrepancy between me and the beautiful others, the time has come to take up staff and bowl and hit the road, I think. Let Glynis have her turn. I must remember, by the by, to tell her about the ugly, big-nosed girl who works for Helsinki Braw. My intuition is she too has the potential to become a dealer in Miracle Products to those who depend upon them.

Helsinki wondered why I was looking for Jinx, and I told her: 'Because she is my friend'. But I had not heard a word from Jinx or seen her in fifteen years, nearly half as long as we had known each other. 'Because she is my friend', if it was true at all, was less true than if I'd said: 'Because she *was* my friend'. And why have I gone out in search of a memory? Curiosity may be enough to inspire a new friendship, but it is not enough to fuel a journey to New York, and then on to this coastal dream-pit, in pursuit of an old and absent friend, no more than the ghost of a friend.

I guess I could puff myself up and pretend I set out to

193

find Jinx because I sensed that she needed help. But the truth is, I was the stationary member of our pair, and if Jinx needed my help in any way, then I was the easier one to find. There isn't much in life as egregiously demeaning all round as help that has not been sought. Jinx was not trying to find me: she did not need me. Naturally, I had wondered about her over the years and thought of her fondly. But why suddenly had I been compelled to look for her? It ought to have been an easy question to answer. But it wasn't.

A day in early spring arrived when I knew I had to find Jinx or I would have no peace of mind. The weather was typically indecisive for the season. Japanese cherries had begun to bloom in their well-meaning but dotty way, like something knitted for a teenaged niece by a pensioner. Trees of pride and stature preferred to keep to themselves a little longer, and when the wind gusted through their bare branches, as it was doing every few minutes, it wasn't hard to believe winter still had a firm grip on London, in spite of the smiling sunshine. It was a Saturday, the day of fervent shopping. Instead of going in to the office, as I almost always did on weekends, I had taken to the streets. I was under an uncharacteristic compulsion, not to buy or spend, but I now realise the same way Jinx used to shop during her marriage to Mo: I was in search of something to *want*. It hardly mattered what I wanted, it could have been a book, a picture, a bracelet, any curio, as long as I could make what I wanted my own and so, for a fleeting instant afterwards, be relieved of wanting. Otherwise, wanting, wanting something, wanting was a constant ache in my heart.

Looking back, I can trace my unfamiliar state of yearning to the day I'd seen Jinx's face smiling off the wall at 'Kisses'. Naturally, over the years I had sometimes wondered what had become of Jinx, and when I thought of

194

her, I did so fondly. But ever since my return from holiday, tenuous and bittersweet within me, more like perfume than an image, was essence of Jinx. Please, don't laugh; but if the mind has an eye, then why not a nose? In its time, the nose was as noble an organ as any other; it certainly saved as many human lives as the eye, possibly more. True, the human nose is so fuddled by chemical perfumes these days its function as an alarm system has been impaired, but it has evolved, and is now largely — among us Feldsteins, very largely — an organ of nostalgia. The nose knows what has passed by more surely than what is under it, or ahead. And in my case, essence of Jinx filled my mind's nose.

Why did I start out on this journey, which now is ending? Because I desperately needed to, and there was no reason on earth to prevent me. I set out to find Jinx, in other words, as I might scratch an itch: because not to would have been torment.

TWENTY-SEVEN

Helsinki's lead did not take me far, only to a modest one-storey house in a neighbourhood of thrifty working people. A tricycle was upended in the drive, and kiddies' clothes were hung out on a circular dryer like the spokes of a beach umbrella upright in the garden. Only a few days earlier in New York I'd seen an item on the news about a post-menopausal biddy well into her fifties who had given birth to a baby girl. The medicos had popped a test-tube foetus into her for incubation. Neat? We may not know how to make a fool of death, but life's a real sucker; it will cuddle up to anything warm and call it mama.

'I love having babies,' the woman told her interviewer. 'And I plan to have another one when I'm sixty.'

There was no reason Jinx could not have had herself fixed up in the same way to make a contribution to next season's orphans. When I rang the spiffy brass bell and heard a child laugh inside, I let myself imagine my friend had finally come to rest in a domestic setting, after her life of glamour. But actually, I knew perfectly well, long before the door had opened, I wasn't going to find Jinx O'Malley there.

The woman who stood in front of me was a plump young Mexican, and it was immediately apparent she was not a servant belonging to the house; the house belonged to her. Orange and crimson decor in the rooms behind her repeated the very colours in her dress, and the spicy smells that came from the kitchen were her own smells, deep in her skin and brushed into her glossy hair. I was not surprised to learn Jinx O'Malley no longer lived at that address. Even when I'd dropped my bags at the hotel and grabbed a taxi to the address Helsinki had given me, I'd had only the merest hope of finding Jinx so easily.

Over cups of coffee that tasted pleasantly of peppercorns, Mrs Gonzalez told me Jinx had not quite moved out when she and her husband had arrived three years earlier to take over the lease. 'She had too many things, very pretty things,' Mrs Gonzalez said. 'And only a taxi waiting to take them all away. Her furniture was sold, she told us. And her husband had taken the money, and the car. She was laughing. But I thought it was not a good story. Understand?' Mrs Gonzalez looked around the room that was crammed with overstuffed chairs and carved Mexican tables. Her eye rested for a moment on a small rug hanging on the wall beside the door, it depicted the American eagle surrounded by gold stars; the sight of it seemed to give her courage to say more. 'For a long time, this house did not feel happy.' She darted a look my way to make sure I was the kind of woman who understood how houses can feel happy or sad. 'Your friend must have been very beautiful once,' she said.

Suddenly a naked brown baby boy appeared in the doorway and stared at me solemnly. I said, 'Hello there,' or something, the way you do, you know; not expecting anything. To my amazement he toddled straight to me on legs that rotated and wobbled like two full fat little tyres. And next thing I knew my arms were full of warmth and sweetness. I was surprised by the smoothness of his flesh, without strings or sinew or muscle and I felt decades of growth compressed into his compact body, bursting to get out. The urge to nuzzle was irresistible, my big nose bent to the job it could have been designed for. I smelled health and life, and when the little fellow laughed, I smelled pure witless joy. A bright hot light flashed over a waste within

197

me, and it was all I could do to stop myself running off with the baby in my arms. I had never held a baby before, remember. The power was phenomenal.

'Your house is very happy now, Mrs Gonzalez,' I said.

She looked fearful, and crossed herself.

Jinx had promised to be back with a forwarding address, but the last Mrs Gonzalez had seen of her, she was driving off in her taxi; trailing silk roses and scarves, I fancied. The Gonzalezes had waited nearly two years, but Jinx never returned or telephoned, and finally they gave away the four boxes of clothes she had left behind. There was a remaining box, however, containing papers and pictures. Mr Gonzalez had wanted to burn it in the back garden, but his wife had felt that was not right. 'Papers are often important,' she said.

She had stored it behind the sofa I was sitting on. It was a brown and white striped box from Henri Bendel in New York, tied with twine, of about the size to have originally contained a fur coat. When I said goodbye and left Mrs Gonzalez, the Bendel box was next to me, sedate and well-behaved, on the back seat of the taxi.

Jinx had never been secretive, her candour about everything made her practically impossible to betray, and as soon as I returned back here to the hotel I opened her box with not the slightest compunction. Papers, letters, clippings and snapshots were jumbled like fallen leaves in the wild. I dug in at random and pulled out a handful of tear-sheets from fashion magazines of the 1950s; there was Jinx looking ravishing even to the modern eye, and in spite of being dressed in some of the most hideous clothes ever designed for womankind. There were later pictures taken in the 1960s and early '70s when she appeared perversely younger, as all women did back then, except those too decrepit or, like me, too plain to join in the fun. Snapshots were jumbled with the pages out of magazines; they showed her mostly with handsome men on beaches or on continental streets. There was one glossy press photo of her standing next to John F. Kennedy, who was looking down at her speculatively; several others showed her with assorted movie stars, sportsmen, and other faces sure of their importance, though I could no longer place them. There was not one picture I found showing her with Jake. No copies, either, of the magnificent photographs Henri Dimanché had taken. Under a pile of romance magazines loosely bound with shoestrings, I found her marriage licence to Mo Gittleman, who was not Moses, as I had assumed, but Mordechai. Also bound together and apart from the other things was a pile of letters, most of them returned to their opened envelopes, written in a vaguely familiar hand which, after a moment, I recognised as my own when I was young.

She appeared to have saved every letter I sent her, most of them from Paris after I'd first arrived, increasingly few from England, where the schoolgirlish curve of my hand-writing had become peaky and assertive. A quick flick through the stack revealed how few letters I'd sent her during her marriage to Jake, and of course, there was not one at all in the past fifteen years.

With a cringing of all faculties, not unlike the fear of darkness at your back when you go down cellar stairs, I started to read in no particular order. At whatever time over the years the letter I pulled out of the pile had been written, its writer was as unknown to me as an unborn child to a mother: within me, and all my own, yet unknown. My ugly baby girl. Why was she so complaining and self-conscious? I wanted to shake her. What had happened that compelled her always to undercut what she meant most to say? Even when her jokes made me laugh, I implored her, please, to stop making them. And when she told Jinx stories I had never heard before about people I would have staked my life I'd never known, the pain of loss at our separation was almost more than I could bear. She had been to places I did not remember; she'd gone into rhapsodies over books I'd never read, films I'd never seen; she had arrived at numerous conclusions with which I most certainly did not agree; she had arrived at others I envied. In a letter written while Jinx was married to Jake, young Marsha wrote: 'Once upon a time in darkest prehistory, love between the sexes kept us going, and saved us from extinction. But these days, love is a mere shadow of what it used to be, a vestige of ancient necessity, with barely any remaining force or purpose: like the vermiform appendix, we're stuck with it. Better to remove it surgically before a long voyage, lest it flare up, and make trouble. . . . '

A prostitute lived on the floor above hers in her Parisian hotel [I had no recollection of any prostitute] they used to pass every day on the stairs without a word. One morning, for no good reason, they stopped face to face. '*Bonjour,*' said the girl, who was myself. And the Parisian whore replied, without a moment's hesitation: 'Men stink!' I remembered no such encounter. But the writer of the letter thought it an appropriate anecdote for her friend, Jinx, with whom she took a generally admonitory tone, and never more so than when she touched on love between the sexes. Who was this little smartass called Marsha Leah? I asked myself. And what is the point of experience if we lose it all in the end?

Finally I threw the letters back into the box, and pushed it to one side, and for the first time in more years than I can remember, I cried. Can you imagine? Like a fool, I cried for the vanished girl who started all her letters, 'Hi, Jinx . . . ', and signed them 'Marsh', until about the time her handwriting changed and she became 'Marsha'. Then, I cried a little more to think that my friend had sloughed me off, and left all she possessed of me along with her wedding licences, and pictures of herself in full flush of hope and beauty.

Before I gave up altogether and went to bed, I dipped into the box compulsively, promising myself it would be the last time. From the bottom I came up with an old photograph mounted on cardboard and frayed at the edges. It showed a tall, raw-boned woman in front of a one-storey house that was little more than a shack; sheets of tar-paper were nailed on the roof, and one window was patched with newspapers. A dilapidated sofa sat out in the front yard; an American flag hung limply from a pole over the porch. I held the photograph close to the lamp so I could study it closely. Next to the woman stood three miniatures of herself in varying sizes, and in her arms was a baby. The baby had to be Jinx; and the photographer, I knew, was Jinx's father. The picture must have been taken days, or even hours, before he flew the coop. He had kept a wary distance from his wife and her pretty chicks, who smiled out at the camera tentatively, like earthquake victims in fear of the aftershock.

Sleepless in bed, another lead occurred to me. I had checked the telephone directory of course, first thing, though at the rate Jinx changed surnames, without much hope of tracing her. I switched on the lamp and reached for the telephone book again. If I could not find Jinx, then I had to find someone who could find her, or who might know where she was. And what could be easier to find in Los Angeles than an out-of-work actor?

TWENTY-EIGHT

Nick chose the restaurant. It was called 'Short's Circus' and
the taxi driver who took me there said it was the place of
the moment in Hollywood. The kitchens were in a solid
building of bricks and mortar, but the dining area was
outside, under a giant marquee with walls of see-through
plastic that added to a general impression of impermanence.
Nick was late, and while I waited for him I studied the
menu. There is a case to make for the menu as a sub-genre
of American literature; the one at Short's featured a dish of
the day called 'Carnival Chicken' which was described as:
'recreating all the fun of the fair in a hilarious blend of
fat-free mayo and low-chol cream that does your arteries
a flavor. . . .' A glance at the business side of the epic
showed that lunch for two was going to set me back around
two hundred dollars. Actors and actresses familiar from
television and movies were all around me; the prettiest and
most famous of them had been placed facing the door, so
the effect on each newcomer was of walking into a field of
flowers blowing in a breeze that showed their flashier side.
Those seated with their backs to the door, and consequently to me, where I had been put just inside the
entrance, were mostly ordinary men in suits. Whenever the
door of the entrance swung open, I watched sly calculation
sweep across the faces of the seated as they debated with
themselves whether to greet the person coming in, or wait
to be greeted first.

I was afraid I wouldn't recognise Nick when he finally
arrived, but I need not have worried. He entered and stood

framed in the doorway long enough to show me how mother nature plays favourites. His hair sported wide silver wings, apparently natural, where women have to fade or dye; and at first sight he looked pretty springy for a man well into his sixties. Briskly, he looked around, and briskly came towards me, waving jauntily right and left to people already seated. Nobody waved back. When Nick kissed the air either side of my face, a smell of Brut and patent medicines filled my curious nostrils. He sank into the chair across from me, puffing a little, suddenly nowhere near as young as he used to be.

'You shouldn't have let them put us here, Marsh,' he complained. 'Nobody sits this close to the door.'

Gone was the 1950s actorish mumble, gone the tv tough guy I remembered from his old series; both had given way to California peevish, c. late 1970s, when a note of discontented whining started to distinguish method actors from the mere others.

Barely seated, and already Nick was fishing in the pocket of his tweedy English jacket, not for a cigarette, good Lord, no! Smoking was forbidden at Short's, as in most of Beverly Hills. It was merely a matchbook he took out to turn and twiddle in his nicotine-stained fingers. His nails were clubbed and ribbed like small seashells, and when he reached for the glass of iced water beside his plate, he shook so hard he had to use both hands to raise it to his mouth. His entrance made, he'd fallen in on himself, like a deflating balloon. Sudden hollows sank deep under his cheekbones, skin sagged around his chin. When he turned to look for the waiter, I could see the vertical gouges at the back of his neck where time takes old men, and shakes them like kittens. Up close, I saw too the minute domes over the pupils of his eyes that turned them bright 'Newman' blue. The colour bothered me more than any other change in him. Blue eyes are for seeing over oceans and fields of

203

snow, brown eyes always look at things through a heat haze of emotion. Jinx had never fallen for a blue-eyed man, and Jake was the only one she'd married.

'What about green eyes?' Jinx had asked me long, long ago, when I'd been sounding off.

'Green eyes see what they want to see,' I told her, teasing. 'And they make a lot of trouble for everyone else.'

'Hi, my name is Robin,' said the nimble boy who sprang forward to refill Nick's water glass. 'And it is my pleasure to be your server today.'

'A drink, Nick?' I asked; obviously, he was parched.

'Shouldn't,' he said. 'Early in the day for me, Marsh. But . . . oh, hell . . . special occasion . . . what? . . . when in Rome.'

Nick was awfully cool about meeting me again after so many years; with greater excitement, he was watching the waiter go off for our vodka martinis. As he studied Robin's progress, he tore strips off the bottom of the matchbook, rolling, unrolling, re-rolling them between his fingers. I gabbled bravely, but he wasn't all there, not until the moment Robin returned and put our drinks on the table, they were in big frosted funnel-shaped glasses on long stems. Nick grabbed his, and poured a third of it down his throat. The alcohol must have vaporised on contact with his gut, and the fumes lifted to his brain; he smiled at me for the first time. That was when I saw a tooth was missing on top, at the corner of his smile. And after that, I noticed the shadow of a stain on his tie, and then how the collar of his shirt was frayed from being scrubbed with a nailbrush at the bathroom sink. But it was mostly the tooth, or absence of it that told me clearer than words Nick was all washed up.

The dread I felt when I saw the small, deep, black gap in his smile melted away quickly, and was replaced by a feeling I remembered from the old days; it was a swelling

204

tenderness, like a pain, that used to fill my heart whenever I listened to Nick bragging about his talents and saw the poor chump all puffed up over himself.

'Well, how you doing, Marsh? Good old Marsh,' he said and his voice was phlegmy with swift sentiment. I mean, this man *drank*. 'Long time no see. Who you working for these days?'

'Call me Supermarsh,' I said. 'Wherever I'm needed, that's where you'll find me.'

'Hey, Supermarsh. Now, that is awesome. Is business good, Supermarsh?'

'Not bad,' I said cautiously. 'Not good. Not bad.'

'I know what you mean, sweetie,' he said. 'It's a great life if you don't weaken.'

We sounded like a pair of travelling salesmen meeting for lunch and cleverly setting each other up for the bill. He had finished his drink and nodded to Robin for a refill. With a significant glance at the menu, he said: 'Hey, we can go somewhere else, Marsha. We don't have to eat here.' He looked at me shrewdly, making sure I got the point: that lunch was really going to be on me, and it wasn't going to be cheap.

Money is a cosmetic, too. I'm a lot less plain nowadays in the eyes of some men than I would have been when I was stony broke. I figured as soon as Nick found out he was lunching with the founder of a business the size of a hamlet, he would, first, begin to boast; and then, as soon as he thought he had convinced me of how well he was doing, he would try to touch me for a loan. Fortunately, I've hung on to the diffidence of a plain-looking girl who has no reason to expect good things from the opposite sex; it has kept me safe from flattering sharks in my prosperous middle age. Straight into his too-too guileless fake blue eyes I told him I was on an expense account, and I had a dozy boss; so as long as we didn't go hog-wild, I could fiddle a decent lunch.

He ordered modestly, the house salad – 'a medley of freshly-picked greens, dew-pearled, under a gossamer veil of nonpolysaturate oils . . . .' While we were waiting for our food, and all the time Robin was serving it, Nick continued a monologue that threatened to cover practically everything that had happened to him since we'd last met. To hear him tell it, life had been a series of betrayals: colleagues made off with his ideas, false friends stole his thunder, women took his money, actors less gifted landed parts that should have been his. Why? Because they lied about him to casting directors, made him out to be difficult. Studio heads cancelled the series 'Nolan and Klein' out of spite and small-mindedness. And when Niccolo de Lisi tried his luck abroad? The very places conspired against him. In frogland, for instance, they seemed to expect him to speak French. Would you believe it? He caught hepatitis from the water in southern Italy. And the only time he went to film on location in London, it rained so long and hard they finally ran out of time and cancelled his big scene. 'Those English "ack-tawrse" are okay for Shakespeare and Ibsen, and stuff. But take it from me, Marsh, they cannot make movies to save their lives. Ever noticed how they spit when they say their lines?'

Tomas Blalack, less than a wavering stain on the ocean floor, sure knew what he was doing in his time. While Nick went on and on, images of him in his youth as Tom-Tom caught him in *Black and White Wedding*, line for line, matched the face before me, that was marked, as Blalack had foreseen, by laziness and disgruntled ambition. Lunching with Nick was a lot like lunching with one of the ageing sex kittens I have come across in the beauty business; old girls, briefly adorable once upon a time, who end up pickled in envy, blaming everyone and everything for their lost and wasted chances. Nick ate hardly anything. Soon he dropped his knife and fork in favour of rolling more bits of paper. And he drank. Wine was on offer, of course. But he stuck with martinis, and I went along with him, at a quarter of his speed. Robin was hovering in exactly the way Jinx and I used to at Schrafft's whenever we had a dangerously big drinker on our patch.

'Robin, old cock, Cock-Robin,' said Nick, suddenly slightly blurry, 'you will deliver us two more vodka 'tinis!'

Robin was going to make a good waiter some day, when he got over believing himself born to be a star; he had known from the start under which saucer he was bound to find the tip. He looked at me, and I nodded slightly.

'The bitch used me, Marsh. I'm sorry to be the one to tell you, but she was a user. She used hell out of me. First, she used me to get at Tom-Tom. Wasn't he a great guy? A genius. They broke the mould. He warned me, you know. Tom-Tom told me she was only using me. "Nicco," he said, that's what he used to call me: "Nicco, that girl is using you!" She used me to get into one of his "Home Movies". And as soon as she got all she wanted, what happened to yours truly? I made her a star, I put my own career on hold for her. And what happened to Mister Nice Guy? She gives me the old heave-ho.'

I sat up straight, stiff with anger. But instantly my anger was overcome by remorse: if Nick could not remember the past to suit himself, he would have to have died of shame. I leaned over and actually patted his hand; it was as thin and dry as birds' bones.

'Memory's continuing story, right Nick? Soap opera for spooks, brought to us this week courtesy of Stolichnaya.'

He wondered if I was calling him a liar. I saw him weighing how much he wanted this lunch, how tired he was of third-rate California plonk to drown the hangovers. I smiled at the jerk, poor jerk, and he settled back, reassured.

'I don't like to say it, Marsh. You know I don't,' whimpered my toothless old Narcissus. 'She was pretty, I guess. She was gorgeous.' He made the very same old maid's mouth Blalack's camera had caught at the altar. 'Those pretty women, they're all takers. I never met a pretty woman who could give. Take. Take. Take. Love. Love. Love. Jinx couldn't get enough, let me tell you, sweetie. She could not get enough. No man in the world, no man, I don't care who, could have given Jinx O'Malley all the love she wanted. I'm sorry to say it, Marsh, but I have to tell the truth. She ruined my life. I don't know where she is. And I don't want to know.'

After a quick, subtle semaphore, done mostly with my eyebrows, Robin brought me the bill. When Nick glimpsed the colour of plastic I put down, his eyes lit up with feverish interest. Suddenly clear-headed, he started telling me about all the irons in his fire – 'Italians are big this season. Maturity is hot. Maturity is making a comeback' – and he straightened his shoulders so the old platinum card could see he was still mucho hombre. While Nick was trying to sell me his bill of goods, I worked out in my head the ratio of a beggar's expectations to the teeth in his head. With every tooth in place, Nick would have dared aim for five figures, and he'd have settled for four. If a lot of teeth had been missing, the meal, the free drinks, and a couple of dollars would have more than sufficed. At the rate he was going, it was bound to be ages before he actually got around to naming figures; I was tiring of grandiloquence. Jinx was out there somewhere, and most of all I wanted to find her. It is an offensive act to give anyone money when something more personal and much more important is what he's dying for. Equally, to offer advice, prayers, or even love, when money will perfectly well do the trick is always vain and pretentious. So I pulled my American chequebook out of my bag. I estimated the solitary evil flaw in his Ipana smile must pitch the figure around two-grand; and I decided, for old time's sake, to double it, then throw in an extra thousand.

'I'm serious about finding Jinx,' I said, interrupting him in mid-flow, and I opened my beautiful Mont Blanc pen. 'I'm pretty sure she's here in Los Angeles.'

Nick gave me undivided attention while I filled in the cheque and tore it away from its stub. I waved it in the air to dry the ink; he watched it flutter.

'Could you find out where she is, Nick? Nobody knows this town better than you.'

Momentarily, LA was in my bloodstream: I was a slinky heiress hiring Philip Marlowe, and I was hugely enjoying it. When I held the cheque out to Nick, he took it warily, looked at it, then did the classic double-take. There appeared on his face, like words on the flicked corners of pages: astonishment, delight, annoyance (with himself for having underestimated me at the start), guilt, suspicion (Would I stop the cheque in the morning? Would it bounce?), gratitude, hatred, and finally over it all, nearly ecstatic hope. Not that I'd given the poor guy a million, not by a long shot. But foresight dwindles in adversity, and it filled him with all manner of happy emotions to see his booze and cigarettes clear for five or six months ahead. He consulted his wrist, there was no watch on it, and drained his glass fast. He needed to get shot of me and bank the cheque, or better yet, cash it if he could.

'Well, let me see what I can do to help you out, Marsh,' he said. 'Niccolo de Lisi is always glad to help a friend out.'

Outside, away from the pseudo-dusk of Short's, Nick paused to light a Marlboro from the crumpled pack in his pocket. For the first time, I was seeing him in daylight. When he looked up and caught me assessing his losses, tears welled up into his eyes, but he did not dare shed them, not while three-hundred-dollar lenses were floating on his eyeballs. Instead, he forced a wry smile.

'Oh Marsha, Marsha,' he said thickly, 'where has all the promise gone?'

And I, who longed to hug Nick every time he boasted like a hopeful ass, I, who had sympathy for his cowardly lies and forgave them, even when they were against my oldest friend, the moment I saw him snivelling like that, not only had I no wish to offer him comfort, it was all I could do not to slam him in the solar plexus with my handbag.

'What promise, Nick, old bean?' I asked as calmly as I was able. 'Nobody promised you, or anyone, anything at all. And besides, the only promise worth a damn in this life is the one we keep.'

TWENTY-NINE

The morning of the day before yesterday, that is, the morning after Nick and I had lunch, I was pleasantly surprised to find a note from him waiting for me at the desk. Sidestepping a thank you as deftly as ever a man had, he wrote that he was on his way to a 'planning session' (how best to demolish a crate of vodka?), and in a week or two he would 'bell me' (as the mouse the cat?) about a deal that I might find interesting. Meanwhile, he'd been able to find no home address for Jinx more recent than the one Helsinki had given me. But through his contacts (of Newman blue), he had discovered Jinx's last place of employment. Heart, break! The name he gave me was of a restaurant, 'Sammy's Real New York Delicatessen', on a big street near Farmers' Market. According to Nick, Jinx could be found there any weekday after ten in the morning and on Saturday after noon. All that was left to say for the time being was bye-bye, good old Marsha Leah, *auf wiedersehen*, *au revoir*, and *arrivederci*. Exit, stage-left, Niccolo de Lisi. By the time he ran out of money and his thoughts turned my way again, I was going to be far, far from Los Angeles. And there was no chance he and I would ever meet again. Not in this life.

Just as I had known Jinx was not going to be at the Gonzalezes' address, it stood to reason she was a waitress again, so enticing and desirable are balance and symmetry in this life. I felt in my bones I would find her at Sammy's. I located Sammy's easily, a barn of a place on a busy street that borders the mock village square known as Farmers'

211

Market; its shop-front windows were hung with big red salamis, and none to clean. If Sammy was aiming for the look of a genuine Manhattan delicatessen, he'd pulled it off too well for local taste. Southern Californians are raised on the surreal, they need their authenticity to be tarted up; unless what's on offer is over the top, they cannot take it seriously. From what I could make out whenever Sammy's door swung open, the place was packed with tourists, most of them middle-aged and portly. Being much too eager, I had dashed out of the hotel with Nick's note in my hand, and arrived in Farmers' Market a few minutes after noon, before the end of the lunchtime rush, when any waitress was bound to be too busy to down her tray, even for an old friend. If American eating habits had not changed since my days in the trade, there was an hour to kill before the lull that commences every afternoon around two, and ends at five thirty or six, when the tourists from Minnesota and the Midwest, and the blue-collar townies of the east, would pour back into Sammy's for the meal they call supper.

Farmers' Market exists for no ostensible purpose but to sell junk-food and souvenirs to tourists; they were milling through the arcades, and stopping at outdoor tables to slurp hot dogs and slabs of pizza. I found a relatively quiet place called 'Ye Olde English Tea Shoppe' and there I sat on a bench outside in the sun, sipping pale yellow American tea – 'We only have it in bags,' the waitress said when I asked for loose tea. She was examining her fingernails as she spoke, and 'take it or leave it' was implicit in her tone of California smug. At least, Sammy's was in my line of vision, and as I watched the customers come and go through its doors, a great excitement took hold of me, and a kind of apprehension: like a child on her birthday morning, I wanted the fun to start, yet at the same time, in my heart I knew that when it did, it could not be as good as my day-dreams. You'd think by this time I would be able to control my imagination, even to dominate it. But I could not stop the barely coherent fragments flying through my mind. One moment there was Jinx in her prime, and the next, Madame Marsha Leah Feldstein, founder of Miracle Products, was striding into Sammy's, and showing off a little for her bedazzled friend before whisking her away from all that, to a more suitable occupation: to manage a boutique on Madison Avenue, let's say — we'd call it Ancient Miracle, for the over-fifties, or Dodo, or Tough Old Birds. And, come to the crunch, how was I going to find Jinx? How would she be? Not gone into drink or drugs the way so many dreamboats do when they can no longer inspire fantasies; no, not Jinx. And she was too much a country girl ever to give animals first place or settle as other desiccated sexpots did, for a sham family of dogs, and donkeys, and stray pussycats. Even in her heyday she had been neither vain nor competitive, and as competitiveness and vanity are the antecedents of envious spite in later life, I knew she would not have gone down spitting vitriol the way disappointed old beauties so often do. The strongest possibility to strike my addled brain was that Jinx had gone overboard for a jerrybuilt imitation of thought, à la Fawn Ellis: tarot cards, crystals, reflexology, some messianic cult, or fortune cookies — it hardly mattered. Whatever folderol she'd found to help her face her losses and put a stopper on the nagging question, why? Why? Why? I made up my mind to tolerate it without derision. What are friends for?

At last, I paid my bill, left an unmerited dollar under the saucer, and started across the street to Sammy's Real New York Delicatessen, where I knew I was going to find my old friend in service. As I pushed through the twanging accents of the crowd, it was uplifting and somehow darkly amusing to think I could be in the very process of advancing a sound theoretical answer to the question, why? Because

213

our very purpose is to be kind to one another under conditions that would otherwise drive us all mad. That's what friends are for.

And Jinx was not there. After the certainty and excitement: no Jinx. What a let-down it was. I sat in a two-seater booth on a leather cushion that slipped and tipped in its frame, and once again I looked the place over: no, she was not there. A handful of customers were finishing lunch, they were all fat and pasty-faced, not a California godkin in the lot; they could have been included as part of the authentic New York deli decor, along with the floor of small white and green octagonal tiles, surely intended originally for a bathroom, deeply worn along the central aisles between the booths. Five waitresses were working the floor, each of them pushing sixty, all of them wives of failed husbands and mothers of neglectful children: five ageing women marked by toil, and somehow preserving a wary, obstinate benevolence. One of them ambled over to my table, her head was like a great dandelion going to seed, all frothy yellow with roots of white. She leaned over me, more in fatigue than attentively.

'What can I getcha?'

I wasn't hungry in the least. The same choking anxiety that killed appetite, prevented me asking about Jinx, and I heard myself say: 'A chicken-salad platter'. It was the way she stood there, too, you understand: wide-hipped and flat-footed, the tray held as if it had been born on her forearm – she was purpose-built for the bringing of food, unable to do anything any longer for me, or men, or anyone, except to wait on us. I sat there, soaked in dire premonition.

'Oh sure,' my waitress said, when I was finally bold enough to ask. 'Jinx, sure, she's out back.' For one giddy instant, I thought she was telling me Jinx had gone to Australia.

214

'Out back. Out back,' she repeated, nodding towards the rear of the restaurant.

There was a door to the kitchen back there, a second door marked 'Rest Rooms', a cigarette machine, and a third door with a push-bar across its width that led, no doubt, to an alley behind Sammy's.

'Having a smoke?' I asked, light-headed with relief, my heart pounding.

'I hope so, dear,' my waitress said. 'Tell her to have one for me, too.'

I had to pay my bill at the counter before I could go out back. My salad platter was untouched: three scoops identical in size – a pinkish one of chicken, white potato salad, greenish slaw – on a bed of iceberg lettuce with wheels of beef tomatoes turning around the edges – a commercial artist's interpretation of food. It would have tasted only of tubed and bottled pigment. As I was going back past my table, I paused and slipped a five-dollar bill under the platter. My waitress stood near the entrance in serious conversation with her co-workers. They stopped talking to watch silently when I pushed open the door to out back.

A long dark alleyway ran between lowering walls. There was a dank, oily, fishy smell in the air, and sounds of heavy traffic beat like a hidden engine not far away. Except that the ground was stable, it could have been the belly of a ship. At one end of the corridor to the left of where I stood, was a fissure between the two enclosing buildings, through it I glimpsed a warmer, brighter dimension where pedestrians were hurrying by, unaware of me in the darkness. Between me and the busy world stood a row of Sammy's rubbish bins. They'd been rolled out on their rims, I figured, by lowly kitchen staff, through the door that was hissing slowly closed behind me. In the greyish opening overhead, time was suspended like an executioner's hand.

215

'It's been years and years, honey. What's it been? Four years?' With a leaping heart I turned to her voice.

'More like fifteen,' I said. 'Jinx . . . dear Jinx . . . .'

The depths of the alley to my right were closed off by the back of another building and practically roofed in by overhanging eaves. Before I made Jinx out in the dimness, I saw a supermarket trolley drawn in close and carefully to one wall. Ribbons and coloured paper were wound round and round the frame; it was piled high with plastic bags, and a furled umbrella stood upright out of one corner; perched on it was a straw hat stuck with paper roses. Jinx stepped forward from behind this jaunty vehicle and started towards me, her arms lifted as if in blessing, or to hug. Thank God, I did not recoil. But a voice within me shouted loud and clear: 'Lice!' At arm's length, leaning back from the waist like two little girls, one much taller than the other, we whirled each other around in circles.

Had I seen her eyes first, and nothing but her eyes, I could have believed everything was much as it used to be. But first I saw her hands etched with dirt, and I felt them rough as fish-skin in my own. And then I saw, oh Lord, how she was dressed. Dun-coloured strata of shirts, pull-overs, several skirts, tights, slacks and socks fell thick around her, gaping unevenly over each other like geologi-cal accretions. A long strip of upholstery trim was wound several times around her head and ended in a pair of tarnished gold tassels dangling behind an ear.

'A girl's got to make the best of what she has, honey,' Jinx said cheerfully. She smiled at me; at least, she appeared to have all her teeth. 'When it happens, it isn't nearly so bad as you'd think, Marsha, honey. So don't you worry about me. I'm okay, honey. Isn't that the darnedest thing?' she said, and she pronounced it 'thang'.

At the back of the alleyway was a broken car-seat propped against one wall. Courteously, she led me to it and

216

motioned me to sit down. Hanging from nails on the rough wall of the building behind me were five or six string bags; as if I led the life myself, I knew right away she put them high up to keep their contents safe from vermin. Jinx sat across from me on a pile of burlap sacks. Between us was an orange crate, upside down to serve as a table; on it a broken fragment of mirror was propped up against a coffee-pot that lacked its lid. Behind Jinx were more orange crates, stacked to serve as shelves for an accumulation of objects, many of them so distorted it was impossible to guess what they had been, but somehow all of them together giving an effect of domesticity. Jinx chose an old biscuit-box out of the jumble and laid it between us. When she opened it, I saw a mass of broken oddments of make-up. I recognised a line of lipstick Miracle had taken off the market a year earlier, and a couple of Capran's mascara wands. She spat on one of them daintily to moisten it, then leaned towards the mirror and began to stroke it on her lashes.

'There was a girl down home', she said as she applied mascara, 'who married a fast-talking Fuller brush salesman, a Gemini, and didn't he go and run out on that poor child, and leave her in New York City . . . ?'

'But, Jinx, darling, that was you!' I cried.

She held the mascara wand still, and thought for a moment. 'No, honestly, honey, I do not believe it was me,' she said at last, and returned to her mirror. A plate was beside us on the ground, piled high with Sammy's left-overs.

'Let me get you out of this Jinx,' I said. 'Oh please, Jinx, please come back with me.'

'Well that's very nice of you, honey,' she said, and she looked where I was looking, at the ends of rye bread and strips of meat smeared with mustard, and cold french-fried potatoes. 'But, you see, I can eat anything I want now. It doesn't matter if I gain weight.'

Circles of rouge blazed like fever spots on the summits of her cheekbones; she held a broken lipstick in her hand, but paused to speak before she used it.

'There was this girl I used to know who married a rich old man. He bought her everything money could buy. But, honey, how many times have you heard me say that money cannot buy love? No, money cannot buy love, and that's the cold, cold truth. Brains can't think love for you, either, and write it down. I have always loved love more than anything, Marsha,' she said, with a smile as dazzling as she had ever smiled. 'I guess I always will. You see, honey, I was made for love after all.'

'But Jinx,' I cried, 'you can't find love here, not in a place like this.'

'How do you know, honey?' she asked me kindly.

When she bent her head to the mirror, she was dismissing me gently but reprovingly back to a world without hope or magic, a world of my own making which I knew in that moment was no longer where I wanted to be, and hadn't been for quite a while. As I watched with what concentration she drew the carmine outline of her mouth, inflating it fetchingly far above the natural lipline, whatever force or grace central to myself I'd mislaid long ago, or doped, or put aside in fear, awoke, and started clamouring. A buzz of youth and purpose stirred again, tingling in every nerve. A million things need doing; I do not yet know what they are, but only I can do them.

Jinx is where she wants to be, and I will not bother her again. She was barely found before I lost her once more, probably for ever. But it's never really the other we're looking for when we set out on a journey, is it? And it's never the other we find.

218

RINGLAND 9/93

STACK 2/96